A Vindication of a Life

A Vindication of a Life

PART 1

STEPHEN BADDELEY

Matador
Unit E2 Airfield Business Park,
Harrison Road, Market Harborough,
Leicestershire. LE16 7UL
Tel: 0116 2792299
Email: books@troubador.co.uk
Web: www.troubador.co.uk/matador
Twitter: @matadorbooks

ISBN 978 1803130 392

British Library Cataloguing in Publication Data.
A catalogue record for this book is available from the British Library.

Printed and bound in Great Britain by 4edge Limited
Typeset in 11pt Minion Pro by Troubador Publishing Ltd, Leicester, UK

Matador is an imprint of Troubador Publishing Ltd

For Lucy

It was in the foyer of the East India Club. We were there to meet our friends. Our friends were the Heathfields. Remember them?

'We' was me, I'm Tom, Annie and Brosie – they were, still are, my wives. Brosie was in her wheelchair. It was raining. It was London. The foyer was full-to-fullish. There was coming-and-going. There were comings-and-goings. Umbrellas were being furled and un-. The 'full-to-fullish' was of well-dressed people.

I went to reception. I asked the lady to ring our friends. She said she would. So she did.

The commissionaire sat at a desk. He wore a uniform. It was extravagant. There were epaulettes of scrambled-egg. There was a name badge – 'Sgt R C Connolly'. He looked at us. He stood up. He walked towards us. He stopped in front of us. He stopped in front of Annie. Annie towered above him. She was six-two, six-two in bare feet, six-two in bare feet with her knees bent. Up straight, in heels she was daunting. She was 'up straight, in heels'. He was daunted. It was from the height of her. It was from the sight of her. The destroyed but beautiful face. The empty eye. 'The thing' from the one. 'The thing' that 'burnt the topless towers of Ilium'.

He swallowed in his daunt.

1

◎   What is it about men, daunt and swallowing?

But he had a job to do.

"I'm terribly sorry, madam, but I must ask you to leave."

"Why?"

"You are wearing trousers, madam."

"So are you, Sergeant R C Connolly."

"Yes, madam, but I'm not a lady, madam."

"Better luck next time."

"Indeed, madam, but I'm afraid it is a club rule, madam."

"Change it."

"I'm afraid that would take some considerable time, madam."

"I'm in no hurry. And don't be afraid, it's bad for the kidneys."

"I'm sorry, madam, but I really must insist."

"Insist away."

The manager detached himself. He came over. He wore a suit. There was a name badge – 'Maj Craig M Sanders'. "What appears to be the trouble?"

"No trouble up my end, Major Craig M Sanders."

He looked up. He looked into the beauty of the destroyed face. He swallowed.

But he had a job to do.

"I fully appreciate the inconvenience, madam, but I am afraid you must leave."

"Don't be afraid, chum. Fear isn't good for the pancreas."

"Indeed, madam."

Then he made a mistake. He put his hand on her elbow. Annie looked at the hand. Major Craig M Sanders looked at the hand. Annie looked at him. He looked at her. He saw 'the thing'. He took – as though burned by a tower of Ilium – his hand away. It was an unusual moment.

Brosie wheeled over. "Eh, you dere. Boss-fella. Wot you a doin' askin' dis charmin' lady in de gorgeous onesie to be leavin'?" She was doing her Caribbean 'ham-it-up' voice. She was good at it. She was from Antigua.

He looked down at her. Into the blackest-of-all-black-faces. Into the wisest-of-all-wise-faces. It was the blackness alone he saw. The wisdom of the ages he saw not.

"The rule book is quite explicit, madam. No ladies in trousers are to be allowed into the club."

"It soundin' like de sort o' rule dose ol' days fellas make, back when yous guys be doin' de rapin' and de pillagin' all roun' de worl'."

"Indeed, madam. But be that as it may, I must ask your friend to leave."

"Dis rule book mus' 'ave lots o' de rules. It mus' 've de rule 'bout keepin' de fuckin' niggers out. Go get de rule book, Dickie Boy, dere mus' be de rule 'bout de fuckin' niggers. None o' you fancy fellas wan' de club infestin' wid no fuckin' niggers." An audience was gathering.

Major Craig M Sanders ['Dickie Boy'] didn't know what to say. The commissionaire didn't either. They stood silent, swallowing. Then Annie spoke.

"Gentlemen, if I wasn't wearing trousers, would that calm your troubled minds?"

"Certainly, madam," said Major Craig M Sanders.

I knew what was about to happen. Annie was my wife. I knew the workings of her mind. So did Brosie.

'De gorgeous onesie' was zippered from her chest to a lot lower than that. And then – quite slowly – it wasn't. And then – quite slowly – it was shrugged from shoulders. And then – quite slowly – it slid down the long and unadorned body to the floor.

"How's that?"

There was silence in the foyer. Umbrellas were neither furled nor un-. Wives steered husbands towards libraries, dining-rooms and stairs. Husbands showed no desire to read, eat or climb.

3

We left. The Heathfields too. The rain had stopped. We stood outside. Passers-by showed a reluctance to pass. Traffic slowed. A policeman walked towards us. He talked to his radio.

"Hello, hello." He was two-thirds of a traditionalist.

"Hello, hello, yourself," said Annie.

"Do we have a problem, madam?"

"Not me. How about you?"

He backed off to the curb. He spoke to his radio. His radio spoke to him. He came back.

"I'm afraid you can't stand here like that, madam."

"Don't be afraid, officer, it's bad for the spleen."

"None the less, madam. You can't stand here like that."

"Like what?"

"Like that, madam." He was having trouble with the word 'naked'. He was young. "I must ask you to cover up."

"And if I was to decline your kind request, officer?"

"Then, madam, my sergeant would be most upset."

"Tut, tut, that would never do. There's no knowing what organ damage a 'most upset' sergeant might suffer."

"Indeed, madam, but if you would cover up, please."

"As you ask so nicely," she said, and slipped back into 'de gorgeous onesie'. His radio crackled. He went back to the curb. He returned.

"My sergeant says thank you and asks you, please, not to do it again."

"You have a polite sergeant."

"Not always."

We walked and wheeled to Pall Mall and then on to Villandry's. The others – Prue, Andy, Zola, Mitzi and Rupert were already there. The wine was open. Zola knew about wine. She was French.

We talked of islands. Not just any islands. Islands in the Calvados Chain off the tail of New Guinea. It was the obvious, if not the only, thing to do.

4

Enter Chorus.

Bert sat in an armchair on the balcony of his home. It overlooked Sydney Harbour – Rushcutters Bay. He wore a Hawaiian shirt & shorts. He wore a smug smile too/also/and as well. There was no reason/obvious or otherwise/for the Hawaiian shirt & shorts – but there was for the smug smile. He wore it in the knowledge that half-of-half-a-ton-of-Afghan-best was hidden away where no one would/could/could possibly find it. Where he was sure/sure-ish/hoped no one would/could/could possibly find it.

Mr Woo sat Buddha-like – because he looked a lot like Buddha – in an armchair on the balcony of his home. It overlooked Repulse Bay. He wore a chángshän. It fitted his generous frame. He wore no visible expression. Invisibly – the expression was one of being 'pissed-off-to-the-max'. A dead monkey lay before him. It was not the reason for the 'pissed-off to the max'. It was the result of it.

The reason for Mr Woo's unhappy/'pissed-off-to-the-max'/ state of mind was that he didn't know where half-of-half-a-ton-of-Afghan-best was hidden away. And because of that lack of knowledge – and because of who he was [who he'd spent his life becoming] and in the knowledge that he should be the only person to know where half-of-half-a-ton-of-Afghan-best was – and thus been free to hide it anywhere he wished – he was [see above] 'pissed-off-to-the-max'.

Mr Woo was 'Mr Big' – and in more ways than one. He was – and had been for longer than he could remember – *numero uno/dï yï* of the Hong Kong drug trade. The sharks of the South China Sea had/on many occasions in the past/been grateful – if sharks are capable of gratitude/which they probably aren't/but it's hard to be sure – for his rise to that prestigious position.

But not so much of recent years. Aspiring competition – aware of the 'sharks of the South China Sea' – now trod-&-skulked with care-&-caution around the borders of his empire.

$$*$$

The 6th Earl of Somewhere-or-other – having recently bludgeoned his children's nanny to death with an iron bar – and leaving it [together with his Savile Row jacket/double-breasted & double-vented] at the scene – was uncertain of what to do next. And because of that uncertainty he sought the company & advice of his oldest-&-closest-friend.

◎ The 6th Earl's name was John. But to refer to him as such would be to introduce unnecessary confusion. It was also the name of the oldest-&-closest-friend.

Now – old friends & close friends/even oldest-&-closest-friends – aren't necessarily the best friends to have. That was perhaps [perhaps even more than 'perhaps'] the case with the 6th Earl. The 'perhaps' was partly/perhaps largely/due to Friend John owning & running a gambling house in Mayfair – the 6th Earl's home-from-home.

And – being his home-from-home – the 6th Earl had spent much of his time & very nearly all of his inheritance there. It was there – with the 6th Earl/down-on-his-luck/fresh from sniffing a line of white powder up his schnoz and depositing [in the apartment upstairs] a viscous off-white fluid into the daughter – a girl with organ-stop nipples that did intriguing things when he did less than intriguing things to encourage them to do the intriguing things they did – of the Shadow Minister for Something-or-other – that Friend John had suggested to him that his 'down-on-his-luck-ish-ness' might be ameliorated by getting his hands on his wife's robust & not inconsiderable [her G⁵ grandfather being an acolyte of Warren Hastings/and thus an enthusiastic co-rapist of the wealth of India] fortune.

And so – in the knowledge of the inheritance laws of England – but with morality +/– common-sense fuzzed somewhat by the booze & white powder – the 6th Earl proceeded home and battered to death the wrong woman.

Returning to whence he came/Friend John suggested that it might be felicitous for him [the 6th Earl] to disappear. He said he would arrange it. Which he did.

⁎

Eli was an 'interesting' man. He was the first/last & only person ever to be conceived in Dachau concentration camp. His father/ Amos Cohen [an artist/Lothario & aspiring poet from Passau] – taking a fancy to Hannah Rubenstein [a young/coquettish virgin from Tuttlingen] who/not minding/not in the slightest/that he did – did to & with her what artists/Lotharios & aspiring poets have been doing to & with young/coquettish virgins [especially ones who don't mind/not even in the slightest] since Eve begat Cain.

It was in the cattle wagon in which they were being 'relocated'.

Never being one to allow hardship/the knowledge of unpleasant things to come [or overcrowding] to interfere with the-needs-of-the-body – and with Hannah sporting a nascent but likewise outlook on life – and in the knowledge of their impending demise & her preference not to die un-shagged – they'd managed/with some difficulty [but admirable determination] to get-their-mutual-rocks-off.

It was as the train was passing through the gates of the camp that Amos' Y-chromosome accepted the invitation to snuggle up with Hannah's X – thus giving birth [not 'birth' but existence] to Eli [short for Elijah].

Some weeks later – long enough for Amos to have turned to ashes – the United States Army appeared over the horizon. Gates were opened/guards were – quite understandably – shot and Hannah Rubenstein – in the knowledge of her condition and the need to project her genome into the future – applied her newly found & not inconsiderable charms to doing just that. It was in this way that – possessing both a naturally gregarious disposition & a good [bordering on remarkable] set of knockers – she'd managed to get mutual-rocks-off with Corporal O'Malley from Boston/Sergeant Schmidt from Milwaukee/Lieutenant Suarez from San Diego & Captain Petersen from Long Island. She was an upwardly mobile girl. She knew-how-many-beans-made-five.

Captain Petersen – his name was Charles ['Chuck'] – was a good man. He'd been away from home/wife & family for too long for him to have any guilt [apart from in an academic sort of way] about getting-his-rocks-off with Hannah.

He took her under his metaphorico-avuncular wing and after a number of weeks – in the mistaken belief that the bulging of her tummy was down to him/and not knowing of any contribution from Amos – he asked her where she would like to go. He asked her that because – even though he was a good man – he wanted her off his hands/out of his bed & a long way away. There was his career in Uncle Percy's bank [as well as a fearsome mother-in-law] to think of.

She said she wanted to go to Israel.

*

Tim Gatting was a young lawyer. He lived in Cape Town. His father owned the country's largest & most lucrative import-export business. His mother – partly because she was partly French and partly because she liked teaching – taught French to girls at the St Ethel's School for Young Ladies. They were largely/

8

but not exclusively/young ladies of the Anglophonic tongue. Afrikanophony was neither shunned nor encouraged.

Tim – during his time at Bishops – a school for young men largely/but not exclusively/of the Anglophonic tongue – where Afrikanophony was [likewise] neither shunned nor encouraged – was something of a freak. He was the only boy in his valedictory year to be in the First VIII [rowing 'stroke']/First XI [batting at 3 and opening the bowling]/First XV [fearsome on the wing]/ and First Aths [400/800]. He'd missed out on 'Dux of School' by a cigarette paper. He was handsome without knowing it. There was an air of disarming naïvety about him. It was a heady mix.

———
*

Noor Coetzee came from the veldt. She was born the daughter of the land of the Great Karoo. And being born the daughter of the land of the Great Karoo was a pretty rotten thing to be born the daughter of. To say that the Great Karoo [her family's bit of it] was marginal land would be an insult to marginal land. It was the pits.

In addition to the land she came from being the pits her parents were the pits too. Her father was an old fashioned & unreconstructed Boer pig. There was nothing good/decent or nice about him. There was not a single redeeming feature [not one] and not even the most unlikeable of dislikeable [or most dislikeable of unlikeable] people liked him.

Mrs Coetzee – seeing the error of her ways/but seeing no other way to ameliorate the effects of it/and through the vector of puerperal sepsis – popped-her-clogs soon after Noor popped out.

Mr C was – of course he was – a staunch supporter of Gene T Blanche and his Afrikaner Westandsbeging – a benign group of men who cared for all men – as long as they were of Dutch/ German descent & not black/brown/yellow or Jewish.

To anyone – to anyone who wasn't one of them – they were about as detestable a group of men as it would be possible to find [anytime/anywhere] on the surface of the globe.

Noor was her father's daughter – perhaps more so.

She liked killing things. The more the merrier/the bigger the better. She once watched a cow elephant give birth and then shot it. Then she killed the calf – she preferred to think of it as 'the baby' [because she liked killing baby things] – with a butcher's knife. She'd slept well that night.

In the morning she went back and skinned the dead calf. She made a handbag – a shoulder-bag/a big one – she carried lots of things/none of them feminine – out of the skin. It became her prize possession.

—
*
—

Chan-ying was a pretty girl. She came from a large-and-thus-poor family. They lived in a small village outside a small town in the small/poor Chinese province of Shanxi. At fifteen – her prettiness changing/as it so often does/into beauty – her father/seeing the chance of continuing to feed his extensive family/allowed a passing Political Commissar – in exchange for tax exemptions & a wad of *rénminbi* – to drive away with her.

The Commissar – whose name was Wang Dengping but everyone called him 'Shieng shong' ['Sir'] – was not as bad a man as the word 'Commissar' tends to suggest. In fact – in many ways/given the restraints on 'goodness' that the system imposed upon him – he was a good man.

He cared for Chan-ying in ways he hadn't for the other girls in his life. So it was sad when – after backing the wrong man for governor – he was called to the capital and not seen/heard of/or spoken of ever again.

Chan-ying – now heavy-with-child – took the long & dusty road home. Her father – an agrarian simpleton and not happy with her heavy-with-childness/and with the *rénminbi* long since gone – was unwelcoming.

◎ The probity & hypocrisy of parochial societies is seemingly universal – [i.e. it's OK to sell your daughter into concubinage but not to accept the inevitable result of having done so].

But her Aunty Boazhai took her in and the baby – a boy/Hai Chang – was born.

＊

Eli struggled his way through Hannah's birth-canal and thus into the glaring light & cold of a moderately uninterested/ disinterested/uncaring & unwelcoming world. He managed the feat just as their ship was docking in Haifa. Being born Jewish was good. Being born in Israel was even better.

There were few of Hannah's extended family to have survived the recent nastiness/but there was one/a distant cousin/Elijah. And Hannah – knowing [see above] how-many-beans-made-five – thought it might be politic/which it was/to name her recently emerged son after him.

Elijah Sr – having been quick to see 'the-writing-on-the-wall' of Mr Hitler [as many of his race weren't] had/long before *Nachts* became *Krystal*/vacated Europe for England. He'd re-established his publishing business in [where else would he] Golders Green.

◎ My grandfather's ashes are in Golders Green. Significance uncertain.

Though prospering there he was not happy there. And the 'not happy there' was in part/but not *in toto*/due to the attitude of home-grown British Jews.

Although – not that long before – being refugees themselves/ and only being let in by Oliver Cromwell because [from the way he saw it] Jews were a lesser evil than Catholics/they had – in the sneaky way common to Brits of any religion – invented a kosher-oid version of England's ancient class-system. They were – and went out-of-their-way to make their more recently arrived Yehudi cousins aware of the fact that they were – a-cut-above the European riff-raff.

The other part of Elijah's 'not-happy there-ness' was because he was a disciple of Herzl and – 'Next year in Jerusalem,' wasn't [and would never be] enough for him. He was not born under a patient star. He yearned for 'Next year...' to be 'This year...'

And so – as soon as it was appropriate to do so – which was before most/because the Jewish race is by necessity a tentative one – he'd unfurled his allegorico-emblematico & figurative flag of Zion and decamped to the Holy Land. He'd thrived there.

He brought Hannah home to his home. He was married [it's a long story] to a Bronx Ashkenazi called Rebecca. There was a daughter. There were servants & a dog. The dog did not please Rebecca.

Soon after arriving Hannah heard her wailing a quiet wail [as only Bronx Ashkenazi wives &/or mothers can wail] "Aye, aye... a Jew with a dog? Either it's not a Jew, or it's not a dog." But she could tell they were [even with the dog] happy together.

It was a big house and there was room for her. She stayed until Eli was one.

The reason she moved from Elijah's comfortable & happy home was that she'd met Aaron Aarons.

◎ I once knew a guy called David David. My sister dated a Benjamin Benjamin. "Oy, vey."

---
*

12

Bert was something of an enigma. He wasn't your every-day/run-of-the-mill/purveyor of chemical happiness. He was born to smart parents and was smart himself. He'd excelled at school and got into Med at Sydney Uni. His father was a radio-astronomer at CSIRO's Honeysuckle Creek. He was part of the team to help Messrs Armstrong & Aldrin get where they got. And/because of that [Honeysuckle Creek being almost as far from civilisation as the moon] Bert spent his school years at Kings – an exclusive & exclusively boys school in Parramatta. This – together with a natural shyness – meant that/by the time he hit Uni/he was not as knowledgeable about those of the alternate gender as he might otherwise have been.

And so – as so often happens – when it happened it happened in a way that wouldn't have happened to someone whose happenings had happened more gradually/relaxedly & step-by-step.

Bert was at college – Wesley – and Wesley was mixed. There he met Trixie. It was – in-more-ways-than-one – a seminal meeting. Without it the course of his life would be different to the point of 'very'.

Trixie was smart enough to get to Uni. But she was only smart in an on-the-surface sort of way and not a-deep-down sort of way.

◎ We all meet [don't we] people like her – people who seem smart enough/but aren't really that smart at all?

She was doing third year Arts. She'd managed to scrape through the first two years – which says more about a BA degree than it should.

Q. What does BA stand for?

A. 'Batchelor of Attendance'.

Q.   What do you say to someone with a BA?

A.   "A Big Mac and Diet Coke please."

Trixie's main problem was not her smartness/or even her lack of the-deep-down variety of it. It was that her parents were mega-rich & separated. Or is that two problems? Anyway – her father was too tied up with moving his wealth from the gigabyttic to the terrabyttic to spend much time on his only child. And her mother was too involved with fornicating her way through the A-Listers of the Eastern Suburbs to do anything other than likewise.

So – Trixie was the up-market equivalent of a love deprived & emotionally child-abused orphan. And so – in an attempt to ameliorate the effects of that deprivation & abuse – she sought solace in the arms of anyone with arms to spare. And there was no shortage of those.

To assuage his conscience for the deprivation [etc.] her father had inundated her/& continued to inundate her/with money. It was done in the belief that that would be enough.

◎   We all know – don't we – that $$$ + (no love) x2 = sadness. And that sadness + $$$ + (a lack of deep-down smartness) = disaster?

And so it was for Trixie.

Deciding to emulate her mother [the only female role-model available] she commenced – in the hope of finding that illusive thing called 'love' – a program of screwing everyone she could. And 'everyone she could' was a lot of people/mostly guys.

The *Neisseria gonorrhoeae* [Gram –ve] *diplococcus* – always keen on new hosts – was grateful to her. Her file at RPA's STD clinic was enlarging steadily.

Sadly – a side-effect of 'the clap' [enough 'clap' to be considered applause] can be the gumming up of female anatomy/ deep-seated pelvic discomfort & general misery all round. Such was Trixie's lot.

Given the deep-seated pelvic discomfort [& with all the $$$ available to her] she decided – quite understandably – to ameliorate her pain/pelvic & emotional/with the lavish administration of available chemicals. She started [like we all did] with cannabis. But [unlike what most of us didn't] she moved on.

She met Bert one evening when he was in need of a break from studying the anatomical structures [of which there are five] to pass through the clavipectoral fascia. It was by the coffee urn in the common-room. Trixie was just back from both screwing her Asian-studies lecturer & snorting a few hundred bucks up her schnoz. She was as-high-as-a-kite and [given the diminutive size of the lecturer's 'Shanghai dicklet'] decided that Bert/a strapping lad/was just what she needed.

Bert – tired of the axilla in general/and the clavipectoral fascia in particular/and having liked the look of Trixie from when he'd first arrived at Wesley [and thus having done sundry things to his person at the thought of 'giving-her-one'] but aware of her lofty third year status & his lowly freshman one/ and in the knowledge that he'd never 'given-one' to anyone/only dreamed [in an academic sort of way] of perhaps making her acquaintance/as a preliminary to [if luck went his way] 'giving-her-one' – asked her/because she was slumped in an armchair nearby/if she would like a coffee.

He was surprised – then pleasantly surprised/then anxiously surprised – when she stood up/came to the urn/draped herself all over him and said – "I don't need coffee… I need a fuck… my room… now."

"OK," said Bert… and swallowed.

*

Hai grew long/remarkably long & thin. 'Thin' was to be expected. 'The Great Leap Forward' ensured that everyone [except for the author of 'The Great Leap Forward'] was thin. But 'remarkably long' wasn't to be so easily explained and no one could. The Commissar wasn't tall and neither was Hai's mother. He was the tallest person in the village.

He was also the smartest person in the village. Not Einstein smart but more than smart enough. Smart enough [by the age of sixteen] to see-&-know that there was no future for a-boy-like-him in a-village-like-that. So he decided to leave it. And/after deciding to/he did.

*

Eli was not an easy child. Hannah blamed that entirely – because there was no available right of reply – on the/presumably/faulty family traits [the second 't' being silent] of Amos.

By the age of ten – with a string of offences for shop-lifting/old-lady bashing & obscene gesturing to police behind him – and an all too predictable future ahead of him – his mother/now Mrs Aarons/as well as Mr Aarons [a normally tolerant & kind hearted man] would happily have paid for him to be taken far-far-away/sold into slavery/or donated to medical research/should [which sadly they were not] any of those options been available to be opted for.

By fourteen – with more of the same behind him – he/to the mutual satisfaction of all parties/left home. By fifteen he was in juvenile detention in Ashdod for stealing cars. By eighteen he was in the Ktz'iot Correctional Facility [big-boy's-jail] for the kidnap of/rape of & general unpleasantness to/the daughter of the Mayor of Nazareth. He got ten years/the minimum – they were lenient. It was because of his age & conception in Dachau. But that's still a lot of years when you're eighteen.

◎ I was eighteen when my sister [twenty-three] told me she was dating a man of thirty. I can remember wondering how come she'd developed a penchant for such old men. Now – in the mid-afternoon of life – tank commanders & policemen look like children. Life's full of relativity.

But they were years well spent. Eli entered Ktz'iot as a pimply thug and left as a fully resourced bad-guy. And that was thanks to Solomon [never Sol or Solly] Hagelstein.

Solomon was one of a rare breed of men who enjoyed being in jail. He would rather be there than not. That was because he was safe there and his enemies/who were legion/couldn't get to him there – even though they'd tried. The prison population [for-one-reason-or-another] were his protectors. All new-comers were suspected of being – and/as the prison cemetery attested/sometimes were – assassins. The governor & wardens were his Praetorian Guard.

He enjoyed a spacious cell to himself. There was a TV & a fridge. There were unrestricted phone privileges. There was tea/chess & chocolate biscuits with the governor every Tuesday. He ran/as everyone knew/his empire from inside the jail.

But it wasn't an 'evil empire' [just 'a little bit evil-ish'] because he shunned dealing-in-drugs & the provision of minors to dirty-old-men. He avoided murder – except when necessary. In addition to that he was financing the governor's son-in-law in setting up his [after the demolition of inconveniently placed Palestinian ones] home construction company.

And-so-it-was that Solomon saw the potential in Eli and took him under his [in metaphor of course] wing.

$$\overline{*}$$

Noor – evil & horrible though she most certainly was – knew/like others in this book/how-many-beans-made-five. She knew that a life on the veldt [especially her father's bit of it] was not the life for her. She was a smart enough & handsome enough [but not quite beautiful] woman. She knew there was more to life than the one she was leading.

She liked the free life of killing things. She liked it [perhaps more of a 'didn't mind it'] when her father forced – not a lot of force being required – himself upon her. But it wasn't rape because [see above] she liked it [perhaps more of a 'didn't mind it'] when he did. She liked it/more than 'didn't mind it'/when he made the grunting noises he did. She liked the grunting noises she made in return. But those things weren't enough for her.

So – one day – after axing him in the back of the head [which gave her just as much pleasure as it did to make grunting noises] she hitched his corpse to the back of the old Land Rover and dragged it out to the base of the *kop* where she knew hyenas were camped.

She drove home/shot the dogs/took the photograph of H F Verwoerd – her hero – the diamonds [still in the Romeo y Julietta cigar tube] the ones her father had extracted from the rectum of the tortured/and then slowly [very slowly] hanged/ kaffir Kimberley mine worker – the bag of gold Krugerrands & the elastic-banded wad of notes from under his mattress. She then rummaged through the papers in the office. She found the deeds to the farm & the 'Last Will & Testament' she'd got him to write the month before. Then she sat in his armchair. Then she pissed in it. Then she set fire to the place. Then she left.

Mr Woo – outwardly calm/but inwardly 'pissed-off-to-the-max' – an understatement of 'Houston we have a problem' proportion/ sat with [just as we left him] the dead monkey before him. It was a family tradition and Chinese traditions go back a long way. His father kept a monkey/& his father/& his father/retreating into the mists of time. Mr Woo harboured no great affection for animals in general or monkeys in particular/but they served a purpose. When things got too much for him [when he was 'pissed-off-to-the-max'] the throttling of a monkey allowed him to remain outwardly calm – a very important thing for drug-lords in general/and a Chinese drug-lord in particular/to remain. It hid the snarling/spit dribbling & murderous intent within.

Mr Woo's XIIIth monkey – a supposedly unlucky number to be/but not in China where [or so I'm told] it's IV – had lived a longer life than most. The early days of establishing himself & feeding the sharks of the South China Sea had seen a rapid progression of monkeys from living to non-.

He knew he must act.

But he wasn't sure of what act to act. It was years since anyone had dared pull a stunt like this. For that reason – the not being 'sure of what act to act' – he called for a man. He called for his Mr-Fix-It. The man entered the room. He was tall/remarkably tall/and thin. He looked smart. He was.

＊

Bert – molested & raped – was molested & raped in all the ways a woman can molest & rape a man.

◎   Which – while not legion perhaps – are more ways than most of us can imagine until [if we are/or were/lucky enough to have been it] we've been it.

Sometime during the process of being pleasantly – although not gently – devirginized [and three times more just to be certain] Bert fell/had fallen/or thought he had fallen – but he hadn't/ not really/because lust can so easily be confused [until we've experienced the real thing] with love – in love with Trixie.

Trixie never – as far as she could remember – having devirginized a man before and not really liking any of the men she hadn't needed to/but liking to the point of 'very' the heady mix of Bert's naïvety & staying power/fell in lust /but definitely not in love [because she didn't have the intellectual capacity for that] with him in return.

Trixie lay on her back in a state-of-sate. But/alas/her pelvis called to her. It threatened the moment. She rolled onto her side and rummaged in her bag. She found what she wanted and snorted it. Bert – coming back from a pee – asked her what she was doing. She told him. She showed him what to do. He sneezed. It was a waste but there was plenty more. By early morning/as the dawn snuck in/he thought of neither the clavipectoral fascia nor the structures purported to pass through it. He was *un homme changé*.

If wedges can be said to have thin ends/and if slopes can be described as slippery [which I think they can] then-so-be-it. Bert's life was over the cusp of whatever-it-was that it had just come to the cusp of. Cocaine & Trixie's sundry/but always welcoming/*fenestrae corporis* came to dominate his life. It was with difficulty on his part – and surprise on his tutor's part – that he scraped his way through to second year.

But then things worsened. Trixie's pain could no longer find panacea from smokables & snortables. She needed something stronger. Of course she did.

$$$ being not a problem – apart from the root of all her problems – she found what she needed. $$$ being not a problem – apart from the root of all her problems – she found the means of administering it.

Being in lust – although not in love – Bert 'helped' her.

◎ 'Helped' being a relative term.

He tightened & released her tourniquets. He found her veins. He washed her syringes & replaced her needles. Being in lust

– but [see above] definitely not in love – she said he should try it. Being in lust [etc.] he did. The thin end of the wedge was no longer thin. The slope was slipperier. He bombed second year.

―
*

Hai left home. He knew not to leave home until he knew where he wanted to go. And where he wanted to go was anywhere other than where he was. And – as an extension to that philosophy – to anywhere that wasn't 'The People's Republic of China'.

◎ Have you noticed that any country that incorporates the word 'Democratic' in its title invariably isn't/and that any country that does the same with 'People's' is more likely to be a nasty little [or in the case of China 'a nasty big'] dictatorship?

Being able to count beans up to five/and well beyond/he knew to head east. 'The West' was where he wanted to be. To get to 'The West' he must go east.

◎ Life's full of stuff like that/isn't it?

Now – China is a big country – we know that and Hai knew that too. He knew he couldn't walk to 'The West'. He knew – because everybody did – about the restrictions on the free movement of 'The People' in 'The People's Republic'. He knew/too/also/and as well/that the rivers of China flowed – generally/by-and-large/ most of the time/and with few exceptions – in the direction of freedom/east. He knew that the Fen River wasn't a million miles from where he lived and that it flowed into the Huang and that the Huang flowed to the sea. He could cadge a lift to the Fen without trouble.

He collected his meagre possessions. He discarded most of them. He touched his mother/aunty/grandparents/friends for all the *rénminbi* they could spare [which wasn't a lot]. And then/ Dick Whittington-like/left home for 'sunnier [hopefully freer] climes'.

Stowing away on grain boats wasn't hard. A lot of his fellow itinerants did it. But it only got him part of the way to where he was headed. He needed a bit of south to add to his east. There was a map in his head and he was following it.

Many adventures befell him on his protracted road to freedom. Some were memorable and some were not. The most memorable – without a skerrick of a doubt – were the years/almost three/he spent in Zhengzhou. It was where he was befriended by an old lady – she was thirty – [ref. sister [twenty-three] p. 17.] – who took pity on his ragged clothes & sunken cheeks.

She was the widow of an air force test-pilot – a 'Hero of the Republic'. A 'hero' [even though he wasn't given the choice about being one] who'd ridden his experimental & woefully designed fighter-plane all the way from the borders of space to ten feet below the ground *and* without a smidgeon of radio-wave complaint. He possessed – so everyone said [because it seemed the appropriate thing to say at the time] 'The Right Stuff'.

His widow – on a larger pension than was usual & with no children of her own to care for – cared instead for Hai. [With 'cared instead' being a euphemism for 'took-him-to-her-bed']. And it was in 'the-bed-whence-she-took-him' that she – of course she did – 'took-her-pleasure' upon his person.

Hai was not – even before the 'cared instead' – without experience in these matters. He – as was only natural and as was to be expected [there aren't one and a half billion Chinese on the planet by chance] had taken his fair share of venereous pleasures with the young ladies of his village.

But this was different. This was a woman almost twice his age and she wasn't/not like the young ladies of his village/an inexperienced/behind the haystack/ten-minute wonder. She would – in the salons of Louis XIV – have made a more than passable courtesan. She knew – when it came to the pleasures of the flesh – how many beans made/or near enough not to matter/10^9.

She showed Hai things & the way of doing things that Hai never thought physically possible. She was a supple woman and he a supple boy. They needed to be.

And then she came to care for him/not just the physical him/ but the other him/the 'spiritual him'/the 'him' that lived within. She clothed him/fattened him & taught him many things. Only years later did he remember 'the one thing' – 'It is the superior part of us that shall survive'.

And then one day [one morning a bit after ten] for no particular or specific reason/but for a lot of general & non-specific reasons [because that's how it often happens] she fell in love with him. It was a sincere form of love and she'd never felt anything like it. Certainly not for her husband who [while being a 'Hero of the Republic' and a supposed possessor of 'The Right Stuff'] was – if-the-truth-be-known/as it *was* known to her – a self-obsessed little wanker.

So – she fell in love with Hai. It was the inner 'him'/the brain of him/that she fell for.

Hai's brain was a good brain and it wasn't surprising that she fell in love with it. When not making love [and it *was* love for her] they talked. They talked – of course they did – about the important things in life.

And in talking about those things Hai fell in love with her too.

◎ What is it about 'talking' and 'love'? Do deaf people fall in love? They must.

23

She was an English teacher before she met her husband/and Hai was an eager pupil. He knew that if he ever got to 'The West' he would need to know that strange & dysphonic/dysgrammatical & exception-ridden tongue. She taught him well.

Having fallen so serendipitously upon easy times/as well as in love/Hai thought seldom about travelling further east to 'The West'. He was happy where he was. He was with the woman he loved. He would be content there forever.

But then she contracted a particularly aggressive form of pancreatic cancer and was dead in three months.

Hai was desolate & desolated to the borders/and beyond the borders/of his sanity.

◎   And that is what happens when love is real.

⸻
*

Eli – firmly ensconced under Solomon's protective wing – learned many things. And as the years passed it became apparent to him that he was being groomed to be Solomon's number one/*numero-uno*/מפקד אחד on the outside. And that/when he eventually got there/was what he became.

There had been – over the years – a number of *numero-unos*. Changing them was never a problem. If Solomon wasn't happy with his current *numero-uno*/מפקד אחד – which happened occasionally – that מפקד אחד came to an often-unconventional end and usually at the hands of the replacement מפקד אחד.

With his exit from Ktz'iot – a happy/sad occasion – Eli went to work.

A newcomer – however much Solomon oiled the machinery for him to do so – was never going to replace the incumbent אחד מפקד without the backing of the-rank-&-file. So – it was the-rank-&-file Eli went to work on.

Innuendo can be a powerful tool. If linked to rumour/lying
& a well-placed *douceur de vivre*/שוחד/bribe/it can be an even
more powerful tool than that. And so it was that the מפקד אחד
of the time – a large & threatening [but unimaginative] man
from Acre – lost the support he needed and became/instead/an
integral part of the northern support buttress of the new bridge
over the Yarkon River.

There was – of course there was – house-cleaning to be done.
Houses don't clean themselves. A new broom needs to flex its/
his muscles – if only to show that it/he has them. Other large
& threatening [but unimaginative] men went the way of their
buttress-supporting colleague.

And so it transpired that 'lack of imagination' [rather than
'size & threatenability'] came to be a hindrance to longevity.

But why the need for house-cleaning? Was it just Eli flexing
his muscles?

No it wasn't/not quite. It was like this.

While more than happy to be taken under Solomon's protective
& instructional wing Eli felt there was potential for expansion.
Solomon was an 'ethical' [i.e. 'old-fashioned'] bad-guy and was
happy to limit his activities to the 'four Bs' – burglary [houses
of the wealthy of]/banks [given by God for the breaking into
of]/booze [the smuggling of] & brothels [babes/boobs & bums
for the fondling, etc. of]. He was happy/as the years went by/to
branch out into blackmail & bribery. But that was all.

But Eli – not being born under an excessively ethical star
– saw things differently. And so – without telling Solomon –
and after putting the fear of an angry Yahweh &/or concrete
sarcophagi into the hearts of any underling with ideas of his own
– he branched out into arms-dealing [supply and distribution
of]/people-smuggling [from anywhere to anywhere of] and
hiding things away [and 'things' meant 'anything'] that anyone
[and 'anyone' meant 'anyone'] wanted hidden away. So – all-in-

all/by-and-large/all-things-considered/looked-as-at-a-whole –
Eli was a bad man – but [as you will see] he could have been/
even a lot/worse.

Then came a terrible day for Solomon.

Without asking him if he might do so – a young & idealistic
lawyer in Tel Aviv decided to reopen the case that had sent him/
Solomon [for-the-term-of-his-natural-life] into the protective
arms of Ktz'iot.

It was a sad thing for Solomon that the 'young & idealistic
lawyer' found that/so many years before/the prosecuting
attorney – long dead & thus unaccountable – was guilty [without
needing to be] of massaging the evidence against him.

So – a miscarriage of justice had been done – not in reality
done – but with the appearance of having been done.

Solomon – to his horror – was released.

It may be said that/or even be that – in the whole of recorded
history – Solomon was the first [if not only] man ever to be
thrown kicking-&-screaming out of jail while loudly professing
his guilt.

∗

Noor drove to Cape Town. She hated the 'idea' of Cape Town. It
was/as she saw it/enemy territory. It was/as she saw it/an enclave
& bastion of Anglophonic and hubristic up-themselves-ish-
ness.

However much power was assumed/taken [more-often-
than-not grabbed] by 'her own people' [i.e. by the worthy –
relativity again – burghers of the Boer Republic] those *Engels
doos* in Cape Town – like they did all over the *fokking* world
– stayed smug in the knowledge of their own Anglican God and
thus their anointed supremacy over the rest of human-kind.

◎ And as Cecil Rhodes – with no suggestion of personal bias or irony – so poignantly put it: "To have been born English is to have come first in the lottery of life."

But she knew it was where she must go. She knew what she must do when she got there.

She stayed at the Mount Nelson Hotel. That *fokking mega-doos* Churchill once stayed there. It was deep inside enemy territory.

She went to the in-house beautician – an *Engels* woman – a woman with a long patrician nose. It was a nose designed to be 'looked down'. And having it to look down – and at the sight of Noor – she looked down it. Noor would/happily & without qualm/have axed her in the back of the head. But she needed to get through this ordeal. Retribution could & would come later – to all of them. It could wait.

Her eyebrows were plucked. The small hairs in her nose were removed. The rough and sun-hardened skin of her face was oiled/creamed & fussed about with. Ludicrous things were done to her fingernails & toes. The whole business was a violation of all that she was and of all that 'her people' [the 'children of the Voortrek' – the 'children-of-Blood River'] stood for. But she told herself – more than once – that it was a necessary first step along the path of 'steps-yet-to-come'.

She went next to the hair-salon. She showed the woman the picture she'd torn from last month's *Cleo*. Her hair was washed/conditioned & cut into the provocative & lopsided [because 'lopsided' she'd decided was sexy] shape she wanted. Then it was [lopsidedly] tinted. She sat in front of the mirror. She looked at herself. She looked ridiculous but [especially with the 'lopsided'] sexy.

She visited up-market dress shops. She tried on farcical things. It was her first time in a dress. She owned nothing but jeans. She was a girl of the veldt. And girls from the veldt didn't waste money on dresses/knickers & bras. Those things were for *die Engelse vroue doos.*

Wearing jeans was what she was used to. But trying on the dresses – she couldn't work out why – did something to her. It sent blood to unanticipated places.

After visiting the 'up-market dress shops' she took a cab to a sleazy part of town. She visited a shop with XXX on the door. She bought an eye wateringly large black thing. Batteries were included.

She got back to the hotel and tried on the dresses. She laughed at herself in the mirror. She then went to the bathroom and shaved her armpits and then/carefully/very carefully/ elsewhere. The man she was after would be excited by that. A shaved 'elsewhere' would – though she couldn't understand why – send a message to 'the man she was after'.

Then she went to her bag. She took out the eye-wateringly large black thing. She clicked the switch to 'ON'.

‾
*
‾

Bert – besotted & bewildered though he was – first by Trixie's imaginative & insatiable desire for sex-while-stoned and second by the cornucopia of smokables/snortables & injectables – was smart enough to see that this wasn't going to last.

While aware that Trixie's endless supply of paternal/guilt-induced $$$ was showing no sign of abatement – he could see that [with the way she was going] Trixie's vital spark was well on its way to being permanently 'snuffed-out'/'cut-off'/'extinguished' & [in every other way] abated.

And – with the certain/certain-ish knowledge of that – he came to the realisation that/with Trixie's inevitable passing/the $$$ would inevitably pass too. And 'then' what was he to do?

So – in light of the above – Bert decided that/instead of buying all the things they bought from the seedy-little-men-in-Kings Cross/he would become a seedy-little-man-in-Kings Cross himself. Instead of buying he would sell. So – that's what he did.

Another thing he did was 'stop using'. That sounds easy/isn't/ but he managed. He came to know how frozen a turkey could get and was never going to go through the misery of defrosting one again.

He was – as you know – smarter than the other seedy-little-men and/because of that/he soon became a seedy-middle-sized-man.

It was at about that time that – having got the dilutions semi-purposefully wrong – he injected Trixie's/increasingly difficult to find/median cubital vein. He watched her with both regret & relief as she died. He was sad [in an academic sort of way] but knew it would happen sometime. And now was/wasn't it [the justification took an hour or two to-get-his-head-around] as-good-a-time-as-any?

This abrupt curtailment of his sex life gave Bert new resolve to climb higher up the distributional tree. Which he did. He reached the top.

As he climbed he gathered 'friends' around him – some to distribute his wares/some to enforce his wishes and others/ always 'beautiful' & always enhanced/to fill in [so-to-speak] for Trixie. He gathered enemies too.

It was late one evening when he received a call from his *numero due*. The last of his enemies was/at that very moment/ providing dinner for the sharks off Ulladulla.

The view from the top of the tree was a pleasing one.

✳

Hai – saddened to the edge of his sanity/but enriched to the edge of credulity by all she'd bequeathed him – found once more his desire to be free. He resumed his voyage east-to-West/with a lurch or two to the south. Only his moral compass knew north.

Further adventures befell him. None of them worth mentioning here.

He arrived – after many weeks [by road/river & canal] in Shenzhen. He was almost there. But 'almost' only counts in horseshoes.

He walked the road to the border crossing. Freedom lay so near. He could almost smell it.

Private MacPherson was on outside-duty that day. He was a Queen's Own Cameron Highlander. This – Kowloon – was his first posting away from home.

He & his brother had once considered a trip to France to pick up cheap booze. They couldn't believe that Glenmorangie was cheaper in Calais than it was in Inverness. But – thanks to the low-church intricacies of British 'Customs & Excise' law – it was. And it was only the death of Uncle Fergus/and their mandatory attendance at his wake/that had prevented them from going.

Private MacPherson didn't like outside-duty. Neither did the others in his squad. There was no reason for it. Why must there be someone outside the gate to 'meet 'n greet' the endless stream of/soon to be disappointed/hopefuls? It was just another one of Captain Campbell's stupid fucking notions. Some nonsense about being kind to the 'slanties'. Why couldn't they just stay behind the razor wire and tell them all to piss-off from back there? And why – it was probably one of fat bastard RSM Findlay's ideas – did outside-duty need to be done in full ceremonials?

Private MacPherson was from the Highlands but had never felt comfortable/not like his father did/in a kilt.

In addition to all of that – he was in receipt [just yesterday] of a 'dear John' letter from Elsie/his girlfriend. It said she was going to marry 'Four Eyes Fergusson' from the post office.

Because of that – and with Private Macalister & Lance Corporal MacDougal in attendance/assistance – he'd got himself slobberingly & tearfully drunk. He had a fearful hangover.

And so – when early on in his outside stint/and as a tall/thin [remarkable of both] young man approached him/he was able [with all the vituperation born of a pounding head and his country's native xenophobia] – and in the knowledge that he wouldn't be understood anyway – to say – "Why don't you just fuck off back to where you came from, you skinny Chink cunt."

It came as a surprise then – not surprisingly – when the 'skinny Chink cunt' replied – "Fuck off back to where *you* came from, you fat pansy cunt in a skirt." It was turning out to be a bad day for Private MacPherson.

He watched the tall/thin [remarkable of both] young man run away down the road/and for a passing moment considered chasing him. But given the young man's more than expected turn of speed/and in the knowledge that his head might explode at any moment/he decided not to. Then/for a further moment/ he considered unshouldering his weapon and shooting the 'skinny Chink cunt' in the back. But something from behind his left shoulder [where a variety of things of an internal nature come from] whispered to him that that might not be such a good idea. He didn't want to turn 'one of the worst days of his life' into 'the worst day of his life'. And so – like many men before him – literature is literally littered with them – sick & discarded/ insulted & humiliated – he did nothing. But not quite nothing. He walked to the side of the road and vomited into the gutter.

RSM Findlay – watching the unfolding of events from the guardhouse – opened his notebook and put Private MacPherson on a charge.

Hai – looking back over his shoulder and seeing the 'fat pansy cunt in a skirt' neither chasing him nor unshouldering his weapon – slowed to a walking pace. He walked back to Shenzhen. He sat on a bench in a park. He was so-near-yet-so-far. What was he going to do? There was no intention – never was/wasn't now/never would be – of 'fucking off back to where he came from'. He sat & he pondered.

⁎

It was a difficult time for both of them. For Eli – because his status as 'numero-uno/מַסְפַּר אֶחָד on the outside' was now elevated/in his mind at least/to the status of 'el supremo everywhere'. And for Solomon – because he was 'away'/ רַחַק for so long and knew no one/not anymore/on the outside. He didn't understand – how could he – the changed & changing nature of the business he was now but the titular head of.

To say that Solomon & Eli no longer saw-eye-to-eye was an understatement of previously mentioned proportion.

The only solution to the impasse [as far as Solomon could see] was to have his once trusted/but no longer trusted/acolyte removed – in a permanent way – from his position of power.

The only solution to the impasse [as far as Eli could see] was to have his recently/but not that recently/revered patron removed – in a permanent way – from meddling-in-affairs-he-didn't-understand.

Eli – being young & energetic/and with the-rank-&-file behind him – got to matters first and Solomon became memorialised – if not immortalised – beneath the basement car park of a new supermarket in Tel Aviv.

Now free from restraints [real &/or perceived] Eli unfurled his wings and – of course he did – took flight. He became a renaissance crook. He became the Leonardo of the underworld.

The underworld – if not the world – was his oyster/and he its pearl. He was having a wonderful time. He was loving it.

It was for the renaissance-ish-ness of his talents that he was known to a man called John. And John [as you may remember] was the oldest-&-closest-friend of a man called John.

*

Noor – recovered [thanks partly to an hour or so with the eye wateringly large black thing] from the violation & tarting about of her body – went out. She took a taxi to a club. A club well enough known to get a mention/more than one mention/several mentions/in *The Cape Times*.

The Cape Times was the only thing with more words than pictures [mostly pictures of naked men doing predictably pedestrian things to-&-with naked women] that her father brought home from the store. She'd read – because/as well as being a voracious killer/she was a voracious reader – every word about everybody who frequented/with any degree of frequency/a club called [somewhat unimaginatively] *Le Club*.

She'd poured kerosene on a pile of *Cape Times* to get the house fire started.

Le Club – she remembered – was described as being 'the place where the literati meets the cognoscenti'. It was 'the home of those on the way up'. It was where – as was decided some time ago – she would start. It was where – as was decided some time ago – she would meet the man she intended to.

She was only a member of the 'literati' if that meant she'd once read all twelve volumes of the 1911 Encyclopaedia Britannica. Her great-grandfather having bought them – while drunk/which he was for much/if not most/of the time – at auction in the '20s. So her knowledge of the world was indeed encyclopaedic [if a little out of date]. She was only a member of

33

the 'cognoscenti' when looked at from the perspective of those who read [as she did] *Guns 'n Ammo*. But 'upwardly mobile' was what she had every intention of becoming.

The door of *Le Club* was held open for her by a man/a white man – *om Christus wil* – in a cap with a badge & a coat with epaulettes [see above/it's universal] of scrambled egg.

Noor couldn't understand why a white man [quite a reasonable-looking white man] would be happy – which he seemed to be – to be doing kaffir's work.

She looked around and selected a table near the dance floor. She ordered a dry martini and then another one. It was as the third was being placed before her that she became aware of someone watching her. She knew not whom and she knew not from whence/but she hoped by whom and from whence.

She was a tall-to-tallish woman [so not remarkably] but taller than most of the women in her neighbouring *dorp*. She possessed 'good bone structure' [whatever that may be] too. And – though she wasn't beautiful in any classical sense – she knew she was 'handsome enough'. She knew those things – the height/the 'good bone structure' & the being 'handsome enough' – were why she'd managed to screw/bonk/hump &-so-on – and be screwed/bonked/humped &-so-on-ed – by more guys than any of her friends. She knew – she was a fast learner/as well as imaginative – how to make guys [and that included her maths teacher] grunt in a variety of keys.

The band started up and played middle-of-the-road stuff. Couples got up to dance. She watched the band play & the dancers dance. It was more wiggling around than dancing. She could do that. She'd attended her fair share of *Jongboere-vergaderings*.

After the fourth martini/a visit to the loo/& in the knowledge that she was still being watched – she decided to dance on her own. Which she did.

Now – a tall(ish)/'good bone structured'/'handsome enough'/apparently lithe enough/fulsome & free moving bosomed enough/lopsidedly & sexily coiffured enough/sexily dressed enough [and especially one 'dancing-on-her-own'] woman is like honey to a bee. Trust me.

And so it was. And the bee who got to her first [and the bee she was hoping would get to her first] was a bee called – you're way out ahead of me – Tim Gatting.

She'd danced close enough to his table – as well as seductively enough to several of his *supratentorial ganglia* – to ensure that it was.

---

*

Oldest-&-closest-friend John made a call. It was an overseas call to prefix 972. The man who answered spoke no-English. He then spoke to a man who spoke poor-English. He then spoke to a man who spoke neither no-nor poor-. He spoke to a man who spoke fluent or [championing the lost cause of the adverb] 'fluently'. Friend John told the man who spoke fluent/fluently – a man who was the only man to be conceived in Dachau concentration camp/and the 'first-and-only' man [even though he wasn't much more than a boy at the time] to screw the daughter of the Mayor of Nazareth/who had [perhaps because of that] gone on to become the 'virago's-virago-from-hell' &/or [it depends on how you look at it] the 'feminist's-feminist-from-heaven' [relativity again] – exactly what he wanted.

They talked preliminaries/generalities/specifics & money. A price was discussed. A price was agreed. Money was transferred. A place was agreed. It was a long way away.

Friend John put down the phone. He spoke to the 6th Earl. He was satisfied. They both were.

Eli Rubenstein put down the phone. He was satisfied too.

Hai sat on the bench. It was in the park in Shenzhen. It was where we left him. A man watched him. The man walked towards him. The man sat down next to him. The man talked to him. Hai talked to the man. They talked for an hour.

Money changed hands. The man left. Hai lay on the bench. He slept until the man woke him. It was dark. They left town. They walked by narrow ways. They walked into surrounding hills. Hai could see a fence. It was high. It was electric. There were towers & lights. The man walked through bushes. Hai followed him. They came to a hole in the ground. They climbed down a ladder. They were in a tunnel. The air was stale. There was an aroma. It was the aroma of freedom.

At the end of the tunnel – it was a long tunnel – was another ladder/another hole/more bushes. Instructions were given. Directions were given. Money changed hands. It was over. He was there. He was free.

He came to a road. He walked along it. It was in the Crown Colony of Hong Kong.

What – he thought – would 'the fat pansy cunt in a skirt' have to say about that?

But [with the fetid stench of tyranny behind him/and a new life of freedom unrolling before him] he didn't give a toss/not in any practical sense/what 'the fat pansy cunt in a skirt' might have to say about that.

*

Bert was faced with/confronted by/a problem. It posed a conundrum. There was half-of-half-a-ton-of-Afghan-best. It was hidden away where no one could find it [where he hoped no one could find it] but somewhere where he knew it *would* be found 'someday'. He knew not when that 'someday' might come. But he knew that – when that 'someday' did come – all-hell-would-break-loose & all-sorts-of-things would hit-all-sorts-of-fans.

And after hell-and-all-sorts-of-things [etc.] were finished doing their respective things he would be considerably out of face/pocket & [just possibly/more worryingly] liberty.

There were two other men/other than himself/who knew [or had known] where it was and they were now – happily for Bert/ but not so much for them – under the plinth of the new War Memorial in Dubbo. But that wasn't enough to keep 'someday' at bay forever.

So – the conundrum was this. How was he going to access his half-of-half-a-ton [which he didn't need to yet/but would do sooner-or-later] without letting someone else in on the secret? There was a limit to the number of new War Memorials required.

Would he be able to retrieve it on his own? It weighed half-of-half-a-ton for-fuck's-sake. And if he did – should he do it all in one go or bit by bit? He didn't want to flood the market & bring the prices down.

He sat looking out over Sydney Harbour – the most beautiful harbour/perhaps the most beautiful place [trust me] in the-whole-wide-world. But its beauty upon-him-registered-not. The view from the top of the tree wasn't quite what it was. He sat deep in thought.

$$*$$

Eli was purring. His whole life was where & what he'd ever wanted it to be. He was a happy man.

He was an even happier man when – after the not particularly sad demise & concretisation of Solomon – he found himself to be the sole beneficiary [the heir] of the Last Will & Testament [because he'd never got round/although he was planning to/ to changing it] of his not overly/or even particularly/mourned mentor.

As well as a number of other things – and for reasons he couldn't fathom – he was now the proud/but not particularly proud/owner of an island in the Calvados Chain off the tail of New Guinea.

"*Food-for-thought*," he thought.

*

Not far from the R514 on the shores of the Hartbeespoort and not far from Pretoria lies the Pelindaba Nuclear Facility. Commissioned in the late '50s – it was there for a solitary & singular purpose – it was there for the production of stuff to make atomic bombs from.

Pelindaba [& thus South Africa] was – hard to believe/ because Jews & Boers share no natural affinity – in cahoots with Israel.

Israel sent them stuff called tritium [just water but heavy] and in return/because Israel doesn't give away anything for free – unless you stray into their air-space – stuff called U-235 came [or went] the other way.

And so it was that Pelindaba begat an unfashionably fissionable material called Pu-239 [weapons-grade plutonium] and sent it a few miles down the road to Kentron where – indeed – six-and-a-bit atomic bombs were concocted from the stuff they were sent.

No one outside South Africa – and not a whole lot of people inside it – knew what was going on.

Not – that is – until a Russian spy satellite wandered its way overhead and saw what was going on.

The Russians – treacherous schoolboys – dobbed them in to the Yanks [Mr Bush Sr] who must have gone ballistic.

◎　A poor choice of metaphor/for which I apologise.

Mr F W de Klerk – I imagine/and can't think why he wouldn't have – must have received a terser note than usual. But – being [although increasingly reluctantly] the protagonist of Apartheid and constantly receiving terse notes from everyone – it might not have disconcerted him as much as it would have/say/you or me.

But because of the/presumed/increase in terseness from Mr Bush [and because Mr Bush was as close to an ally as he & his country was ever likely to get/and after the stuff that hits fans had settled] all six bombs were decommissioned.

But that is of no interest to us – because what is of interest to us is the 'bit' of the 'six-and-a-bit'.

What happened to it?

I'll tell you… later.

☰
*

Hai – as to be expected – made his way to Victoria Island [the real Hong Kong]. He thrived there. His smartness/his height & his comely disposition helped.

In Hong Kong – the home of short guys – being as tall as Hai was made him stand out. Standing out made him noticed. Being noticed was what he wanted. What he wanted was to be wealthy/famous & good.

But getting to be 'wealthy/famous & good' would require sacrifices – mostly moral ones. Mostly ones at the 'good' end of the moral spectrum.

To become wealthy/famous & good he needed to work for wealthy & famous men – none of whom [as far as Hai could see] were good. But he – his memories of the woman he loved held like a banner before him – managed. She kept his moral compass pointing north.

But then one day that all changed. He was working – temporary work/replacing a sick servant work/sent upstairs to do 'servant's work' type work – for a Mr Woo. He was cleaning behind a partition. He was overhearing things he didn't want to.

◎   How come we didn't evolve 'earlids' like we did eyelids?

Mr Woo was talking to a man. Hai couldn't see/or be seen. He stood still & stiff & silent. He didn't want to listen. He didn't have a choice. He didn't want to hear what he was hearing. He didn't have a choice. He didn't want to know what he now knew. He didn't have a choice. He didn't want to be heard hearing what he was hearing or knowing what he now knew. Being heard/while he heard what he heard and now knew/would be the end of him.

He slept poorly that night. In the early morning – in that strange place between asleep & awake – his lover spoke to him. She said things to him/things he knew were true/and [in the knowing that they were true] he knew what he must do.

The next day he worked hard. He did more than any servant could ever do. For a week he did as much as any servant in the history of servants & servanting ever did.

At the end of the second week his predecessor/now recovered/was relocated to the kitchens and Hai was one step further along the path to the Celestial City of Goodness.

To *be* good was to *do* good. To *do* good was to destroy bad. It was simple/mostly/and it was good.

‗*‗

Noor – never being exposed to decorum of any sort/and never being initiated into the conventions of 'polite' society/or being reared to [and in consequence subjected to] the arbitrary constraints of a world where the word 'proper' held sway – and [because of 'all-of-the-above'] was unaware that to do more than

40

kiss on first meetings was to be seen as/labelled as & considered to be a loose woman.

So – in the lack of that knowledge – she invited Tim back to the Mount Nelson for a nightcap.

Tim – being exposed to decorum all his life/as well as being initiated into the conventions of a 'polite' society/and reared in [and in consequence constrained by] a world where the word 'proper' held sway – and being totally aware that for a woman to do more than kiss on first meetings was for her to be seen as/labelled as & considered to be a loose woman – knew that Noor was just/maybe/ and perhaps/the sort of woman he'd been looking for all his life.

He'd slept around a bit – of course he had. He was a young & handsome man and a highly thought of sportsman. He was a wonderful tennis player. He was a wonderful lawyer. There was a near-certain ascent to 'silk' & judicial appointments before him. He was every young woman's/every prospective mother-in-law's/perfect catch & match.

But all of that didn't – and none of that did – sit comfortably with his 'inner man' [the man/woman we all have hiding somewhere down inside us].

Inside him was another man – not a worse man/not a better man/just a different man. This man was a man who no longer wished to live his life constrained by all things decorous/polite & proper. He wanted to 'live' and Noor's offer of a euphemistic nightcap/together with [in the back of the taxi] the tongue she stuck halfway down his throat/suggested to him/most strongly/ that his life was about to change. And how?

They entered her room. She said she needed the bathroom. Needing it/she disappeared into it. Tim – admiring the view from the balcony – heard her return. He turned to admire the view – even more – of an approaching & charmingly dressed [in nothing whatsoever] Noor.

She poured two large – very large – vodkas. She handed him one. He couldn't remember being handed vodka – very large or otherwise – by a woman so charmingly dressed.

She pushed him firmly/rather than gently – Noor wasn't much good at 'gentle' – into an armchair. She sat opposite. She sat in a provocative pose.

They sipped from their glasses. She stared at his face. He didn't at hers.

He wasn't accustomed [probably because he never had been] to being undressed by a woman – naked or otherwise – and [probably because of the 'naked' rather than the 'otherwise'] he enjoyed the experience a lot/quite-a-bit/immensely. He then enjoyed being pushed – firmly rather than gently – onto the bed. He then enjoyed – whatever it is that's more than immensely – having her stimulate to-the-max his *amygdala* [and all the other things that needed to be stimulated so that she could 'stimulate to-the-max his *amygdala*'].

And – as was to be expected – after stimulating him to-the-max – she annexed certain parts to certain parts. And those parts were the parts we were [unless we are irretrievably & irredeemably naïve] expecting her to.

It was a memorable night for Tim.

Noor – happy with how things were going so far/but in the knowledge that there was still a way to go yet – put [but only in metaphor] her best foot forward. She knew that this was her big chance/perhaps her one big chance/perhaps her one-and-only big chance/to get where she wanted.

In the knowledge of that – she unleashed her talents – lascivious & lubricious/lusty & licentious/lecherous & lewd [which were legion] upon him.

They were talents gained – partly from talking to her friends/ partly from the porno magazines her father kept in the bottom draw of his dresser/partly from humping every boy in her class as well as the maths teacher and partly [but you don't know about this yet] from humping/and thus being humped by/a goat.

Tim – by dawn – sated & satisfied/lay on his back. He 'pondered life's uncertain passage'. It was pleasant pondering.

Not much of the world's pondering is pondered in pleasant ways – but Tim's pondering was an exception.

He pondered what might happen when Noor awoke. Would it be more of the same? He didn't know. Would she/when she awoke [recovered from the libido stimulating effects of four dry martinis and a large/very large/vodka] shed tears of remorse? He didn't know. He hoped not. In the 'hoping of not' he thought he should find out.

Noor lay supine & sleeping beside him. He could hear the purr of her breath. It was in contrast to her night of snorting & epithets.

He looked at her breasts – they were like Goldilocks'/neither too small/nor too big/but just right. Caressing them [etc.] he knew – from a long night's experience – was fun. It was more fun when she moaned/which she did when he did.

His previous girlfriends – reared to be 'young-ladies' – moaned seldom. Some of them/quite a lot of them/perhaps even most of them/never did. But with Noor [whose threshold for moaning/as well as epithets/seemed low] the things he did/the things he was encouraged to do/the things he was asked to do as well as the things she did in return/as well as all the moaning [etc.] were the things that had made that most memorable of nights so memorable.

Her breasts glistened in the bedside light. They called to him like sirens. But they were to be disappointed. There was the clarion-call from other parts.

He lifted the sheet that lay sprawled/in Abstract Expressionist fashion/across her belly. He made a decision – it was an easy decision to make – to reacquaint himself with the mother of all anatomies.

Noor woke to pleasing memories of the night. She woke to a sensation more pleasing than that.

It was Saturday and for neither of them – certainly not for Noor – was there anything more pressing or better to do. They 'PLEASE DO NOT DISTURB'ed the door handle and stayed in bed for the rest of the morning. 'The rest of the morning' became the rest of the day. 'The rest of the day' became the rest of the weekend.

By Monday morning Tim thought he might be in love.

By Monday morning Noor hoped he might be thinking that.

—
*

Hai – without needing to ingratiate himself to Mr Woo – did just that.

His lost love – in parallel with her loving and teaching him English – had taught him witticisms from English history. He remembered them/how could he not?

Things like – "Sir, you will either die on the gallows or of the pox." To which had come the reply, "Sir, that will depend upon whether I embrace your principles or your mistress."

Things like – "The honourable gentleman is a modest man. He has much to be modest about."

Things like – "The honourable gentleman is a sheep in sheep's clothing."

Things like – "Everyone likes flattery, but when it comes to royalty, lay it on with a trowel."

It was that last aphorism that came to mind now and with Mr Woo there was no limit to the size of Hai's trowel.

He fawned/he scraped/he adulated & admired. All in High Mandarin – another of his lover's teachings.

Mr Woo – he could tell – was a mongrel from Canton. He knew that [while giving the outward appearance of dispassionate calm] his boss would make note of & perhaps be impressed by

Hai's eloquent tongue. Which indeed – without showing that he was – he was.

Hai went out of his way to be informed. He read widely of Hong Kong/Chinese & world affairs.

He dropped small [but poignant] snippets of information into the short conversations he had with his monosyllabic boss.

He rose – slowly at first and then more rapidly – through the hierarchy that surrounded his decreasingly laconic master.

He became in succession and then all of them together/ Groom of the Wardrobe/*domus providentiae*/*domus magnificentiae* & [finally] Lord Privy Seal.

He never expected to lose sight of the Beacon-on-the-Hill but somehow – somewhere between the Wardrobe & the Seal – he did.

$$\overline{\underset{*}{}}$$

The 6th Earl – used to the comforts of Belgravia & Mayfair – took longer to settle into his new surroundings & diminished state-of-being than most of us would. He was [and why wouldn't he be] happy for Friend John to arrange the continuance of his unfettered existence/but he missed the things he'd taken for granted since childhood.

His G^3 grandfather had been responsible for one of the great [perhaps greatest] cock-ups in all of British military history [i.e. when he'd ordered a whole lot of light English guys on light English horses to charge a whole lot of heavy Russian guys sporting heavier Russian cannon]. And because the only way to hush up a FUBAR of that magnitude was to claim it as a great victory and thus/& obviously [because it was such an outstanding 'victory'] to decorate the FUBAR's author [the author of such a 'glorious' event].

By tradition – and the Brits love tradition – the greater the FUBAR – and it was indeed one of epic/even poetic/proportion – the greater the decoration.

It was in that way that G³ grandfather became the First Earl of Somewhere-or-other and his descendants – right down to Descendent John the 6th – became/continued to be [because lack of cerebro-synaptic function was their family's *sine qua non*] a pack of arrogant & talentless pricks.

So – in the knowledge of his lack of cerebral-wherewithals – it might be offered as some sort of a mitigatory defence that the 6th Earl had little or no option but to be a talentless prick. But that did not/however/excuse the arrogance of the prickishnesh that was hard-wired into him/his father/his grandfather [etc.] all the way back to the first arrogant prick and that fateful day on the Heights of Wherever-it-was.

It was ever thus.

So – he was finding it hard to adjust – especially when having to 'do' for himself.

He'd never needed to 'do' for himself before because there was always someone around to 'do' the things that needed doing. And even in the knowledge that the alternative – to sit in Wandsworth with an Afro-Caribbean smack-dealer as cell mate/as well as being buggered up the Khyber [because there was no way of avoiding the communal showers] by nasty big men with tattoos and an unreasonable chip-on-their-shoulders about the English class system – was several orders-of-magnitude worse than where he now found himself – he still harboured feelings of indignation [bathed in self-pity] at his present & humbled circumstance.

He was not – as you can guess from the 'battering to death' – by either nature/inclination or training – a good man. He was a-country-mile from being one of those. But no man [not even the arsehole who stole my bike last week] is a fully/totally and in every way evil man [a man with no scintilla of goodness within them]. And so it was with the 6th Earl.

His 'scintilla of goodness' hid below – quite a long way below. It hid somewhere between his *nucleus habenular* &

nucleus emboliformis. There wasn't [as neuroanatomists among you will surely know] a lot of room for it/but it was sufficiently small for there to be only minimal crowding.

Stamped across the front of the scintilla – in Calibri 8 because [see above] there wasn't a lot of room for it – were the words:

'Acceptance of Fate'.

And that is what the 6th Earl did – he accepted his lot. And even as he railed against the dire chance/cruel fate & general cock-up of life/his life [e.g. having the dinghy he was given overturn in the surf on first outing] he accepted that his present circumstances were the almost ['almost' because for a short while he thought he might get away with it] certain result of picking up the iron bar in the first place.

As he sat – alone/disconsolate/but free – on the beach of an island [an island in the Calvados Chain off the tail of New Guinea] he felt/without knowing it/the same as Dreyfus did after they dumped him on Devil's Island.

At last alone – and in the knowledge that his next food drop would be in six months' time – he stood up & stripped off down to his 'smalls'. He wished not to damage any further his really-in-need-of-a-good-dry-clean-and-press Savile Row suit pants – the jacket/double-breasted & double-vented – being left [see above] at the scene of the crime.

He removed & folded the neck-grimed shirt from 'Hawes & Curtis of Jermyn Street'. He didn't know [and would have been surprised to learn] that neither article of apparel was ever to grace his body again.

He commenced – because there was no choice in the matter – the task of carrying the mountain of crates & sacks of this-that-and-the-other/the mountain of things Friend John had arranged for him/up to the protection of the palm trees.

After erecting – with difficulty/because he wasn't cut out for doing things like that – his one-man no-brainer tent/he removed his 'smalls'/swam in the evening sea and decided/because there were no reasons of propriety for him to do so/or not to do so/not to put [double-negatives confuse me too] them back on again. He didn't know – and would be surprised to learn – that these articles of apparel were never to grace his body again.

He found with some difficulty – because they were under all the sacks of rice/boxes of dry spaghetti/crates of baked-beans/ravioli-in-tomato-sauce/canned tuna/corned-beef and Fray Bentos steak-and-kidney pies/the cases of Chivas Regal his oldest-&-closest-friend – God bless him from here to eternity – didn't forget to include.

He opened a bottle. He sat on the trunk of a fallen tree. He drank. But that's not quite right/because he didn't [not in the way you or I would think to] 'drink'. He gulped. He sat gulping as the sun rushed down to the sea. It was the equator. The sunset went out like a light. There was no green flash. There never is.

He stumbled to his tent/gulped a last gulp/and experienced the most uncomfortable night of his life. Then – just as the dawn came – so did the sand flies. He was a long way from Belgravia.

*

Bert was worried [mega-worried] about what to do with his half-of-half-a-ton-of-Afghan-best. He thought-to-the-max about what to do with it. He'd heard rumours of men/a man/'the man'/who might help him. He made discrete enquiries.

With bilateral discretion assured – he rang a man in a country with prefix 972. He talked to a man with no English. He talked to a man with poor English. He talked to a man with neither-no-nor-poor. The man-with-neither spoke fluent or [see above] 'fluently'. There was a slight accent that was difficult to pick/but – with the prefix 972 – Bert guessed [it wasn't/I guess/

48

that difficult a guess to guess] that the man he was talking to strode the hills of Jesus.

They talked preliminaries/generalities/specifics & money. A price was agreed. Money was transferred.

In the fullness of time – which wasn't a long time – a dilapidated barn some miles from the almost-but-not-quite-ghost-town of Manangatang and just down the road from the full-nine-yards-ghost-towns of Chillingollah & Chinkapook was visited and the floor dug up. Half-of-half-a-ton-of-Afghan-best was transferred to a truck/from the truck to a boat/and from the boat to – you guessed it – an island in the Calvados Chain off the tail of New Guinea. Where else?

*

Eli was seldom worried – and to say that he was worried now would be an overstatement. There was little for him to worry about. He had all the things he'd ever wanted. He was everything he'd ever hoped to become. He was powerful & respected [perhaps feared more than respected] & wealthy. His secret was [and always had been] to stay 'hands-on'. It was *his* organisation now. Decisions were made by *him*. Things that needed doing were done by *him*. He didn't deal through middle-men – not like Solomon had. They wanted 'him' so that's what he gave them.

"Always give the customer what they want." He would apply the same philosophy to selling fruit or cutting hair. He was a market-place-man at heart. It was/almost certainly/in the blood.

So – it wasn't a worry – it was a problem/and the problem was this. There were two things to hide but only one island to hide them on. They were both things needing an island to be hidden on/and somewhere that wasn't an island would never do. But that wasn't the real problem because two 'treasures' hidden on the same island wouldn't/not normally/be a problem. But the 'wouldn't/not normally' didn't apply in this case because one of 'the treasures' was a walking/talking & cognisant Peer of the Realm.

It would be easy to bury the half-of-half-a-ton on the island with the Peer of the Realm's corpse lying beside it – but that wasn't how his business worked. That wouldn't be 'Always give the customer what they want' – or anywhere near it. He was a-fair-trader and that was what/largely/had helped him get where he was.

Mr John [he preferred not to deal in surnames] was a man of wealth & influence – largely gained from 'knowing where the bodies were buried' – and was the oldest-&-closest-friend of the-Peer-in-question and he/Eli & Mr John had a deal. Any suggestion that he/Eli might/in some way/nefarious or otherwise/precipitate the premature demise of the Peer would send ripples [if not waves] of discontent through the ranks of current & prospective customers. It was not the way to do business.

So – that was the problem. How was he to get Mr Bert's half-of-half-a-ton-of-Afghan-best onto & buried into the/his island? How was he going to do it with the Peer of the Realm roaming around it?

But it was a problem that [like most problems] had a solution.

Noor knew she was on-a-winner. She knew the traps of being-around-the-traps [admittedly rural/Afrikaans and thus far from sophisticated traps] enough to know when a man's 'hots' were becoming more than just hot.

She was used to this. It was what happened with boys at school. It was what happened with a few/more than a few/quite a lot/ of the town boys. It was what happened with the maths teacher. Almost unbelievably – it was what happened with the goat.

She'd enjoyed screwing the maths teacher – not because he was anything special because he wasn't – but because letting him screw her and then telling her friends about it was fun.

And after letting him screw her for most of third term [thus getting the best grades anyone was ever going to believe] he declared his eternal love for her. But that was far from being right because – after she told him to 'Fuck off and take your piss weak dick with you' – he drove out onto the veldt and shot himself. So much for eternity.

She knew it would be different with this Gatting character. She knew she needed to play-hard-to-get. She knew that sticking her tits in his face [much as she now knew he liked that] wasn't going to get her to where she wanted to be. And where she 'wanted to be' was – for sure – with her tits in his face [because he was a better lover/which wasn't that difficult/than anyone before him] – but with her tits in his face *and* a ring on the appropriate finger of her left hand.

So – when he rang on Monday and asked her to dinner – she said 'No'/not even 'Sorry, no'. She said 'No' on Tuesday & Wednesday too. Come Thursday – she said she might be able to fit him in [so to speak] on Friday.

She – being a strategist as well as a good lay – wanted to work on him for the whole weekend. It was the same the week after that and the week after that.

But – 'full' as Noor's weekends now were – she wasn't wasting her celibate 'Mon-thru-Fri'. There were daily elocution lessons and spending time in the library. She was doing a crash course in how to change from a *jong dame van die land di veldt* into a 'lady'. A 'lady' that Gatting's parents – they were the next hurdle – would approve of/or not *disapprove* of. It was hard work but she was – with difficulty – shedding the guttural Rs. She was improving – as was her knowledge of all things *Engels*.

Tim – never having been in love before and only reading about what it would feel like when he was – and in the only recently realised realisation that John Donne was a twerp but that Lord Byron wasn't – was sure that he was. And that was a shame –

51

because he wasn't. But the way he felt when he thought he was/ but wasn't/was almost – but not really/not quite – as good as the feeling of being truly in love.

◎ That – or so I'm told/or so I'm led to believe/but don't believe/and neither do you [do you?] – can happen.

Not quite being in love/but thinking that he might be – but not being sure because without being in love before it was impossible for him to be sure that he was/or that he wasn't – was more than a little confusing.

Love – as we all know/because we get told often enough – can be 'a very splendid thing' – but it can be a complicated & confusing business too. And so it turned out to be for Tim.

But not for all of Tim – because the Tim who lay on the surface/the Tim who suspected that he might be [and on occasions convinced himself 'beyond-reasonable-doubt' that he was] in love/was [without knowing it] in conflict with a deep-down Tim. A Tim from the dark places/places where the knowledge of what makes love lives. This Tim was a Tim who knew – with a certainty more certain than the-surface-Tim's certainty that he was – that he wasn't.

So – with the-surface-Tim/rather than the-deep-down-Tim/in charge/and after a month-or-two of spectacularly unconventional sex – Noor was invited to meet the Gattings. She was moving along nicely. She was ahead of schedule.

$$\overline{*}$$

Hai – wishing to become/trying to become/and then becoming indispensable to Mr Woo – became two thirds of what he'd vowed his dying lover [he kept a small bag of her ashes around his neck] he would.

He was now 'wealthy' & – within a small fraternity of 'not-particularly-pleasant-men' [an understatement of some magnitude] – 'famous'. With the HKPD in general – and with Inspector Fang of the HKPD in particular – he was 'infamous'. But in no way was he approaching the concept of being 'good'.

But there was still a *soupçon*/a suspicion/a smattering – something a bit larger than a scintilla – of goodness within him.

Arranging for others to do the dark & devious deeds they did [because under the eye of his lover he was unable to do them himself] became second nature to him. He spent his days dispensing [as the middleman he was] the avaricious/vicious/vindictive & plain nasty-for-the-sake-of-being-nasty will of his master.

He never/of course [see above] got his hands dirty. He did/however/spend much of his time – because that was his undescribed job-description – arranging for others to do just that. He didn't do what was done but he knew what was done. He wasn't the author/more the ghost writer/of the dastardly & despicable deeds done.

But alone & at night – lying in the dark with her ashes held gently in his hand – he recorded for future use all the things he was instructed to do that day. He knew about Inspector Fang. He knew they might/probably would/almost certainly would/meet one day.

With the coming of the light he returned to the dark.

✳

Gene T Blanche & his Afrikaner Westandsbeging – the product of a low but fevered brow – were neither-nice-nor-good. They were especially 'neither-nice-nor-good' if your ancestors weren't on the Voortrek/didn't do their bit at Blood River/didn't worship the memory of Hendrik Verwoerd and didn't think Andries Pretorius was the bees-knees. They were more than especially 'neither-nice-nor-good' if you were black/brown/yellow/any shade of colour in between… or Jewish.

To say that he & they were 'neither-nice-nor-good' would be right up there with 'Houston [etc.]'

But they were men/lots of them/& women/a few of them/ who believed in things. And the 'things' they believed in were: A.) That white people in general and: B.) White Afrikaner people in particular and: C.) White Afrikaner people who were members of the Dutch Reform Church [a nasty sub-set of 'Christians' who would happily have kicked a swarthy Yid like Jesus out of the promised land] in even more particular – were the White Tribe of Africa & thus the chosen of God.

They believed that the rest of Africa should go-fuck-itself/were saddened when Southern Rhodesia decayed into Zimbabwe and lamented Ian Smith going the way of all martyrs.

But – not-nice-men though they most assuredly were – they weren't stupid/not in everything. They could do the maths. They – 'the good guys' [how subjective life can be] were four-million in a country of forty and a continent of eight-hundred.

And so – after doing the maths – their natural paranoia was turned-to-the-max.

They were outnumbered two-hundred-to-one – and while they knew that fifty kaffirs were about equal to one of them – the odds were still stacked against them.

They knew [because they knew things like that] what went on at Pelindaba & Kentron. They knew that the *doos* de Klerk – just to ingratiate himself to that *fokking doos* Mandela – had given it all [but not quite all] away. A nuke – wouldn't it – would even the odds nicely?

So – *wat de fok* were they going to do about it?

*

The right side of Bishop's School chapel was packed. Gattings by the dozen came from far-&-wide. Tim's friends by the score came from farther-&-wider. His 'best man' flew from London so as to be it.

The left side of the Bishop's School chapel was not packed – with the solitary/triple-solitary/exception of Tim's three sisters who – under instruction from their brother – occupied the front pew. It looked even emptier that way.

◎ We all know that [sometimes] trying to hide something [cover something up] makes it all the more obvious. But we still do it.

There were no relatives that Noor knew of/apart from an aunt & uncle in the Transvaal. They reared pigs-&-potatoes/ate pigs-&-potatoes/thought of little else but pigs-&-potatoes and – from what she could remember – acted like pigs with the brains of a potato.

And neither were there friends to fill her side of the chapel. There were girls she knew – of course there were. They were the girls from the *dorp*/the girls she went through the rigours of adolescence & puberty with. They were girls whose fathers reared mutton-&-potatoes/ate mutton-&-potatoes/thought of little else but mutton-&-potatoes [etc.].

But in the case of her *friends* – while they too thought of mutton-&-potatoes – they also thought about/and more than just *thought* about/getting drunk & getting-laid – and not just by their fathers.

She didn't want them getting drunk at the reception – which she knew they would – and/having done so/regaling the groom's family-&-friends with anecdotes from her highly anecdotable past.

She didn't want to hear – not on that particular day – the story of how/at one Midnight Mass/with the congregation drunk on Christmas Spirit & cheap schnapps/she'd secreted herself in the pulpit and given Pastor Cronje [in the full flight of his sermon & knowledge of everyone present] a blow job.

She didn't want Hanneli du Plessis to tell the story about how she/Noor – for a hundred-rand bet – went with the girls from her class to the de Kock farm/stripped-off-to-the-skin and got Old Man de Kock's prize goat [after a bit of *stimulatum per manum* & much up-in-the-air bum wiggling] to do what prize goats are known for.

She'd spent the *'n honderd rand* getting star-bursts tattooed around her nipples. It was the most painful experience of her life. The second nipple took guts.

That night – in the midst of taking his *droit de seigneur* – her father/tearing open her shirt/seeing what he saw/and after finishing her off in extra quick time/*sjambokked* her until she bled. Her revenge had been to add dog shit to his dinner the following night.

But she'd been quite taken with the goat and the money their coupling made her. She could see the potential in it. She made it a regular for the class on Fridays after school. Then the word got out and the crowd started to grow. She was making reasonable money for doing nothing more than getting down-on-all-fours/ doing a bit of bum wiggling – more for the audience than the goat – and then letting Billy [she called him Billy] do what he obviously enjoyed doing and no longer needed any sort of *stimulatum* to get him going. But then the doctor's son/but only after his sixth visit/dobbed her in and it all came to an end.

But now-and-again – when there wasn't much else going on – she'd drive out to de Kock's and spend the afternoon with Billy. There was affection on both sides. She liked the way – after he'd done what he was so good at doing – he would nuzzle her star-bursts and lie with his head in her lap.

She wasn't worried about her closest-of-close-secrets getting out because – except for Ellie Botha who went with her – no one knew. They both knew that – if the story ever did get out – they would have to emigrate.

Their secretest-of-secret-secrets was how they drove to the kraal by the river/picked up a couple of young kaffirs/took them to a barn on the Botha farm and spent the afternoon defying every 'racial-purity' law there was. They were both good daughters of the veldt but they were curious and wanted to 'try-a-bit-of-black'. They'd both enjoyed it and so had the boys.

A week later Noor dropped round to Ellie's to find one of the lads strung up – minus organs of procreation – from a tree. Ellie's father had caught him climbing out of his daughter's bedroom.

Both of them were expecting a thorough *sjambokking* but it never came and nothing was ever said. Ellie's father didn't want to emigrate either.

And so it was that the emptiness of the left side of the chapel made thinkers prone to thinking think. And that's not always/seldom is/even rarely is/almost never is [especially if you're the one having thoughts thought about you] a good thing. And that was because the thinkers thinking thoughts thought there must be something wrong/or at least something unusual/with/about this young lady (sic) woman.

And among the thoughts they were thinking about this young woman were thoughts about why she was here with neither family nor friends and that someone – preferably someone else [because they/people of elevated thinking/didn't want other people to think they were the sorts of people who would think lowly thoughts about prying into the private life of this particular young woman/ however pleasantly prurient the prying might potentially prove to be] should look into it.

But just this once/just in this case/because it *was* a bit of an exception/and if no one else was prepared to 'look-into-it' then they [clandestinely of course] would.

And that's what happened – just as Noor knew-it-would – and because she knew-it-would/and right back at the start she knew-it-would/before she planted the axe in the back of her father's head she knew-it-would/she was way out ahead of them all.

She was no longer – and hadn't been since she'd arrived at the Mount Nelson – 'Noor Coetzee from the Great Karoo' – but the solitary child/daughter [Carlotta van den Boetzlaer] of Baron van den Boetzlaer [thus accounting for her intermittently guttural & throat-clearing accent/as well as the absence of relatives & friends].

And with the name – adequately researched & purposefully concocted – came the news that her parents/the end of a minor Dutch/almost unheard of/line had succumbed [at a sadly early age] childless apart from Carlotta/and in every other way relativeless/to a rare tropical disease while searching for blue morpho butterflies in the Amazon basin.

So – with the quietly disseminated story/myth/fabrication/ lie of Carlotta…

◎ To avoid unnecessary confusion we will continue to call her Noor.

…being moved from one foster-home/surrogate-parent to another – she hoped [and was successful in doing so] to put likely sleuths/amateur & otherwise/off her track.

That night – with her diamond engagement ring/it was more than a full carat/anchored securely in place by the gold wedding band – she/unlike others from both history and fiction [i.e. brides-on-the-make] did not withhold nuptial pleasures from her so recently betrothed-become-husband. Quite the opposite – because she/having both needs of her own as well as a wish to celebrate the successful achievement of this 'next rung up the ladder'/did with & to Tim everything conceivable from the annals of prurient invention.

When she woke/she woke to the not unpleasant sensation of Tim gently removing the large/eye wateringly large/black thing from where she'd insisted he put it. It was still going.

She rolled over and counted her-lucky stars – which were legion.

‾
*

Mr Woo – now/once more/pissed-off-to-the-max – sat overlooking the bay. His chángshän was stained with breakfast. He'd refused Hai's offer of a change. When pissed-off/now/once more [see above] to-the-max/the state of his chángshän was of little interest to him. Hai knew that but thought he should offer anyway – just to make it known that he cared – which he didn't/ but didn't want the-fat-*lä shĭ* to know that he didn't.

The reason for the 'now/once more/pissed-off-to-the-max-ish-ness' was that he now knew where/as well as to whom/the half-of-half-a-ton-of-Afghan-best had gone. The knowledge of those two things/knowledge brought to him by Hai/brought to Hai by his man in Canton/brought to Hai's man in Canton by a man who wasn't/but soon would be/Hai's man in Kandahar/ should & would normally have brought a smile to Mr Woo's *faciem internum*.

And the reason why those two smidgeons of info were not doing what they were meant to do was that the two men he/Mr Woo had sent to sort things out [his best-of-the-best/though not his best-of-the-best-of-the-best] were gone but not disappeared. And/more galling than that/they were 'gone but not disappeared' in a most unacceptable [& galling] manner.

'Disappearing' would be bad enough – but these two men hadn't disappeared in any of the ways a disappearance could be achieved without causing embarrassment to their boss – to him/ to Mr Woo.

And what was more-galling-than-gall was that they'd managed to 'disappear' in a way that made them/and thus Mr Woo/newsworthy. They'd managed/quite spectacularly/to have themselves – what was left of themselves [because they were no longer attached to their hands & feet] – hung/more crucified [that's what the newspapers said] over the front of the Bondi Beach Pavilion/where they were/by early morning joggers/ extensively e-photographed – with the *Sydney Morning Herald* being in receipt of those before the police arrived at the scene.

But the galliest-gall-of-all-galls – given that the photos found their way onto page three of the *South China Morning Post* – was that the corpses were adorned with a blood-smattered & blood-written sheet that read/most clearly – 'FUCK OFF WOO OR YORL GET YORS'. It was a specific message with little in the way of ambiguity about it. It was – thought Mr Woo through the red haze of his gall – a message in need of reply.

"*But perhaps not,*" thought Hai – who could both read the-fat-*lā shǐ's* mind as well as think for himself.

He cleared away the remains of monkey XIV. He was deep in the thinking of his own thoughts.

*

The 6th Earl – as expected – had gone through a night of mourning. Not for dear-dead-Nanny [of course not] but for himself. All he'd wanted was his wife's money. Wasn't he within his rights? Wasn't what a woman brought to a marriage automatically her husband's? If it wasn't then it should be. Why did she refuse/time-and-time-again/to let him have some of it? Just a bit of it? He didn't ask for all of it. Why didn't she have faith in him? Why did she need to carp on-and-on about how much he was losing? He was going to win big one day/so why couldn't she believe in him? Why wouldn't she give him the money?

Maybe killing his wife – right then/right that night/even though he'd ended up killing Nanny by mistake – hadn't been such a good idea. Maybe he should have waited and done it later when he could have got rid of her without too much trouble. Maybe a boating accident – but he'd sold his boat/his father's old boat. He'd needed the money to get through that bad streak last year. Maybe a shooting accident in Scotland. Jimmy Baird always invited them for the Glorious Twelfth. Accidents can happen on grouse moors/ everyone knew that.

His wife was a good shot/better than him – maybe it was the tremor from all the booze. It was another reason why he didn't love her/not even like her.

But Nanny was a mistake – he admitted that. It was up there with marching on Moscow.

◎ It was up there with bonking a woman called Jan. It was up there with expecting her not to talk about it. We all make mistakes.

But it was dark and with all the booze & coke he wasn't seeing/ probably not thinking/too well.

Anyway – it was all over-and-done-with now – wasn't it? It was all just-water-under-the-bridge – wasn't it? There wasn't really any reason to feel too bad about it – was there? Everyone has to die sometime – don't they? Maybe Nanny would have gone on to have a thoroughly miserable life. Maybe killing her was doing her a favour. Who's to know?

But – after the expected/if not mandatory/sleepless night of self-pity & righteous indignation at his lot – something stirred within him. It wasn't a big stir/just a little one/one that would be easy to miss if it wasn't stirred at the moment of being looked for.

Was it the cold [School By The River] showers that were giving him this/not to be expected/not in a hundred years/

stiffening of the spine? Or was it his subaltern year in the Guards? The year he did because he couldn't find a way to get out of it/because it was a family tradition going back to the 1st Earl and his glorious cock-up. Or was it just the simple realisation that unless he pulled his oligoneuronal & chinless-wonder finger out things might not bode too well for the future.

And so – with the banner of his [medium-rare rather than well-done] resolution held aloft – he set about ruling his far-flung kingdom.

The first thing he did – which was a sensible thing to do – was to find out what he was the ruler of.

The second thing he did – which was not a sensible thing to do – was to find out what he was the ruler of without putting his clothes back on.

He headed off clockwise/as good as the other way/along the beach. He thought he should circumnavigate [in a terrestrial sense] his little kingdom. That was a reasonable approach.

He set off before dawn with the sun soon to appear in what he knew – his years at the SBTR weren't a total waste of time – must be the eastern sky. He was told that it wasn't a large island and was expecting to be back after an hour/two at the most.

But his realm – although small in a planetary sense – wasn't-as-small-as-all-that and after toiling from beach to beach/clambering from rocky headland to rocky headland/and with the sun now at its zenith/he began to feel a certain tingling of the skin.

But being reared of sterner stuff/but not *much* sterner stuff/and certainly not smarter stuff than the stern stuff of the other men of his minimally talented family/and in the tradition of the 1st Earl [the simpleton who started it all] and in his own habit of leaping-before-looking [not thinking-before-doing] and thus – it had become something of a habit – clutching-defeat-from-the-mouth-of-victory/he soldiered on.

And so it was that – as the sun sank towards the western sea – King John VI returned to his tented palace a little the-worse-for-wear. To say he resembled a lobster would be close to the mark. To say he resembled a man simmered to the point of being declared *al dente* would be even closer. King John VI was sunburnt – this was the tropics for Christ's sake – in places where none of his forebears had ever been sunburnt before.

It took a few/several days to subside and in the course of those few/several days he came/quite rapidly/to the knowledge that sand-flies relished crimson skin.

He skulked under the palms & hid from the sun/just as any seasoned troglodyte might. He ameliorated the discomfort of the sunburn & sand-flies – of course he did – by getting drunk & staying that way. By Day 4/or was it 5/he couldn't remember/ he was ready to sober up. By the end of the week – the hangover having largely abated – he was ready to explore further.

He knew from his circumnavigation that the stream he was encamped by was the only stream on the island. So he followed it into the interior. He decided to follow the left-bank – which for some reason aroused memories of summer lunches at *Les Deux Magots* & winter receptions at *Le Palais de Luxembourg/* but not for long. The brook he was following had about as much in common with *la rive gauche de la Seine* as he did with the man he once was. It wasn't that the man he was now was a diminished man – if anything the contrary. He was a man, not of substance – unless a six month's supply of subsistence rations can be called 'substance' – but of an increasing inner substance. It wasn't a lot of inner substance at that stage/not to start with/but [as you will see] it was substance destined to become more substantial.

The ground rose steadily/but not spectacularly/before him. There were to be no snow-covered peaks or glaciated valleys but [see above] the ground rose steadily/if not spectacularly/ before him.

He'd never starred at school – in the same way he hadn't anywhere else. He was once told by the geography master to read to the class [a thing that always made him sweat] a passage from a book about islands. He'd come to the word 'archipelago' and/after staring at it for some-time he – in the spirit of sending light English guys on light English horses to charge heavy Russian guys sporting heavier Russian cannon – pressed onwards – 'Half-a-league, half a league,' [etc.].

He'd come up with his own version of how the word should be pronounced – which was – 'are-chip-a-lay-go'. Smarter boys sniggered – which only further entrenched the 6th Earl's lifelong hatred of swots-and-anyone-smart.

But-be-that-as-it-may – and possibly due to the heightened senses of the moment – he did remember the difference between an atoll & an island [the one being brought forth from the sea floor by the sterling efforts of countless little coral workers and the other bearing more substantial bits of the earth's crust at their centre]. He knew/by extension of that rarely retained bit of knowledge/that he must be on an island and not on an atoll.

The sizable rock from under which the stream somewhere between gushed & gurgled confirmed the island status of his fiefdom.

He clambered to the top of a gaggle of rocks. He looked down upon his island-not-atoll-fastness. It was in much the same way that Ralph & Piggy must have done on theirs – but perhaps not – because [as I was taught at school and possibly you were too] Ralph was allegorical 'civilisation' & Piggy 'intellect'. The 6th Earl was neither of those.

He could see palm trees in the distance. He could see palm trees in the middle-distance. He could see palm trees close by. Like Robinson Crusoe before him/he knew he was alone – but unlike Robinson Crusoe before him – he felt alone without feeling particularly lonely.

His days of recovery from the sun were bringing forth a realisation in him that he didn't [not really] like people/and that it was 'people' who were the cause of his hardships/failures & resultant feelings of worthlessness & inadequacy.

Standing on the highest rock and surveying his domain – and in the knowledge that there was no one else around to fuck-it-all-up – he was engulfed by determination – a thing he was never engulfed by before. He was going to do something right for a change. He was going to make a success of things.

Which – as you will see – he did.

—
*

'The-Bit' – 'The-Bit' of 'The-Six-and-a-Bit'/'The-Bit' left over after 'the Six' had gone [with much posturing & virtue-signalling from the disarmament lobby] to atomic-bomb Valhalla – is the bit we are now interested in. What happened to it? Where did it go? Where was it? Who had it?

I'll tell you.

As 'The Six' were basking in the glory of their own destruction – 'The Bit' was pushed [in metaphor but not allegory] to one side. And the 'metaphor but not allegory' was down to the fact that it/'The Bit' was loaded/in the dark & quiet of night/onto a truck. It was taken [and I'm sure you won't be surprised to hear this] to the farm of a Mr Gene T Blanche.

And 'the farm of a Mr Gene T Blanche' was adjacent to land that was once gold mining land/and that had – when the gold ran out – returned to cattle country. But the mineshafts remained/and it was in the depths of the deepest & darkest shaft that the Afrikaner Westandsbeging came to view 'The Bit' [their bit] of an atomic bomb. But what to do with it now?

Well – what they did with it was this.

They contacted a man they knew/not really 'knew'/but

'knew of'. He was a man – Eli of course – who knew men who knew about atomic bombs and how to turn 'bits' into 'wholes'.

—*—

Eli's problem – the one with the half-of-half-a-ton-of-Afghan-best – was solved.

Late one rainy & thundery night [when all self-respecting Peers of the Realm should-be-&-would-be-&-were huddled up & sleeping] a cruiser of some 70-ish feet/lights out/all navigational bells-&-whistles working overtime/nudged its way through a narrow opening in the reef. It unloaded & buried – in a large-to-largish steel chest & between two quite distinctively bent palm trees – Mr Bert's half-of-half-a-ton of you know what.

Only the sound of the islanders' – the ones brought for the digging & hiding – heads being blown apart [it was done with one of those Dirty Harry Things/and they make a terrible mess] might wake a light-sleeping Peer but/as expected/because it was a fair way away/it didn't.

He/the 6th Earl was in dream-land. He was dreaming dreams of a girl with 'dream-about-able'/as well as 'do-to-able'/parts.

—*—

Noor was as happily married as an unhappily married woman could be and still give the appearance of being happily married. And being a happily/unhappily married woman was the reason she needed to work as hard as she did at the appearance of being a happily/happily married woman.

◎ Being happily/unhappy is not as easy as it sounds... or so they tell me.

The reasons for the 'happily/unhappy' were two-fold. She was happy-ish with all the gentle – Tim was always gentle/too gentle – things he did for her/to her & with her. The '-ish' of the 'happy-ish' was because – being a good daughter of the veldt – she wasn't reared to the enjoyment of 'gentle'. She knew nothing/not a thing/about it. She missed – more than she thought she would – the world of ravishment/riot & goats.

Fold-2 of the 'two-fold' was that she was unhappy – more than unhappy-ish/to the point of being mega-pissed-off – with other things.

Being a good daughter of the veldt she was unhappy with anything that smacked of appeasement towards the other 90% of her countrymen and the other 99.5% of her continent. She was a white supremacist among white supremacists. She was supremely convinced of the supreme rightness of her/their/the Afrikaner cause.

And in the knowledge of that she knew that Tim/his parents & his friends [now 'her friends'] did not share in the supreme rightness of her/their/the Afrikaner cause. They would – if they knew the unremitting certainty of her beliefs – be horrified. She knew the simpering ways of the weak. She knew that it would be [unless something cataclysmic was done] only a matter of time before 'her' people/'haar' mense – with the blood of Blood River coursing in their veins – would be ejected from their hard-fought-for land and the descendants of the mighty/the God-like/the Voortrekkers/would be forced – like the Lost Tribes of Israel before them – to wander an uncertain & unwelcoming world.

But – unhappy as that unhappy part of her was – she didn't show it. She was a reasonable-bordering-on-good actress and became better with time. She could entertain the enemies of her people & her heart. She could do it with no sign of the sneering & contemptuous loathing she held tight-leashed within her bosom.

She suspected – on occasions – that Tim – on occasions – suspected. But she wasn't sure. He was able [as none of the other men she knew were able] because/apart from the maths teacher/they were all dolts – to hide from her the true nature of his thoughts.

She was a woman who prided herself in knowing the minds of men. But [as statisticians might point out] she'd only known ['known'] a 'skewed-sample'. The men she'd known before she came to know Tim were – apart from the maths teacher – a homogeneous lot. They were men and [because they were a 'skewed-sample'] they were easy to read. They were men of simple tastes & simpler thoughts – with their simple tastes & simpler thoughts being not dissimilar. Their tastes & thoughts ran pretty much predictably to eating/drinking/kaffir-beating & *fokking*. But Tim was not simple to read. He was not simple to know.

Tim ate & drank – of course he did – but dwelt little on either. He lived his life – as much as it fitted with work – 'In praise of lofty intellect'. He [like Mahler] could be a little pompous at times/but not often & not too much. He enjoyed art galleries. He liked the opera. He enjoyed plays by 'the lesser Tudors'. He read the classics.

But he enjoyed too – without a doubt – all the things they did in bed/sometimes on the floor/sometimes draped over the furniture and once [when she'd been leaning over the balustrade of the Garden Suite and he'd been reinvigorated by the sight of her moonlit bum] with her head & one leg in a hibiscus bush.

Tim – in his time at Cambridge/at Caius – had read about women like Noor. He suspected – on occasions – the existence of her dark-side – but the consolations-of-the-flesh kept his doubts in check.

He was a capable lawyer and with the knowledge of/& elation at/ Noor's pregnancy he decided to go to the bar. It was what his family

& friends knew he would. He was a man/a husband/a soon-to-be father & a 'man on the way up'. A man to watch. A man to put your money on. A man destined for great things/if not greatness. A man with the highest offices of the land within his remit.

That was – of course it was – why Noor chose him in the first place.

*

Bert was now happy-ish that his half-of-half-a-ton-of-Afghan-best was no longer hidden where it might be so easily found [i.e. so easily found by any passing man with a back-hoe who just might/at a whim/take to the pleasure of digging up the floor of a disused barn in 'the middle of fucking nowhere']. Stranger things have happened.

But because of the 'happy-ish' there was still disquiet [unquelled & unallayed disquiet] within him. There was something of an out-of-the-frying-pan-&-into-the-fire-ish-ness about where he now found himself. Now there was Rubenstein to worry about. He didn't like kikes. He didn't know why he didn't. He just didn't.

'OK/OK' – Rubenstein came highly recommended/highly spoken of/an honest broker/a man with a reputation for never double-crossing the crooks he dealt with. But [a big BUT] as Bert so surely knew – a-crook-was-a-crook-was-a-crook. Or was in the world Bert lived in.

So – now his half-of-half-a-ton was hidden away/buried [and there were photos & coordinates to 'prove' it] on an island in the Calvados Chain [he thought Calvados was some sort of poncy Froggy booze] off the tail of New Guinea. And the only other guy [he was assured] who knew where it was/was sitting back home in Tel Aviv.

But Bert didn't like trusting people – especially not people like himself. And so [by-&-large] he didn't.

With that in mind he drove to the Sydney Yacht Squadron. He asked if there were maps [and was told that/because there weren't any roads on them/they were called 'charts'] of the Calvados Chain.

It surprised him to learn that there were such things/but there were/and they had them. So he bought them.

He enquired/*en passant*/about the availability of motor yachts – the larger the better. There was – the salesman said [as he nearly wet himself with joy] one such 70-ish-footer in the marina.

Driving home Bert realised that he'd just spent – but certainly not/hopefully not/perhaps not/wasted – the equivalent of three-months profit from the NT gunja trade. So-be-it. He needed to keep an eye on his investment.

After a day of planning & plotting he arranged to meet a defrocked navy Commander – defrocked when found wearing nothing but a frock & an under-age [but only 'somewhat' under-age] girl. And the 'only 'somewhat' under-age girl' he was wearing – or so the navy's report said – wore neither frock nor [apart from a wide-eyed look of bemusement at how this could be happening to her] anything else.

He/Bert – having read the report [money can buy anything] – knew that the Commander's defrocking was at the higher end of defrockings and [because of that] came with the loss of pension/medical/entitlements of all kinds/as well as any realistic prospects of future employment at sea.

He/Bert knew – because the business he was in was conducive to him knowing things like that – that he held the defrocked Commander by the-short-and-curlies & held his balls in the palm of his hand.

He/Bert asked – in the knowledge that refusal was unlikely – the defrocked Commander to give him navigation lessons/ and then to take him out on the harbour and show him how to handle his new toy.

Which he/the defrocked Commander – knowing what Bert held in the palm of his hand – did.

Their day on the harbour was memorable. Bert wasn't this turned on for years – not since Trixie snuffed it.

⸻
*

Mr Woo – determined to repair the damage to his reputation and status as *il capo di tutti I capi/lǎo bǎn – lǎo bǎn* of the Hong Kong drug trade/as well as the premier feeder of sharks in the South China Sea – gave tacit/only tacit/only implied instructions to Hai. His failure to do otherwise was possibly/in all probability/ almost certainly/due to the emotion & negative-vibe evoked by the page three photos. This – 'FUCK OFF WOO OR YORL GET YORS' – was a challenge to his manhood/his potency/his machismo/his *force majeure*/his virility.

Well – perhaps not his virility/not really – because Mr Woo hadn't got-it-up [not in any meaningful sense] in yonks. The closest Mr Woo got to 'getting-it-up' was when he was strangling a monkey.

And so – because of that/the challenge to his manhood [etc.] – the instructions he gave Hai were far from specific. They were more like guide-lines/suggestions. They left Hai with wiggle-room & room to manoeuvre.

⸻
*

It wasn't the first time Noor was pregnant – of course it wasn't. She'd been up-the-duff before – of course she had. She couldn't remember how many times it was/but it was quite a few. Twice to her father – for sure. Once to the maths master [but it could have been half the class] and once – almost certainly/because she could remember being on heat that day – to one-or-other of the kaffir boys.

71

She knew a woman in Oudtshoorn – far enough away – who'd dealt with all of them/but that one/the kaffir one/in particular. A daughter of the veldt with a kaffir's kid was a death sentence. You didn't even get a chance to emigrate.

Now she was having an *Engel's* kid but she could put up with that. It was for the greater good. *Her* greater good and – maybe one day – for the greater good of something else. But she wasn't sure about that/not then.

Having an *Engel's* kid was better than having a black kid or a kid with two heads who looked like her father. She was inside the citadel now. She was just where she planned to be.

She'd liked the freedom & killing of the veldt/but it was a hard life. Being knocked-about/knocked-off & knocked-up by your pig of a father/but no more of a pig than Milly Paetz's father who knocked-her-off/knocked-her-up and then – when he heard she was knocked-up – knocked-her-about until she lost the baby/wasn't a whole heap of fun.

It was an easy life for her now. There were servants – kaffir girls she could give a hard time to. She had everything she wanted.

When the time came – according to the doctor – to stop partaking in-&-of 'the pleasures of the bedroom'/she decided not to take his advice. She wanted to 'partake' right up to the time of whelping. Why not? The little *Engel-sprog* could do with a bit of his own back. He'd been kicking her guts out for weeks.

Noor was the daughter of a harsh people/a harsh place & a harsh time. So – should she be forgiven for being harsh? It's hard to know.

So – while Noor wasn't a 'good' person in the way any of us might think of as 'good'/she was about as good as we should expect her to be.

But be-that-as-it-may – she was still a 'bad-mother' [as well as a bad mother]. She was not someone you would want to meet – not at three in the morning/not in a darkened alley.

$\overline{\underset{*}{}}$

Tim was besotted with the wonders of fatherhood and why wouldn't he be? Being a father was up there with winning an impossible case in front of the Supreme Court of Appeal. Perhaps even better.

He took to fatherhood like the proverbial duck. He was good at it. He did things/all sorts of things.

There were women to do the things he did/but the act of doing them gave him more pleasure than in watching them done.

He didn't know it/but he was doing [and having done to him in return] that thing called 'bonding'. That – there's no doubt – is an important thing to-do-&-be-done-to. The value of it can't be overestimated. The lack of it can't either. It's what happens/has always happened – back-and-forth/parent-to-child/child-to-parent – since man climbed down from the trees.

He knew his wife had no intention of breast-feeding – however much she was told that she should. They argued about it sometimes. She yelled at him one night – "They're my *fokking* tits and I'll *fokking* decide who gets to *fokking* suck on 'em."

Tim arranged for a nurse during the day and he did/because Noor was never going to [was she] the bottles at night.

He got into the habit – whenever young Peregrine cried at night/which was every night/like we all did – of getting up/ warming a bottle and sitting in the study with his son on his knees. He enjoyed listening to the contented slurping while he read.

'Peregrine' was one of those old family names that went back through the generations. It was Tim's father's name and his father's too. Tim was never quite sure how-or-why he'd missed out. But he liked being Tim/it fitted him/he felt like a 'Tim'. He had trouble imagining himself as anything else. But he liked the name Peregrine.

Young Perry – because he was/wasn't he/always going to be 'Perry' – didn't know/not then [how could he] how much his father loved him/which was a lot. He didn't know – not then [how could he] how much his mother didn't/which was not at all.

But the love of one parent [so they say] is enough.

And/so Perry was loved & adored – and whatever it is that might be more than that – by his father/ but not at all by his mother. He didn't need to be more than a few weeks old to come to the appreciation of those two things.

◎ The knowing of being loved is hard-wired into all of us in just the same way that the ability to love is hard-wired into us too – or isn't.

Perry was lucky to be loved. Tim was lucky to love. Noor was unlucky with love. It wasn't her fault. There was never much luck in her life and certainly – because both Tim & the maths teacher were confused by lust – no love at all. She was the product of the time/the place & the people who'd produced her.

She wasn't a 'nice' person and would possibly/probably/ almost certainly never be one/whatever her time/her place or her people. But who can be certain of that?

Tim – besotted as he was – was slow to realise that Noor didn't love/or even like/their son. It wasn't a realisation he wanted to realise and/because of that/he hid it. He hid it where we all hide the things too painful to see the light. He hid it away in the deep places of his soul [whatever & wherever that may be].

As Perry grew – as he took his first step & as he said his first word/Tim was there to see it & hear it.

They did things together – almost everything together. When Tim wasn't at work he was at home and Perry was never far from his side.

Tim knew [as you know] that his wife didn't love him or Perry either. He found that hard to understand. He hoped things would get better. He hoped she would learn to love them both. He hid his hopes in the deep places.

＊

Noor knew there was something missing inside her – her capacity to love. But as you will see – her capacity to love wasn't missing in the way a 'missing tooth' is missing. It was missing in the way car-keys go missing. It wasn't 'missing-missing'/just 'lost-can't-be-found-yet' missing. There's a difference.

But be-that-as-it-may – she possessed little-or-no love for her husband & none-whatsoever for her son/and that [you won't be surprised to hear] didn't worry her in the slightest. She was reared without love and was OK without it. She was getting what she wanted from life so what was all the hoo-hah about? All that Beatles crap about 'All You Need Is Love' could go stick its head up its own *fokking* arse. She was doing just fine without love.

But was she?

She had everything she could wish for. A big house/servants/a Mercedes sportscar & money to spend – her husband's money to spend – on anything she wanted.

She was learning to tolerate her husband/his friends & their wives. She knew – especially after the baby – that they wanted her to join their circle. She knew that – if she was to get further up the ladder she was climbing – she would need to play along. So – for a while – she did.

She knew they played bridge/so went and took lessons. She'd played tennis at school/a bit [when there weren't boys waiting for her behind the bike sheds]. She went to lessons for that too. She knew – however much she despised the whole rotten pack of them – that she must do all she could to fit in. Her husband was going to the top of the pile and she was going there with him. There were things for her to do when she got there.

So love? So what? She could do without it. It only complicated things. And – in some ways – she was right.

But – 'in some ways – she was right,' means that in some ways she wasn't [which means that 'in some ways – she was wrong'].

She didn't love her husband or her son and she knew her husband & her son knew it. She never made efforts to pretend that she did. It wasn't that she was callous or cruel – even though she was. It was just that [for now] she was empty.

She had her plan and she was going to stick to it.

But life doesn't always go the way we plan – does it?

The 6th Earl/King John VI/was ruler of all he surveyed. But wait – no he wasn't. And the reason for 'But wait – no he wasn't' was that/when he stood at the top of his island/he could see more than *his* island. He could see other islands as well. There were two of them. But not islands like his island. They were more like atolls. Did his island and the two atolls comprise an 'are-chip-a-lay-go'? He wasn't sure. But they might.

He finished his exploration of his island. He returned to his camp by the beach. He sat staring out to sea. He couldn't see the atolls from this side. He was thinking. He thought for some considerable time. Neither a mayfly considerable time nor a galactic considerable time but for a considerable time somewhere in between. It was the longest time he'd ever thought about anything.

After thinking he acted. He was a man born new. *Un homme nouvel.* There were things to do. Several things/more than a few. He would move off the beach/other things too.

Then – before doing any of the 'several things/more than a few' – he went down to the sea. He rowed the dinghy to the edge of the reef. He clambered over the coral and stared down into the water that has no bottom. He wasn't sure why he did that.

Exit Chorus.

‾‾
*

We walked with the Heathfields. We walked back to the East India Club. The policeman was patrolling outside. He saw Annie. He smiled.

"Hi," he said.

"Hi yourself," she said. "And say 'Hi' to your sergeant."

"I will."

We went inside.

We all went inside. Annie went inside. In 'de gorgeous onesie' she went inside. Mitzi in flared pants went inside. Zola in culottes went inside. Prue in jeans went inside. Sgt R C Connolly was needed in the library. Maj C M Sanders was needed in the dining room.

We went to their room. It was big. Rooms were big when the clubs of Clubland were built. They were built for big men with big dreams. Men whose wives never wore pants.

They unfolded the charts [there were no roads on them.] and lay them on the bed. It was a big bed. Beds were big when the clubs of Clubland were built. They were built for big men with big dreams. Men whose wives never wore pants.

"That one's mine," said Mitzi. She pointed at the chart. "The one you borrowed."

"Yes." I was a man of few words.

"Where you hid the girls." .

"Yes." I was always a man of few words.

"Before we went screwed that asshole right good 'n proper."

"Yes."

"I love that island just for that."

"Yes."

She looked at Macaulay. "Where's yours, Mac?"

"Right there." He pointed to where he was pointing. Jess looked wistful.

"Who owns that one there?" She pointed to 'that one there'.

"Some Jewish guy," said Jess.

"Do we need it?"

"Yes."

"Why?"

"It's got water."

"Who's the Jewish guy?"

"Some Israeli guy."

"What's his name?"

"Elijah Rubenstein."

"You're joking, not lover-boy Eli?"

"More than one Elijah Rubenstein," I said.

"Dare say. Specially in Kikesville… anyway, what would lover-boy want with an island?"

"Why? Who is he?"

"Just a guy I knew, guy who does stuff."

"What stuff?"

"Any stuff you want."

—
*

It was a dream, I guess, Tommy's and Brosie's and mine. It was a good dream and as good as dreams get.

It started out as Jess's dream. It started out in her head and then went viral into ours. Then went viral into everyone else's. Now on a bed in a room in London, with the fucking rain fucking falling again, it was about making the dream come true.

Zola, as we all knew, was richer than Croesus on-a-good-day. Prue was likewise with what she got from Peter and Andy was likewise from his Wisconsin uncle. Tommy was likewise from his arsehole of a father.

So, we were richer than just being rich, and that, for good fucking reason, worried us.

The Heathfields were richer than rich, just not in money. They were rich in more important stuff. They were rich in dreams, and dreams cost zilch.

They were dreaming of stuff they could do.

And the stuff they wanted to do was stuff they wanted us to do. Stuff we could do together with all the frightening fucking money we had. It was stuff they said we could do to make the world a 'better place'. And, because it would be a 'better place', it would be a 'happier place'.

We knew, the ones who had it, that the money was too much. We knew, since before the *Ile du Levant*, that it was going to harm us. We'd wanted to find stuff to do with it, stuff that would make the world a 'better 'n happier place', and in doing that we would stop it from harming us.

Jess was the marine biologist, the polychaete girl, the diver and the driver of it all. The marine park was her idea, the uni was mine, the hotel was Tommy's, the rehab centre was – whose do you think?

They'd be world-firsts because they'd be world-bests.

She, and because of that we, didn't want un-fucked-up sea and un-fucked-up coral to be things of memory.

None of us was comfortable with talking about the money, but we needed to. We added up what there was and that, in a good way – if there is a good way of being frightened – frightened the crap out of me. I think it frightened the crap out of Tommy too.

Money, we reckoned, if it wasn't being used, was dead. And money, only used to make more money, was deader than dead. Money only came alive, we reckoned, when it got used to make the world a 'better 'n happier place'.

But I guess what makes a 'better 'n happier place' depends on 'the who' and what 'the who' thinks makes a 'better 'n happier place'. For Bill Gates it was a world without polio. For us it would be looking after the sea. When we wrote it down it sounded as pompous as hell/but-so-be-it. It was a good idea.

There was no lack of means and no lack of intention. We knew what we wanted and knew where we wanted it.

Mitzi, as you know, owned an island in the Calvados Chain somewhere off the tail of New Guinea.

Macaulay had inherited one nearby. That's called serendipity, or fucking good luck.

The other one we needed was 'the other one'. The one with water.

So, we decided to find out more about this Elijah Rubenstein guy.

And that, as you might imagine, was the start of 'interesting times'.

—
*

Enter Chorus.

Noor – devoid of all wifely & motherly emotions – felt free to do whatever she wanted. And what she wanted to do wasn't what her husband [or the seemingly inexhaustible numbers of 'family & friends'] would expect or want her to do.

She knew she must be careful. She didn't want what she did to become known – not in any way. There was her comfortable life to protect. But she was a daughter of the veldt and the needs of a daughter of the veldt were not to be denied. Why should they be?

The thing she liked about Tim – the one thing she liked about him more than any of the other things other people liked about him – the thing that bound her/although somewhat loosely/to him was what they got up to in bed/on the floor/ draped over the furniture/hanging over the balcony of the Garden Suite [etc.].

But there was a problem even with that.

He was too gentle/too kind/too loving. Or was that three problems?

Noor liked to be – because/or so I'm told/some women do/ which sounds pretty ghastly – 'thrown about a bit'. She wasn't into black eyes & fat lips or anything like that/but she liked the feeling of being/and all the sensations associated with being/ mildly brutalised. She was [see above] no stranger to that. She liked being 'thrown about a bit' before being thrown into throes. It was her default position when it came to getting laid. She needed pain to get her to where things were best – just like most women/or so I'm told/don't.

She hadn't enjoyed – a major understatement – the months of being pregnant and she hadn't enjoyed – an even greater understatement – the twelve-hour labour. There was an heir for her husband and that was enough. She was never going to go – and why would any woman ever want to – through that again. She was on 'the pill' now and with no intention of ever coming off it.

There was a strategy for getting what she wanted & needed. She would wait for her husband to leave for work/get dressed in provocative fashion/drive to a suburb – a 'her people' suburb/

not a 'his people' suburb – and sit in a cheap café/of which there were several. She would show a bit [quite a bit] of thigh & a bit [quite a bit] of cleavage and wait. The longest wait had been an hour but it was/mostly/much less than that.

Afrikaans is not a pretty language to hear but Noor missed its guttural/throat clearing cadences. It made her feel warm to hear it. So – when a man started up a conversation – she would invite him to her table and then give him both barrels of her more/most prurient libido. She'd only been turned down once.

Then she would take him to a cheap hotel where she kept a room.

She wasn't – and being a daughter of the veldt never was – keen on foreplay. That gentle warm-up stuff was for the effete *Engels doos*.

Within a minute of being in the room she would be out of her clothes and with his spirits sufficiently aroused/and with his balls held tight in her hand [to ensure concentration and remove any doubt of who was in charge] she would give him his instructions/together with an eye wateringly large black thing with batteries.

It was often mid-afternoon by the time she walked/ sometimes limped/into the house.

But on one particular day it didn't go like that. Not like that at all.

$$\overline{\underset{*}{}}$$

Tim – becoming increasingly aware of Noor's shortcomings as both wife & mother – still 'thought' he loved her. Even with the increasing awareness of other shortcomings/of which he could count quite a few/he still 'thought' he loved her. He didn't think he loved everything about her – of course not/no one does – and perhaps not even much about her – but he still 'thought' he loved 'something' about her.

If asked to say what the 'something' in the 'something about her' was he would have had difficulty putting what that 'something' was into words. He enjoyed making 'love' to her – of course he did – he enjoyed doing the things she asked/told him to do to her body/as well the things she did to his in return. But he knew that 'that' [the doing to & being done by] was lust – which was pretty good all-the-same – rather than love.

If asked to enumerate his wife's non-bedroom talents he would have had difficulty knowing where to start because there wasn't much to start with – but he still 'thought' he loved her.

Perhaps love is like that. Perhaps 'love' doesn't always need a reason why. Perhaps it never does. Who's to know?

＊

Mr Woo was intent on his right-of-reply. He wanted people dead. Lots of them. The-more-the-merrier. Every last @#$%^&* one of them. Every last @#$%^&* shorts wearing/rubber flip-flop-wearing/singlet-clad/smelly-arm-pitted/hairy-chested/adverb averse Australian. He wasn't this inwardly angry for years. He was going through monkeys at-a-rate-of-knots.

＊

Hai – ever calm – inwardly & outwardly – could see where his boss was headed. He saw the fires of acrimony lit & the bloody banners of confrontation held high.

He knew that monkey strangling – while calming the inner man – did not bring out the best in his boss/and certainly not in his decision-making. He knew no good would come of all this anger & damaged pride. He knew that sharks/swimming around happily somewhere/were in for an unexpected treat.

In the knowledge of that he became a little/if not a lot/less loyal than he otherwise might have been.

He knew – and had known since the demise of monkey XVI – that there would be people/a lot of people/who would be 'going-the-way-of-all-flesh'. He did not intend to be one of them.

With two of Mr Woo's best-of-the-best adorning the front of the Bondi Pav the hypothesis of 'goings' & 'flesh' was confirmed.

So – what to do? Well – he knew what to do and because of that he did it/some of it. He knew the 'how' of [as well as the 'why' of] how & why the half-of-half-a-ton-of-Afghan-best never came to where it was meant to. That information he'd long since passed to his employer – thus triggering the demise of monkey XIII and the start of the present saga.

And now – through men/his men/men in far flung places [places no man of sense/discretion or discernment would ever wish to visit] – he knew 'who' it was who'd/craftily & cleverly – Hai admitted that – diverted the half-of-half-a-ton to whence it was. That information he'd also imparted long since to his employer – thus triggering the demise of monkey XIV and the ill-considered & unnecessarily precipitate actions that culminated – as Hai suspected they might – in the demise of the best-of-the-best/although not of the best-of-the-best-of-the-best.

The information he did not impart to his/now in name only/ boss was the whereabouts of the much sought-after half-of-half-a-ton. This information Hai had gained through unorthodox & circumlocuitous channels involving a disgruntled employee [of short-ish life expectancy] of a man called Bert.

And so it was that – on-a-dark-&-stormy-night – the almost-but-not-quite-ghost-town of Manangatang was passed through by a group of oriental gentlemen in a truck. Three hours later the same truck passed back through the town. It containing a group of – now disgruntled/weary & mud-spattered – oriental gentleman … but @#$%-all else.

The reason for the '…but @#$%-all else' – as well as the 'disgruntled/weary & mud-spattered' – was that at the bottom of the hole they dug/in the floor of the dilapidated barn where they dug it/they found a sheet of tin inscribed 'FUCK OFF WOO OR YORL GET YORS'. It was a specific message [though somewhat repetitious] with little ambiguity about it. It was clear & to the point.

On receipt of this information Hai went quietly to his room. He lit a joss stick and meditated until dawn.

On the morrow he knew what he needed to do. He knew of/he'd heard of – although they'd never met – a man called Eli Rubenstein.

*

The 6th Earl – for the first time in his life – was making things. They weren't things that were much good/not to start with/but they were getting better.

He made himself a hut out of fallen palm fronds. And/during a night of moderate wind/the fronds fell once more – this time on top of him. Crawling out from under them he did not [as he had when something analogous befell him in Belgravia] swear & stamp his [metaphorical] foot or look around for someone to blame. He vowed – instead – to do better. And he did.

He – using the basic tools he was cast away with – sawed & chopped & dug. It was the first time he'd ever built or made anything.

He wasn't even – in his previous existence – able to finish the model Spitfire he was given one Christmas. So – when some days later he stood in front of his little hut – a warm glow of creative satisfaction suffused his *paraventricular nuclei* as/on such occasions/it does.

He – with the muse of creativity heavily upon him – dammed the little stream. He did it twice before the realisation [that sand & sticks were not perfect damming materials] struck home. He travelled to the hinterland and brought back rocks. It took days/but time was not-of-the-essence.

It wasn't an Aswan or a Hoover but it was a dam none-the-less. It was a dam all of his own design & making. It was a pool all of his own design & making. Once again the *paraventricular nuclei* were suffused.

> He – 'the 6th Earl of Somewhere-
> or-other' – built an ingenious fish trap.

That's quite a sentence to write and that's why it has its singular status. The word 'ingenious' had never appeared/not before/ in the same sentence as/or in the same thought bubble as/'the 6th Earl of Somewhere-or-other'. And for good reason/but no longer.

He couldn't claim all the credit because sometime – he couldn't remember when – he'd watched a television programme. There were natives – 'Awfully, awfully black looking chappies' – who'd buried circles of sticks in the sand. And then – 'Almost like bally magic' – with the coming in & going out of the tide – 'Hey presto' – a load of flapping fish.

The 6th Earl knew nothing – because he didn't know much of anything – about protein & iodine. But with the fish came an abundance of both.

He was changing in unexpected ways. He was walking 'his' beaches & swimming 'his' lagoon. He was rowing 'his' seas. He was building & collecting. He built a second hut for the supplies – then a third one for no reason other than the pleasure of building it. Paths into the hinterland were forged and lined with shells. In all ways possible he was – in the parlance of his 'set' – 'going native'.

Having recovered from his first encounter with the tropical sun he took greater care. He didn't return to clothes/because they were being used for other things. Strips of Jermyn Street secured the roof trusses of his huts and remnants of Savile Row wiped his pots and pans. He tanned deeply/probably/possibly because G³ grandma was the progeny of a dark-eyed Spanish beauty. [A long story of 'Wellington-in-front-of-Badajoz' – another time perhaps.]

The 6th Earl came from that stratum of society that equated tanning of the skin with either manual-labour or the lower-class habit of holidaying in Spain and lying prostrate on beaches. He came from that class – whatever higher than 'upper' is – where the only acceptable tanning/never around the eyes of course/ was to be seen after skiing in Verbier.

He was – after the canned nature of his earlier diet – eating well. His fish traps were producing. He found a plant growing on the banks of the stream. It tasted delicious and was efficacious for the bowels.

He was – in addition to tanning – tightening & tautening. He would – for the first time in his life – like to look at himself in a mirror. The reflection of his pale & dystonic torso had never done much for him when he could.

It amused him to look at his willy. Saddle-leather brown on one side and sickly anaemic on the other.

But there were some things he missed from his old life/not many but a few. He certainly didn't miss his wife. God – bitch – why did he marry her? That's right – for the money. But look where that got him.

But he did miss sex. The last woman he'd had sex with was the girl at the club. She had/somewhat surprisingly [see above] turned out to be the daughter of a Shadow Minister of Something or other and came from 'the North' without pedigree. But – against-the-run-of-play of his earlier years – he'd liked her regardless. Their affair – she called it an 'affair' and he thought of it as an 'involvement' – was into its second year when dead Nanny finished them up.

He'd liked her because of her non-judgemental attitude to things. She'd accepted him for what he was. He suspected

– rightly as it happens – that she knew what made him tick/ and that was something his wife never did or even tried to do. Maybe she knew him better than he knew himself. He suspected – rightly as it happens – that some women could do that.

She drank from his glass & sniffed his line. They were kindred spirits. Babes lost in the same dark woods.

He'd liked things about her body too. It was maybe not a spectacular one/but a pretty good one/and the things he liked most about it were her organ-stops and the intriguing things they did when he did less than intriguing things to get them to do the intriguing things they did.

There weren't many other things he missed and the things he thought he would were things that – in the clearing haze of the pointless life he used to live and those of his 'set' were condemned to live – he now saw to be the fatuous & futile things that they were.

He didn't know it – and might even have disagreed with anyone who mentioned it – but he was becoming a more reasonable human being. There was a way to go yet/but he was on the road.

$$\overline{\underset{*}{}}$$

Noor did her usual things. She dressed her provocative dress. She drove to her cheap café. She displayed her cleavage & showed her thigh. She didn't need to wait. Almost not at all.

The man at the next table turned around. He took in the cleavage & the thigh.

"May I join you?" He spoke Afrikaans.

"You may." So did she.

"You are Noor Coetzee?"

"I am."

"Your father was a friend of mine."

"I doubt it."

"Why do you doubt it?"

"My father didn't do friends."

"I knew him."

"He knew people. There's a difference."

"There is."

"How do you know my name?"

"I know a lot about you."

"Like what?"

"Like you come here to pick up men."

"That a crime?"

"Not at all, understandable."

"Understandable, why?"

"A change from being fucked by 'n Engelsman."

"Maybe, what's your point?"

"You sold out to 'n Engelsman."

"You know nothing."

"I know lots."

"Like what?"

"Like you killed your father."

"He deserved it."

"I know."

"How do you know?"

"I told you, I knew him."

"Come to the point."

"Let's leave."

"Where to?"

"To the room you keep."

"How do you know I keep a room?"

"I know lots."

"Why should I?"

"You like to fuck."

"I do."

"Good, we'll do that first. Then I have things to tell you."

"What?"

"I'll tell you after we've fucked."

"OK."

It was an interesting morning & afternoon for Noor. She liked the way the man threw her around and then did all the things she liked. He did the things he did in the ways she liked them done. He did them without being told the ways she liked them done. It was as though he knew the things she liked and the ways she liked them done. He even knew what to do with the eye wateringly large black thing. She'd been researched. She knew that. She wasn't stupid.

After doing all the things he did/he told her things. After doing them again/he told her more things. And then/at last/with the doings done and the tellings told/she knew a lot of things.

They arranged to meet again. Same day/same time/next week. She looked forward to more things done & more things told.

*

Mr Woo – not appearing to cope at all well with his inner angst – was temporarily out of monkeys. He was in no mood to be reconciled to the loss of 'his' half-of-half-a-ton. He was in no mood for taking advice from Hai or anyone else.

But things were changing in the Woo household. Mr Woo was – or so everyone believed – 'losing it' and 'losing it' big time. Mr Woo was – or so everyone believed – becoming a liability and was – or so everyone believed – on-the-way-out.

And as I'm sure you can imagine – in the business Mr Woo reigned over there was only-one-way-out for someone who was on-the-way-out. And so it was.

Hai talked to the best-of-the-best-of-the-best. He asked them [just as they were expecting him to] to arrange the 'only-one-way-out' for Mr Woo.

Although being born a gentle boy – and with his lover to teach him the ways of a gentle man – Hai had spent too long in the company of Mr Woo.

He'd observed/over many years & close at hand/the gratuitously unpleasant things he did. For that – as well as for a number of other reasons/including a lifelong affection for monkeys – Hai asked the-best-of-the-best-of-the-best/when giving thought to the 'only-one-way-out'/to give thought to lowering Mr Woo [in full *conscientia sui morte impediente*/in full awareness of his impending doom] into the South China Sea wrapped/if at all possible/in horse intestines readily available from the Chakwal meat markets. The sharks would come-from-far-&-wide for that.

The-best-of-the-best-of-the-best gave thought to Hai's request. Their answer implied – in the inscrutable way 'the Orient' has of implying things – that they would comply.

Hai went home to his simply furnished apartment. He looked down on Repulse Bay. He watched as the first flames curled up around the walls of Mr Woo's mansion.

He then went to the shrine of his lover and sat lotus-like – Padmasana – until dawn. He prayed for her forgiveness.

In the morning he did other things.

*

Bert – having second thoughts about where his half-of-half-a-ton now was – wondered if he couldn't set things right by going and getting it back. And in the 'wondering if he couldn't' [i.e. 'if he could'] he decided he would.

There were old barns all over the country just crying out to have half-of-half-a-ton of anything/let alone half-of-half-a-ton-of-Afghan-best/buried beneath their floors.

And what was it that made him go trusting a fucking kike in the first place? Jesus fucking wept. He needed his fucking head read.

If there was a monkey to hand there's no telling what Bert might do.

As Bert knew – and as Mr Woo was supposedly finding out right about then – in a business where if you took your eyes off the ball for too long you might wake up without eyes to put back on it.

There were 'trusted' lieutenants – of course there were – none of whom he trusted. They were men who/when he becked-&-called/did becking-&-calling. But he wasn't where he was because he lived-in-cloud-cuckoo-land. He was where he was because he was a hard-nosed/pragmatic & not infrequently violent realist.

He knew the sorts of men he'd gathered around him/because the sort of men he'd gathered there were men just like him – just not as smart. That was/always was/Bert's edge. And he knew it.

The world of drug trafficking wasn't/isn't/will never be awash with men smart enough to get to Med School. It was knowledge he held dear to his heart.

So – he couldn't just swan-off to the back-of-beyond to pick up the-half-of-half-a-ton. When he got back Mac &/or Jimmy – his most/least/'trusted' lieutenants – would be on their way to taking over.

His was a hands-on business – and he was afraid of sharks.

And then one evening he saw the solution. He would take them with him.

He was too busy with what he did to read much and for that reason the writings of Sun Zen were unknown to him. But he knew by instinct [and because it's not rocket surgery] to keep his friends close & his enemies-posing-as-friends even closer.

<hr />

＊

The 6th Earl was in his element. He was happy. He was enjoying his own company for the first time. It was something he never had before. Few people [his oldest-&-closest-friend & the daughter of the Shadow Minister of Something-or-other excepted] had ever enjoyed his company. Now – as the weeks turned to months and the months to what they do – he was starting to understand why. As he morphed from what he was 'then' into what he was 'now' he came to see more clearly the pompous/asinine & totally useless jerk – up until about now – he'd always been.

It was a wonder that oldest-&-closest liked him at all. He couldn't think of anything worth liking. Perhaps it was because they were schoolboys together. Perhaps it was because they went through puberty together. Perhaps it was because of all the things they did together [just as all the other boys at the SBTR 'did' together] as they went through puberty together. Perhaps it was because oldest-&-closest felt sorry for him. Perhaps his own success in Mayfair made his friend's failure in Belgravia something to feel sorry for. He didn't know. All he did know was that he was lucky to have a friend.

It was a wonder then that the daughter of the Shadow Minister of Something-or-other liked him either/and that he [because the Shadow Minister sat on the Labour/Lefty benches] liked her in return. Perhaps it was because he – not having been breastfed by his [way above such vulgar undertakings] mother/ and thus developing – [just as the author did/but for different reasons/ref. A WITNESS TO A LIFE p. 28.] – a life-long & abiding breast fixation – liked/liked a lot/and thus didn't laugh at/as other men had/the way her organ-stops did the intriguing things they did when he did the less than intriguing things he did to encourage them to do the intriguing things they did.

The 6th Earl – as well as being-in-his-element & happy – had time to ponder on things. He'd never [not even with all the empty time his life in Belgravia afforded him] pondered on much. What he pondered on now – like many before him [including the author & possibly you] was on 'life's uncertain passage'.

What a waste – he pondered/more certain than un – of all those years of doing sweet-fuck-all. What a waste of his youth. What a waste of the-best-years-of-my-life. What – he pondered with reluctance/but pondered none-the-less – a shit he'd been. But – he pondered with resolution [for which we should give him credit] it was all going to be different now.

No longer would he – or indeed did he – look upon the island as his jail. No longer would he – or indeed did he – feel incarcerated in body or in mind.

He felt liberated/set free. And he was. No longer was he strapped into the straightjacket of having 'to-do-the-right-things'/having 'to-think-the-same-things'/having 'to-think-the-same-things' as everyone else. Now he could thumb his nose at all the pointless rules of the polite – but only superficially polite [because underneath it was a swirling pool of avarice/malice & jealousy] upper-class English society. The society he once thought himself so lucky to be born to.

Now he could do & think whatever he wanted/whatever he damn well wanted/whatever the fuck he wanted.

Some of it – of course it was – was childish. He was like a schoolboy set free. He walked home-beach yelling "Bum!" & "Tits!" and later [when he'd got into the swing of things] "Fuck!" & "Cunt!" and all of it as loudly as he could. In a funny way – a way he couldn't explain – it made him feel better.

When thoughts of the Shadow Minister's daughter got too much for him he would lie down and 'play with himself'. He was happy to do that. It was a feeling of freedom.

But there were other things too. More important things. The chuffed-ish-ness he felt when he built his huts fired in him the same thing that fired Hiram of Tyre. The little huts and the things to come after them [while not being in the same league as Jerusalem's House of God] were the offspring of the same Masonic creed.

One childhood Christmas he was given a book – 'The Swiss Family Robinson' – and/just like the Spitfire/it didn't do much for him. He'd certainly never read it/but he did flick through it. And because it was the child's version there were pictures. Some of the pictures were of the treehouse they built.

And so – with the Square & Compass of Hiram lodged/in an unknown and purely academic way/firmly in his mind – he set about his task. It was a learning process that took – of course it did – time/'but time was not-of-the-essence'.

His first attempt at a ladder was not a success. But he persevered – a thing he'd never done before. The things he built – ladders especially – improved. Things got better. Collapse rates were decreasing.

He harboured within himself – contrary to all conceivable evidence to the contrary – skills he never expected to find [skills found only among the lower strata] – [i.e. strata that survived by 'doing things' and even by 'making things']. They were the strata he & his 'set' – who rarely stooped to 'doing things' and certainly never to 'making things' – were taught to/and were happy to/ and were perhaps even obliged to/look down upon.

He came to understand that what made Englishmen – his sort of Englishmen – so English/was the alacrity with which they [and the pleasure they derived from doing so] 'looked down' on someone/anyone & everyone else. He came to realise that it was what – up until then/and with the encouragement of his family & 'set' – he'd spent his life doing.

The skills of carpentry have – as we all know – been evolving since a Neanderthal man/woman – circa 150,000 years ago – first hammered a stick between a couple of rocks to hang up his or her mammoth-skin overcoat. By the late twentieth century things were further along than that.

But the 6th Earl – knowing nothing of what went before – was under pressure from necessity. He packed endless millennia of invention/innovation & ingenuity into a significantly shorter time. To say it was a steep learning-curve would be an understatement – up there with 'All things considered I'd rather be in Philadelphia'.

Without knowing it – he reinvented the mortice joint & the concept of 'tongue-&-groove'.

He sawed & he chipped & he hammered. He decamped to an alien world – a Xanadu of 'doing things'. His imagination flowered & flourished. He knew little – because he knew little of anything – of the things that fired Brunelleschi. But that mattered not-a-fig. In his own way he was doing what all great dreamers & artists/all great architects & builders throughout time have done. He was giving substance & flight to his imagination.

And then – one day – he saw a ship. It wasn't his supply ship. That wasn't due for months. This was something different. It was bigger than the supply ship/much bigger. And it had a crane.

*

Noor – no longer needing the provocative dress/cleavage/thigh or any other artifice for getting-laid by a stranger – was now getting-laid in just the way she liked getting-laid by a man who was no longer a stranger. She knew that this man who was no longer a stranger liked laying her in just the way she liked getting-laid. And – what's more – the getting-laid was now a bi-weekly event with 'all the things he told her' thrown in.

Then one day – with the eye wateringly large black thing just where she liked it – he said – "There are people I want you to meet."

She enjoyed [more than most of her friends did] being gang-banged. And being a good daughter of the veldt was no stranger to being it. But the thought of being gang-banged by men like this one did something unusual to the serotonin levels in specific parts of her *prosencephalon*.

Inspector Boris Ulysses Mansfield – his father a fan of Mussorgsky & his mother of Joyce/but with neither of them giving thought to what acronymically minded schoolboys might do with it – was worried. He was worried because he was good. He was the youngest inspector in any of the many & varied branches of New Scotland Yard. 'Chief Inspector' was but a short time away. He would/one day/be to British policing what Tim Gatting would/one day/be to the legal profession of South Africa.

His worry was this – he didn't like loose ends and the business he was looking into was littered with them.

He had been seconded/by request/his request/to 'Unsolved Cases' and this one – the one he was interested in – was about as unsolved as 'unsolved' can get. It was a doozy.

There was a dead nanny. There was a metal pipe. There were an Earl's – *the* Earl's/the 6th Earl's – prints all over it. There was a 6th Earl's Savile Row jacket – double-breasted & double-vented – but no 6th Earl. And the 6th Earl that was lacking had been lacking for years.

He/Boris went through the file with a comb that made fine-tooth-combs seem coarse. The case notes of that time were thorough/up to a point. The interviews of that time had been well conducted/up to a point. No 'apparent' stone had been left unturned. But what about the 'not so apparent' ones? Did they – all those years ago – get turned? Or were some of them left un-? He would need to – which he did – find out.

As a preliminary to finding out he repeated things/ everything – the forensics/the prints/the blood on the pipe/ the hair on the pipe/the Savile Row jacket/the cause of death [etc.].

He reviewed the grisly photos – a battered body on a slab/a dissected brain.

He interviewed friends/boyfriends/ex– & otherwise. They – without exception – wanted things opened [re-].

Boris – as you know – was a good copper. He knew when he was being lied to. None of 'the friends/boyfriends/ex– &/or otherwise' did.

He interviewed the Earl's wife. She didn't either.

He interviewed the Earl's mother. She didn't either.

He interviewed the Earl's younger son. He didn't either.

He interviewed the Earl's elder son. He did.

His lies weren't big lies/or a lot of lies – just a few & small/ but lies none-the-less.

He was the 6th Earl's elder son and thus the 7th Earl [one thing the nobility *can* do is count] and an arrogant man. He – like his father – had been schooled/to no obvious advantage/ at the School By The River. It was where generations of similar Earls were/likewise/taught (sic) to little end.

To Boris – an insightful man – the 7th Earl was very much the same as the picture he was building of his father. He was a bird-of-little-brain who – faithful to his avian brainless-ness – tilted his head back/stuck his beak of a nose in the air/folded his hands/wing-like/behind him and spoke in the silly & affected chirping of his *contrade civetta* ['set']. "Thank God" – thought Boris [a grammar school boy] – "for grammar school boys."

He left the 7th Earl of Somewhere-or-other chirping his laughable chirps. He drove back to London. He felt/he realised/a slight/bordering on moderate/disdain for Earls from Any-old-where & of any-old-number. But he came to realise – as he reached his M25 turn-off – that the lies he was told/told him more than the truths he wasn't.

He went the next day to a gambling club in Mayfair. He interviewed a man called John/the [as you know] oldest-&-closest-friend. He was told nothing but.

In knowing they were 'nothing but' Boris knew they were lies being lied by an expert/a man who lied with ease/a man who preferred to lie than to not.

Boris knew this man & men just like him. He was a man for whom 'telling the truth' smacked of the 'sophisticate-un' & the gauche. Lying was second nature to him. He lied for practice. He lied to keep-his-eye-in.

But be-that-as-it-may – Boris [able to read men like the oldest-&-closest-friend because he'd had practice in spades] took more away from the interview than the oldest-&-closest-friend thought he might.

That evening – in the dining room of *Nel Gwyn's Knockers* – Boris drank lightly & ate sparingly. He talked to his wife less than usual. He pondered – as [once again] so many of us have a tendency to do/or are forced by kismet/fate & circumstance to do – on 'life's uncertain passage'.

And the 'life's uncertain passage' he pondered upon was not that of his own life/or of his wife's life/but of the life of the 6th Earl of Somewhere-or-other.

He was asking himself – as a result of the pondering – questions. And the questions he was asking himself were: Q. 1. Was the 6th Earl still alive? Which he was pretty [but not absolutely] certain he was. Q. 2. If he was/then where was he? Q. 3. If he was where he was – which he would be – how did he get where he was? Q. 4. If he was where he was – which he would be – who knew he was where he was? Q. 5. If he was where he was – which he would be – who helped him get to be where he was? He thought he knew the answer to that one.

They walked home holding hands. He always walked on the gutter side of the pavement. He was a grammar school boy & a gentleman. He went to his study and pondered further. He pondered further upon a singular life/upon uncertainty in general and one uncertainty/singular in nature/in particular. He pondered upon passages to places unknown. But only to places 'as yet' unknown.

He rose earlier than usual. He got to The Yard earlier than usual. There were things to be checked. He sat at his desk. He checked things. He wrote things. He went to his Super's office. He wasn't in yet.

⁂

Two men left Israel. They travelled to South Africa. They didn't fly.

The reason they didn't fly was that few/if any/airlines were-or-are happy to check sufficient plutonium [Pu-239] for a 20-kiloton atomic bomb.

So – the men left Ashdod by boat. It was quite a big boat/but not big enough to be a ship. There was no baggage allowance. Their hand-luggage – bulkier than usual because of all the tools & stuff [stuff that would never fit into that metal frame thing at 'Departures'] – was no problem.

Israel & South Africa – while poles apart in their attitudes to skin colour/race & religion – were happy bed-fellows when it came to the clandestine production of atomic bombs [or were up until F W de Klerk spat-the-dummy/threw-a-hissy-fit & took-his-ball-home – see above].

South Africa/for years/had sent unrefined yellow-cake to Israel/& Israel – a little later – had sent some of it/in refined & usable form/back. But that mutually beneficial/state sanctioned/ trade was no longer.

Now – as necessity dictated – a man whose name was Eli as well as Rubenstein was brought – as you probably suspected he would be – into the story.

'Sufficient plutonium [Pu-239] for a 20-kiloton bomb' isn't as much as you might think/about 10 kilos/and with weapons-grade Pu-39 being significantly heavier than gold/10 kilos of Pu-239 doesn't take up a whole lot of space. You could – for example – fit it in a briefcase or backpack – although neither of those options would be sensible options to opt for. Not if you didn't want to be thoroughly irradiated & die [sometime later/but not a long time later] from pancytopenia & other nasty things.

So – it's the surrounding kilos of lead/receiving & nullifying the alpha particles/neutrons/gamma rays & even one or two beta particles [as they do] that puts you over the baggage limit. Hence the boat from Ashdod.

But [I can hear you ask] where did the Pu-239 come from in the first place? What was its provenance?

Well – Israel had/at that time and still does/more nuclear reactors than-you-could or can-poke-a-stick-at and you couldn't & can't stroll through the Negev without tripping over one. But – be-that-as-it-may – Israel wasn't & isn't in the business of giving away the products of its productive & industrious industry. They were & are – after all – surrounded by enemies who would like nothing better than to see/promote & host a replay of the Holocaust.

Israel's Pu-239 was Israel's Pu-239 and the only way they were [ever were] going to give it away was through the bomb-bay of a Phantom. They'd made plenty/more than enough to go around. There were & are plenty of places to send them.

So – where did *this* ['*our*'] Pu-239 come from? Well – while the world was happy to see the end of 'The Cold War' and applause for Ronnie/Maggie & Mikhail was lifting rafters from Reykjavik to Pago Pago – there were downsides. And one of those 'downsides' was that there was a scary [truly scary] amount of fissile material swilling around unstable parts of the world [i.e./e.g. 'The Stans' – bits of the old USSR/CCCP that now weren't].

So – that's where *it* came from.

But how did *it* get to Israel?

Well – *it* got to Israel – of course it did – through the tireless efforts of a Mr Eli Rubenstein. It was a matter of personal pride [as well as smart business practice] that should a client want 10 kilos of Pu-239 then a client should have every right to expect – in exchange for a considerable sum of untraceable but readily redeemable currency/or other/of which there were several available/financial instrument – 10 kilos of Pu-239.

Things like that were 'what he did' and/because it was 'what he did'/he did it.

Hence the boat/not quite a ship/from Ashdod.

<hr>

*

Inspector – now Chief Inspector – Mansfield [but we'll call him Boris from now on] presented to his Super [when he at last/ because he was late/because/or so he said/he was tied up with taking his wife to the hospital to have her haemorrhoids – which can/as you may know/or may have heard/be pretty painful – fixed/arrived at work] what he had.

And his Super – being aware of Boris' talents/as well as his expected & express rise through the ranks/and being only eighteen months from retirement/and considering the whole matter to be in the-too-hard-basket – made the obvious decision [which was to make no decision at all]. He kicked-it-upstairs. Wasn't that what Chief Supers were paid for [sorting out too-hard-baskets]?

The Chief Super listened to what Boris said. He looked at all Boris showed him. He said he'd sleep-on-it/and he did – for three weeks. It was only at the end of the three weeks – after being pestered by Boris [that was the way he saw it] on a regular basis/and considering the whole matter to be in the too-hard-basket – that he made the obvious decision [which was to make no decision at all]. He kicked-it-upstairs. Wasn't that what Ass Comms were paid for [sorting out too-hard-baskets]?

Now – Chief Superintendent is the highest & last of the non-political ranks of the British police force.

Above that – for an Ass Comm/a Dep Comm & a Comm – the rarefied airs & sodden fields of battle are fraught with the barrage balloons raised & the mine fields laid by the Mandarins of Whitehall.

And it comes as no surprise to any of us – because it's simply human nature – that an Ass Comm aspires to be a Dep Com/a Dep Comm aspires to be the Comm & the Comm aspires to the House of Lords. Like every soldier in Napoleon's *Grande Armée* they carry a Marshal's *baton* in their knapsack.

And so it was that the Ass Comm listened to what Boris had to say to him. He looked at what Boris had to show to him. He said he'd sleep-on-it/and he did – for three weeks.

It wasn't an easy matter for the Ass Comm. He was a Secondary Modern schoolboy from Northolt and had [somehow] 'made good' – thus impressing mightily his family & friends. He knew exactly/right down to the last one/how-many-beans-made-five.

He was a closet republican at heart – although no one knew that – least of all his wife who talked in her sleep and who/he knew/was having an affair with the Dep Comm.

In matters of 'the nobility' – however ignoble they might show themselves to be – it was best to tread warily. A law-abiding pleb [especially one from Northolt] taking down/planning to take down/or even thinking about planning to take down/a nob [even a murdering swine of a nob] was a sure way of making enemies in high & wrong places. The nobs weren't awash with worthy attributes/but closing ranks [they called it loyalty when it was simply self-interest] was the one thing they did well.

He couldn't – for obvious reasons – talk to the Dep Comm/ and the Comm [one foot already in the Lords] wouldn't/couldn't/ not possibly/sanction anything like what he was suggesting.

And so – like Latimer & Ridley before him – with 'rare-to-medium' [occasionally sizzling to 'well-done'] misgivings as to the cupidity of life/the dire chance of life/the cruel fate of life/the general cock-up of life/he stepped forward into the flames and did what he knew to be right.

He gave Boris everything he was asking for.

*

Noor was disappointed. She was up for 'all sorts of things'. She'd spent the previous night dreaming of 'all sorts of things'. And now the men she was introduced to – or so it seemed – only wanted to talk. But after an hour of talking she came to realise that these men wanted more than to do 'all sorts of things'.

They wanted her for 'all sorts of other things' and part of the realisation she was realising was that she was being enlisted – if she was happy to be – for 'higher things'/'all sorts of higher things'.

They were big/bluff & rough looking men. She could see the faraway look in their eyes. They were out-doors men/sons of a hard land. They weren't weak/namby-pamby *Engels*. They were men of her own tribe.

And so – after an hour of talking/questioning & answering/ she was inducted in secrecy that would – of course it would – [because the consequences of it 'being not' were made clear to her] stay secret – into the wonderful world of the Afrikaner Westandsbeging.

After that and somewhat unexpectedly – because there were four of them – but certainly delightfully – because there were four of them – they did 'all sorts of things'. And the 'all sorts of things' were 'all sorts of things' she'd never had done – not in the way they were done/and not for as long as they were done – to her before.

As she lay on the bed/as fulfilled as a woman [a woman like Noor] can be/she came to the realisation – as well as to other things – that she'd never been happier in her life. And she hadn't even needed the eye wateringly large black thing to get her there.

She hobbled into the house. She insulted the cook/then the maid/then the laundry girl. She lay on the sofa in the lounge room. She thought thoughts. They were good thoughts [not *good* thoughts but pleasing thoughts] to think. She lay and thought thoughts for the rest of the afternoon. She rose with some difficulty. She insulted the maid again/drank half a bottle of schnapps/refused dinner and went to bed. Her husband rang to say that his Durban case might finish up tomorrow and he should/with any luck/be home by the weekend.

She slept – like a great man once slept before her – 'the sleep of the saved and the thankful'.

＊

Hai knew about the man called Eli. That was because – in the business he was in – everyone knew about the man called Eli.

Hai's knowledge of [more 'awareness' of] the man called Eli was because the man called Eli was a man who could do things/ arrange things/find things/hide things/move things around and make things disappear. He/Eli was thought to be – because he was – the best at what he did. And in the knowledge that [more 'awareness' that] Eli was the best at what he did – and in the knowledge & awareness that there was someone wishing to hide half-of-half-a-ton-of-Afghan-best – Hai made the assumption [something we know we should try to avoid/but on occasions have no choice but to make] that the man wishing to hide the half-of-half-a-ton-of-Afghan-best would [in all likelihood] contact the man called Eli and would [in all likelihood] ask for his help.

In the assumed knowledge of this assumption Hai decided to find out as much as he could about the man called Eli.

Now – there is more on the public record about all of us than any of us [other than the conspiracy-theorists/who are only wrong most of the time/which means not wrong all of the time/which means right some of the time] can imagine.

And there is – in addition – more on the private record about all of us than any of us [other than the conspiracy theorists, etc.] can imagine.

Hai – in the knowledge of both of those things – set about knowing as much has he could/from the public & private records/about a man called Eli.

But he/Hai knew that there might be and – in the case of a man called Eli – almost certainly would be/things altered in/ added to & removed from/the public & private records.

Hai set about finding those things.

$$*$$

The boat from Ashdod – big /but not quite big enough to be a ship – arrived late one night [which was early one morning] at Lambert's Bay in the Western Cape/in the R of SA. The crew didn't tarry. The 10 kilos of 'you know what' – surrounded by a paranoid amount of lead – was unloaded onto a truck.

The truck driver didn't tarry either. He drove north-east. The boat sailed away. Only the town drunk saw anything and he'd forgotten by morning. The harbour-master – rising late as one does in a sleepy little town like Lambert's Bay – saw truck tracks on the quay. He thought nothing of them.

$$*$$

Boris talked to Detective Sergeant Titus Ishmael [as in 'Call me...'] Taylor. Everyone – of course they did – because 'Titus' was reminiscent of Titus Oates/and 'Titus Oates' was reminiscent of dark times [ref. 'The Popish Plot', Pollock J, 1903] which 'Ishmael' wasn't – called him 'Ish'.

He – just as Boris was – was a man on the rise. They would – in-the-fullness-of-time – come to occupy adjoining offices on the top floor/but no one knew that then. And they still don't/because it hasn't happened yet.

They talked for some time and much of what they talked about – Ishmael being privy to his boss's thoughts on 'The Case of the Missing Earl' – were things they'd talked about before. But/in the talking about them again/they'd modified & nuanced [but never cemented/because 'cemented' thoughts are the death-knell of good policing] their ideas about what to do next/next after that/next after that and-so-on.

After talking for some time they called the team together. They talked more. Leads were discussed/dead-ends considered/duties allotted & responsibilities conferred.

Ishmael went home and failed – even though he never failed – to watch The Seven O'clock News. Thus telling his wife – an insightful & intuitive woman/as women so often are – that there was something on his mind.

He went to the pocket-handkerchief garden. He sat under the hawthorn tree. He thought about ways/best ways – because that's what Boris asked him to do – to find out things that were things about a certain man. And the certain man was – of course he was – the oldest-&-closest-friend of the 6th Earl of Somewhere-or-other.

Boris sat alone in his office. It had been a long day. He was as deep in thought as it is possible to be deep in. He knew there was one thing he must do himself. Something he couldn't delegate.

Noor was happy to be briefed – as well as/sometime later/'debriefed' – by men of gradually increasing importance. She was happy to share in a 'union of the minds' but happier still to share – as seemed to be the habit with members of the Afrikaner Westandsbeging – in a 'post-union of the minds'/'union of the bodies... or two'.

She came to realise – like many women before her – that just the thought of getting 'union of the body-ed... or two' by men of power was a potent stimulant of her libidinous id.

She was – like many a starlet before her – humping/bonking &-so-on-ing her way to the top. And the top was Gene T Blanche. Although/sadly/when she got there/he turned out to be the most disappointing hump/bonk &-so-on she'd ever had. She didn't know about – and had never before met a man suffering from – *ejaculatio praecox*.

There were other things though – more important things – more important than being humped/bonked &-so-on-ed. She wasn't here solely to be 'sex-toy-to-the-powerful'. Mr GTB – lousy lay though he might be – was a man of vision/superb vision/because it was her vision too.

The AWSB – he told her – needed more than farmers to give it the power it needed. It needed power – he told her – to be listened to in the 'Corridors of Power' [the ones in Pretoria]. And the best way – he told her – to be powerful and thus listened to in the 'Corridors of Power' [the ones in Pretoria] was to be feared. And the best way to be feared – he told her – was to possess something frightful.

He didn't tell her/and she couldn't guess/what the 'something frightful' might be. But she was happy that 'her people' were soon to get something that was. She knew that having got 'something that was' they [her people] would be feared/powerful & listened to in the Corridors of Power [the ones in Pretoria].

And eventually it would come – it went without saying – so no one said it – to putting the fucking kaffirs & all the fucking *Engel* kaffir lovers back in their place.

That – 'the putting back in their place' – Mr GTB told her – was why she was chosen.

⊤
*

Tim – having gone to the bar as his family expected he would – was as much a star as the star-bursts around his wife's nipples. To say he was a success would be an understatement of previously mentioned proportions.

As the also-rans of his profession might [and occasionally did] sink-without-trace – Tim did the opposite – he soared. He became a legal megastar. He was as much sought after as a Mandela autograph/a night with Madonna [it *was* some time ago] or a kilo of Périgord truffles. He was the-bee's-knees of the bar and/in being the-bee's-knees of the bar/he got all the best cases.

His polite & self-effacing manner belied the acute & incisive intellect that lay below. He could hold a jury in the palm of his hand. Superlatives surrounded all he did. His handsome & boyish humility made every man like him and every woman want him.

Then [one day] he got a call from Pretoria. A man from a four-letter acronym wanted to talk to him. Tim asked – "What about?" The man said he couldn't talk on the phone. Could Tim come to Pretoria? Tim could. So he did.

They met in the foyer of Tim's hotel. The man was nondescript & average in every possible way of being 'nondescript & average'. Tim assumed – having researched the four-letter-acronym – this to be an advantage in the man's/assumed/line of work.

◎ He was the sort of man you might meet at a party and then/ if asked to describe him/wouldn't be able to remember a

109

thing about him. We meet men like that don't we? Perhaps some of us *are* men like that. I don't think women can do quite the same thing. There's something about a woman that makes her non-nondescriptable. But/being a man/I may be wrong about that.

They drove to the Department of the Interior/recently – for reasons of wanting a less austere countenance – renamed the Department of Home Affairs. The previous administration hadn't cared [not a brass razoo/not a jot-or-tittle] about the severity of its countenance/if anything/quite the opposite. The more severe the better/the more threatening the better/the more threatened the more compliant. It had worked well – up until lately.

They took the lift to the third floor/a long corridor/a small office & an uncomfortable chair. A wall/faded paint where a picture once hung. What/who? Tim could guess.

Opening gambits – "Thank you for coming, I know you're a busy man, I know your time's valuable."

Tim didn't say but thought – because he was a busy man and his time was valuable – *"Get on with it, man, what's this all about?"*

As though he could read Tim's mind the man said – "What this is about, Mr Gatting, is your wife." And that concentrated Tim's mind in just the way the nondescript man wanted it to be.

‾
*
‾

The 6th Earl looked at the ship [a real ship and one with a crane]. He wondered whose it was. He wondered what it was doing here. He watched it steam [if ships still 'steam'] up the channel between 'his' island and the atolls. He watched it drop anchor and/because of that/stop.

"Fuck," he thought. And because he'd been on his own for years and because his internal-censor – that thing that stops us from saying "Great boobs," to a woman we pass in the street –

110

was no longer needed & long since retired he said it out loud…
and loudly.

He watched as a boat was craned over the side. He watched
as people got in/four of them/and motored his way. "Fuck," he
thought & said again. But then the boat turned and headed away
towards the atolls. "Thank fucking Christ," he [etc.] once more.

He was – as were his family/friends & 'set' – raised in the
traditions of the church. And – just like his family/friends &
'set' – he found/like a bastion against the knowledge of his own
less-than-mediocre mediocrity/some solace in the security &
certainty of God & the church.

But not just God & 'the church' – 'The Church'/The C
of E/The Church of England – the church where God was
indisputably/undeniably & without doubt/an Englishman. The
church where Englishmen/Christian Englishmen – little lower
than the angels – looked down & with suspicion on anyone
& everyone they could. And/without doubt/on anyone who'd
arrived since Chaucer was a lad.

God's incarnation as Christ-the-Son [because God-the-
Father was a bit scary & judgemental/and the Holy Ghost was a
concept way above his head] was never far away from him. And
while thoughts of performing 'acts of Christian charity' never
strayed much into his thoughts – 'He' was still 'one of us'.

So – "Thank fucking Christ," was not a phrase that would
– not in his previous incarnation as a Belgravia cad/cadge/
Christian [take your pick] – normally have come readily to
mind &/or tongue.

It was evidence of the changes within him. And the changes
within him were legion.

He watched the boat swing around the stern of the ship and
head off towards the atolls and away from him. The 'and away
from him' being the critical phrase in the last sentence.

"But what the hell," he thought. *"What if they come here next? I'll be fucked."* And then – together with his thoughts of 'hell' & 'being fucked' – he thought another thought which/in the confusion of his other thoughts/was a good thought to think. He thought he should hide.

$$\overline{*}$$

So – when the nondescript man showed Tim the things he showed him/as well as the thing the nondescript man said to him [told him] it/they more than concentrated Tim's already concentrated mind.

He was shown photographs – lots of them. They were of her/Noor. She was sitting in a cheap café. It was in the 'wrong part of town'. She was dressed like a tart. There were men sitting with her. They were the 'wrong sort of men'.

So – there she was/dressed like a tart/sitting with the 'wrong sort of men' and sitting with them in a cheap café in the 'wrong part of town' – why?

And why – thought Tim/as one might expect him to/did the 'wrong sort of men' have their hands/more often than not/resting on her thigh?

Then there were other photographs of her – lots of them. She was no longer sitting in a cheap café in the 'wrong part of town'. She was lying on a bed in a cheap hotel – Tim assumed as a correct assumption to assume – in the 'wrong part of town'. There were men with her/the same men/the same 'wrong sort of men'. There were parts of the 'wrong sort of men' quite clearly occupying parts/ 'the wrong parts'/of her. And in one of them he could see/quite clearly/the end of/but only the end of/an eye wateringly large black thing.

Horrified – inwardly but not outwardly – Tim didn't know what to say. But/being a lawyer/not for long.

"How did you come by these?"

"Routine surveillance."

"Routine surveillance of what?"

"Of our country's enemies."

"My wife?"

"No, the men."

"Who are they?"

"That one," he pointed to the photo on the top of the pile – "is Pieter Linaar."

"Who is he?"

"A farmer."

"From where?"

"Sterkaar."

"Why was he in Cape Town?"

"He goes every week."

"Answer the question."

"He's recruiting people."

"What for?"

"The AWSB."

"What?"

"The Afrikaner Westandsbeging."

"Blanche's trash?"

"Yes."

"Why was he talking to my wife?"

"We thought you might be able to tell us."

"*Fuck*," thought Tim – whose internal-censor was working just fine – without saying it.

He knew very well [how could he not] that his wife sported a healthy appetite for *tous les chose de la chambre*/as well as elsewhere/and that there were parts of that 'healthy appetite' that were a little less healthy than they might have been.

He was used to doing the private/kinky & intimate things she liked him to do to/with & for her. And he'd grown to quite like [even more than quite like] doing them. But to look – in the company of a third party – at a seemingly endless series of pictures of his wife having those things – their private/kinky & intimate things/but now not-so-private/kinky & intimate things – done to/with & for her by the 'wrong sort of men'/ discombobulated him to the point of 'very'. But he didn't let it show.

"What do you want from me?" he asked.
"Your cooperation."
"In what?"
"Keeping tabs."
"On what?"
"Your wife's comings and goings."
"You seem to have that down pat."
"Small things, you know, things between husbands and wives, jotted notes, tender asides, things like that."
"My wife doesn't do 'tender'."
The man looked down at the photographs.
"So I see."

Tim returned to Cape Town. He was a different man. The Scales of Saul were fallen from his eyes. He was a new man/*un homme changé*/a man on a mission.

—
*
—

As it was once/and still is/said – 'All roads lead to Rome' – but as Eli was starting to notice – all roads were now [or so it seemed] leading to him.

Being a worldly/astute & intelligent man and with a 'clearly unclouded' – rather than [to avoid the schoolboy sin of hendiadys] a 'clear & unclouded' – picture of the sort of men his world was full of/and with a healthy desire to make it through to old age without being fed to a variety of carnivores/

or becoming part of some new housing project on the West Bank/he kept his [and always had done] metaphorical ear to the equally connotative ground. And/in addition to his own ear/he employed a number of men & women to keep their ears to the ground for him. And it was thanks to this 'ears-to-the-ground policy' that he became aware of people asking questions about him. Not questions about how he might be of assistance to them/ but about other things.

He'd wanted for some time for it to be quietly known that it was he – Eli Rubenstein-the-Great – who'd spirited away the 6th Earl of Somewhere-or-other to Somewhere-or-other else.

But he knew what hubris led to.

Friend John – a man he'd done business with before and a man who sent business his way – was a man for whom loyalty-&-friendship [the only noble traits – the second 't' being silent – he possessed] were paramount.

Any leaked suggestion that he/Eli – even in some small way – was involved in 'The Case of the Missing Earl' would not/as it might appear at first glance to be/be good for business. Any suggestion/however small [because even small suggestions go viral] that he was a breaker-of-oaths &/or confidences and that by letting it be known that it was down to him/he/Eli that the 6th Earl remained extant [but unfindable] would be the opposite of what Friend John wished to promulgate and had paid handsomely for him/Eli to promulgate [i.e. that the 6th Earl was pushing up the daisies somewhere] and would be the opposite of what he/Eli would want/and would be deleterious to his reputation as the go-to-man-of-the-world.

And so – he/Eli kept – in all the ways it is possible to keep – mum.

He'd enjoyed – of course he had/how could he not/but many years before – an affair with Mitzi Johnson. It was before she put-her-brain-into-park/went sapiently AWOL and agreed to become Mitzi [i.e. Lady] Prouse. It was that long ago. He first met her at a party on the Upper East Side. The affair lasted months/a year. It lasted until she got married.

Then he'd met her again – it was years later – at her home in Eaton Square. It was when he was doing business with her husband. He didn't like her husband – he wasn't honest.

Sir Peter Prouse was [as you may remember] a dishonest & disgusting villain/and honest ones like Eli/who weren't overly numerous/knew not to trust him.

There was – Eli knew – only one way to be a successful crook and that was to be an honest one. If a crook couldn't trust another crook then what-was-the-world-coming-to?

So – he hadn't liked Prouse. He'd known he was planning to cheat him/partly because he was the sort of man who planned to cheat everyone and partly because Eli was a Jew. Prouse [Eli knew] would enjoy crowing about it in his – 'No Jews Allowed' – London club. Prouse [Eli knew] would crow about 'playing-the-straight-bat' & 'beating the swarthy Yid at-his-own-game'.

But everything about Prouse was anything but straight and that was why Eli – there was little choice but to – pulled out of their once-in-a-lifetime deal. But not before pulling out of [which infers that he'd pushed into/just for old-times'-sake] Mitzi/and many more times than once.

So – what was it with Mitzi now? Their time together was years ago. She can't have kept a-torch-burning-for-him this long. He knew – because he prided himself in knowing things – that she was shacked up in New York [sometimes in London] with a guy called Rupert Something-or-other. A guy he/Eli had/ sometime before/made a mental note to keep a mental eye on. Rupert [he knew/more than suspected] was a guy who was going somewhere/somewhere-up-top/someday.

Why – he/Eli wondered – was she making enquiries about him now? Why/even more/was she making enquiries about islands? What was going on? Did she know something? And if she did know something what was it that she knew? What was it all about?

And what about Hai-the-Chink? What did he want?

Eli knew about Hai-the-Chink. He knew he was smart/even for a Chink. He knew a few smart Chinks and this one was a whole lot smarter than his boss.

That fat וזנה Woo had been 'smart' but only smart through the era when being smart meant: A.) Being more brutal than the next guy: and B.) Being more brutal than that. But it was a different world now.

Eli knew – and he knew Hai-the-Chink knew – that you needed to 'do subtle'/brutal on occasions/but subtle all the time. If you didn't 'do subtle' you didn't do much. If you didn't 'do subtle' you made a splash and fed sharks.

So – what did Hai-the-Chink want? Well – he knew very well what he wanted. He wanted the half-of-half-a-ton-of-Afghan-best. But he was coming to the wrong man. He had a deal with the Australian וזנה Bert – and Bert [Australian & a וזנה though he maybe was] had been straight down the line with him. There was no bullshit/no negotiating then renegotiating the price/no side deals. A good crook/his sort of crook. If only there were more crooks like Bert then the world would be a better place. That's what Eli thought.

He would keep his bargain with Bert and Hai-the-Chink could go לצזאל himself.

Anyway – more to the point was – how did Hai-the-Chink know/because no one else did – that he knew anything/let alone everything – about the half-of-half-a-ton? Because he/Eli *did* know everything there was to know about it – right down to it being a bit less than half-of-half-a-ton – right down to where it was buried – right down to what sort of steel chest it was buried in – right down to what combination was on the lock on the steel chest it was buried in and right down to the coordinates –

coordinates down to the last tenth of the last second of the last minute of the last degree of the world's circumference – down to the last/give-or-take/yard-&-a-half of where it was buried.

And because Eli was blessed – which was unusual in people of his wartime provenance – with a wicked-&-wacky sense of humour/and because he'd seen his fair share of pirate movies/ the spot – the exact spot – was marked by a more wacky-than-wicked 'X'.

But did – and if he did how did – Hai-the-Chink know that he/ Eli knew those things? Perhaps it was that Hai-the-Chink knew that – when it came to hiding half-of-half-a-ton of anything in need of hiding – the world would beat-a-path to his/Eli's door and/in addition to that/he/Eli would be there to greet them.

So – Hai-the-Chink knowing that he/Eli would know the whereabouts of the half-of-half-a-ton wasn't such a big deal. Hai-the-Chink could go-לצזאל-himself. No problem there.

But then there was the English copper. What was he up to? How come he was making waves and asking question where questions didn't need to be asked. What-the-לצזאל was that all about.

———
*
———

Ishmael talked to Boris. Boris talked to his Ass Com. His Ass Comm – who didn't want to admit [certainly not to himself] that the Dep Comm was bringing an extramarital bloom to his wife's [all four of them] cheeks and in the knowledge that the Comm [their Lord & Master] was too far above the firmament to be concerned with such trivial/mundane & earthly matters – decided to go it alone.

And – in this way – the processes of the law-upholders ran fair-&-square into the swamps/quicksands & circumlocutions of the Halls of Justice.

The Ass Comm – just as Boris had asked him to do – applied for a Judicial Clearance – Section something-or-other/Subsection B/para whatever of whatever part of whatever code they needed to look at – to be given permission to tap-the-phones and have access to the bank records/back very nearly to the flood/of [you guessed it] oldest-&-closest-friend John.

The judge – who harboured an atavistic as well as inexplicable dislike for the police – would normally/as was his want/have refused the application. But because – at a cocktail party some years before – he'd spent an hour being bored stiff by the Shadow Minister for Something-or-other – he didn't.

It [the cocktail party and what he'd been bored stiff about] was about the goings on/the snorting by & the screwing of his daughter [the Shadow Minister's daughter] in the rooms above oldest-&-closest-friend John's gaming establishment.

And so – having a young(ish) daughter of his own [who was showing reluctance/bordering on 'great reluctance'/to remove herself from the financial safety-net of her father's state-guaranteed & not inconsiderable income] he'd granted it.

And so – the things Ishmael & Boris got to listen to & read of made interesting listening to & reading of indeed.

*

A few miles outside the non-teeming & non-metropolitic town of Groblershoop [a town in Griqualand/in the Langberge & not far from Bechuanaland] sat the farm of Meneer Minnaar.

M Minnaar was a farmer who farmed/on his father's old farm/the usual things farmers in the farmland of Griqualand farmed.

But – not picking up the knack of farming or/it has to be said/much else – he farmed his farmland less successfully than his farming neighbours farmed their farms.

And so – in an attempt to avoid the slings-and-arrows-of-outrageous-insolvency – M Minnaar had taken to repairing farm machinery instead.

One requirement – obviously – for the repairing of farm machinery was [is & always will be] a large shed. And a large shed was just what M Minnaar possessed.

And it was into this large shed that/the day after leaving Lambert's Bay/rolled a truck.

Not surprisingly – you're way out ahead of me again – nearby & occupying a spacious space on the floor sat 'The Bit'.

Men – men from prefix 972 – looked at what they were 'about to receive'.

One of them – but only one of them – was anything but 'truly thankful'.

$$\frac{\overline{}}{*}$$

"Where in fuck" – thought & said the 6th Earl – "am I going to hide?" – because there was nowhere he could. But then [in the manner of *fiat lux*] an idea sprang – eureka-like – to his mind.

His family's ancestral pile/his *paterna patria*/was in Wiltshire. It stood hard by a village with a pub called *Cromwells Wart*. It was – like most family piles – nowhere near the 'Somewhere-or-other' of his family title. The rambling/shambling house – endless rooms where no one ever went – was old when the 1st Earl was young.

It was built for a Catholic – a 'fire 'n brimstone' recusant nob/Lord Such-and-such of Somewhere-or-other-else – who/in the knowledge of what Cromwell's Major Generals [Majors General] were in the habit of doing to Catholic priests [which weren't particularly nice things and usually/somewhere along the line/involved red-hot pokers] had arranged for an easy to find priest-hole to be fashioned inside the house & behind a panel halfway down the main staircase. And another – a not-so-easy-to-find one – dug under a rose bed in the ornamental garden. And it was in the 'not-so-easy-to-find one' that John – yet to be the 6th Earl – had hidden from his tutor when the thought of reciting Latin declensions overwhelmed him.

And so – in the memory of all that – he set about a reproduction of the one in the garden. But where?

Having learned/by-trial-and-error/and in the memory of the all too predictable [but only in hindsight] failure of his first prototypical ladder(s)/that it was better to spend time looking & thinking before jumping & leaping/he – deciding to do just that – sat & thought.

The singularity of his thought was [see above] 'where?' And – with the singularity of that thought carried before him like the bones of Saint Peter – he roamed his island in search of 'the right spot' which/more easily than he thought he would/he found. It was a spot of soft ground between two quite distinctively bent palms. He started to dig. He was surprised at how easy it was. He was down nearly two feet before a realisation – surreal in its reality – dawned upon him. He wasn't the first person to dig where he dug. Digging had been dug by diggers who'd dug here before. And the diggers who'd done the digging had done the digging not that long before.

Continuing to dig he dug down further. Two feet further the spade went 'clunk'.

*

Bert – anxiety over his half-of-half-a-ton getting the better of him – decided/if only for the sake of his gastric mucosa which/with all the stress/fags & Rogan Josh was taking a beating/to go and check things out for himself. He didn't – as perhaps he should have done/and as propriety would suggest he might & ought to have done – let Eli know where he was going & why.

He/Eli – being a man of the world & the underworld in particular/and being fully cognisant of the worries & frailties of his fellow creatures [especially where the protection of their wares & wherewithals was concerned] would have understood fully if Bert had said he wanted to see/first-hand/how things were/where they were/how deep they were [etc.].

But not being told/asked & then finding out later would raise – quite understandably – the idea in Eli's mind that Bert didn't trust him. And that/for Eli – who trusted Bert – would be hurtful to the point of 'very'.

With the passage of the years – and with the knowledge of the respect he was held in – Eli had become a benign/very nearly/ almost fatherly figure. Only occasionally – rarely now – did he need to flex his global muscle. The flexing of which would send – with reluctance – the performer of some unacceptable act to Jehovah's Stygian shores.

 How's that for the juxtaposition of mono–& poly–theism?

But Bert – sadly – did not share his anxieties & concerns with Eli. Instead of doing that he boarded his 70-ish-footer/together with Mac & Jimmy [his not-so-trusted minions] not so much for company but to keep them where he could see them/and 'sailed' out through Sydney Heads. He turned left/to port/north/ towards New Guinea – of course he did.

*

Boris was having trouble. He was sifting chaff and finding no grain. He knew only haystacks with no needles. For his Augean stable there was no Alpheus. He was knee deep in ox shit. And so – as wise men do in circumstances like that – he sought the fountain of all wisdom. He went and talked to his wife.

She – being a woman with special-ish powers/as so many women are/except when it comes to reading maps/knowing which way's north [etc.] could sense her husband's inner turmoil.

He told her in general terms – but not in specific terms – what ailed him. And what ailed him was the conundrum of a man's existence [he didn't say whose] in the face of his widely accepted [although not by Boris] non-existence.

He poured out his troubles.

Now – it is said/by the more cynically inclined/that 'behind every great-man stands a woman with a surprised look on her face'. But that wasn't the case with Boris & his wife. She was a paediatrician at The Westminster and as-smart-&-as-wise as only smart-&-wise people would agree was smart-&-wise. She could – if asked – 'smart-&-wise' for England. She knew full well the goodness & future greatness of her husband. She had faith in him. It was a faith that went well beyond the-faith-of-the-faithful.

"So, you don't know where he is?" she asked.

"No."

"Or even if he's alive?"

"No."

"But you think he is?"

"Yes."

"But you're not certain?"

"No."

"Is his mother still alive?"

"Yes."

"Why don't you ask her?"

"I have. She says she doesn't know where he is. Says she hasn't heard from him."

"Did you ask if he was alive?"

"No."

"Why don't you then?"

"How would she know? She hasn't heard a word from him, not for years, not since he disappeared."

"She's his mother. She'll know. Mothers know stuff like that."

"How?"

"Trust me, we just do."

So – in receipt of what his wife told him – he went to see the 5th Countess of Somewhere-or-other once again. He didn't ask – as he had the first time – if she knew where her son was. He simply asked her this:

"Countess, is your son still alive?"

To which she answered – "Which one?"

To which he answered – "Your elder son ma'am. John, the 6th Earl."

To which she answered – "If the 6th Earl was alive, young man, my grandson wouldn't be the 7th Earl, now would he?"

To which he answered – "But the 6th Earl was only declared 'legally' dead, ma'am, at the request of the 6th Countess."

He could see that the simple mention of her successor was in danger of curtailing his – up until then – moderately cooperative reception. So – taking subliminal cues from his wife who/while many miles away [and performing a tricky 'exchange-transfusion' on a premature baby from Chelmsford] was emitting waves of ESP and/in accordance with her suggestions – he tiptoed away from any further mention of the 6th Duchess.

He looked her straight in the eyes and – even for a seasoned copper – it was a daunting experience to experience.

But – daunt or no daunt – and after swallowing/he continued.

"Ma'am, is the 6th Earl still alive?"

"Don't be a stupid young man," she snapped. "Of course he is."

He drove home. He didn't need to tell his wife what the Countess said – she knew.

That night – the passion of their always passionate passions were more passionately passionate than usual.

Noor knew there must be a reason for her rapid [suspiciously rapid] rise through the rank-&-file of the AWSB. She was asked to join barely three months ago and was already sitting on Central Committee. She'd already humped/bonked &-so-on-ed – as well as been humped/bonked &-so-on-ed by – everyone on it. But she knew it wasn't just her uninhibited attitude to '&-so-on-ing' that they wanted her for. She knew there was some other reason.

She wasn't sure 'why' she was where she was/but getting to 'where she was'/and how she'd got to 'where she was'/had been fun. She'd enjoyed the experience(s) of 'horizontal-starlet-ing' her way to the top. She knew – she could feel it in that place where things like that get felt – that she was being groomed for something more/and that the 'something' in the 'groomed for something more' was something special. But there was no hint/ not yet/of what the 'something' in 'something special' might be.

＊

Keeping tabs on Noor wasn't as easy as Tim thought it would be. He was a busy barrister. He had a large and enlarging practice. It took him all over the country. He was often away for days.

The nondescript man said he knew that and that all 'our people' were asking of Tim was for him to be as vigilant as he could. He was – because that was what they'd asked him to – to look for signs of conflicted loyalty.

The term 'conflicted loyalty' took on a schizo meaning for him.

Which was more important for her to be loyal to? To him or to the country? Because – from what the man had told him and what the man had shown him – there wasn't a whole lot of loyalty going on to either.

He wasn't proud of doing the things he did. No man can feel proud of spying on his own wife. The AWSB was – after all – a legal entity/a legal political party – so what was wrong with belonging to it – apart from all the obvious things? She was a foreigner after all. Dutch. Perhaps she didn't understand what sort of men she was getting involved with.

But then he remembered the photographs and came – quite understandably – to the conclusion that she knew exactly what sort of men she was getting involved with.

He knew he didn't know his wife – not fully. Not down to the bed-rock of what made her tick. He knew there were closed/hidden/'no go' places/places where no one – and certainly not he – could ever go. But he'd thought he knew her better than he obviously did.

＊

Hai Chang wanted to know things. The things he wanted to know were things about 'The Man' – a man called Eli Rubenstein ['Eri Lubenstein']. It was the same as he'd once wanted to know things about Mr Woo.

'Knowledge is'/after all/'power'. It was knowledge & power – the power he'd gained from the knowledge – that had helped remove his erstwhile boss.

He'd learned the thing about 'knowledge & power' at school. He was told it was the wisdom of Sun Tzu.

Only later did he learn/from his wise & educated lover/ that it was the wisdom of a round-eye called Thomas Jefferson. And that had come as a shock. He'd never thought: 1). That a foreigner/a round-eye/a big-nose/a paper-tiger/an enemy of *Zhong Gou* & an enemy of The Middle Kingdom could ever say anything so profound: and 2). That his teacher might not know that: and even worse 3). That his teacher might know that but would [because of honourably/dishonourable patriotism] purposefully mislead him/them/the whole class/the whole school/year-after-year.

The day his lover told him that – the thing about Thomas Jefferson – was the day he started to question everything else he'd been told. And the answers to his questions weren't – because they never are – what he thought they would be.

But – be-that-as-it-may – to know more about Eli Rubenstein/ to know what his part in all of this was/would be a good thing to know.

And so – with-this-in-mind – he set out to find out about all the things he could find out about Eli Rubenstein.

＝
*

The 6th Earl – astounded by the 'clunk' – was astounded more by the cause of the 'clunk'. And the cause of the clunk was a metal chest. But he was more astounded than that – more horrified than that – to find decomposing bodies lying beside it. Two of them.

He sat – after a fulsome vomit/two of them – and pondered. This wasn't something he could put off pondering/not something to ponder later/not something to put off pondering until he had the time to ponder. This was something that called for an urgent ponder because – he pondered – the thing to be pondered upon was seemingly imponderable.

And so – like many men before him – to before Cro-Magnon man pondered the riddle of the stars – he pondered upon 'life's uncertain passage'. He pondered upon who these men were. Who they were before they weren't. And in that pondering he pondered upon himself – on who he was now/now that he wasn't who he was. He pondered his 'aloneness'/his 'might just as well be deadness'/his 'no witness to his lifeness'/his own 'judgement on his lifeness'/his own 'verdict on his lifeness'/the 'valediction to his lifeness'/with no hope of a 'vindication of his lifeness'. He felt wretched.

He would give his own worthless life that these men – whoever they were/however bad or good or otherwise they were – might live. He knew not who they were/but they would be men with lives & loves and now they were – as he wasn't – dead.

So – he pondered – he would give his life that these men might live. It would be – he mused/in sentiment but not in words – 'a far, far better thing I do, than I have ever done before.'

He sat. He pondered. He decided what to do. He took up his spade and filled in the pit. He walked away. He leant on his spade. It went deep down into soft soil/softer soil than it should have been.

He then – of course he did/because there was no choice but to – dug further. He dug in a déjà vu-ish sort of way. He uncovered – of course he did – two more bodies. More recently alive/riper/more disgusting/bodies. They lay beside another metal chest.

◎ Sorry about this. The time-line's got all screwed up. I don't know how it happened. But it all works out in the end – trust me.

He filled in the second pit. After that – after recovering/which he did – he walked down to the sea and washed his body/if not his soul.

And then he decided/because it seemed the logical thing to decide/to take a look at what was going on in the channel.

He climbed to the top of the island.

The ship was where it was before. The boat trailed behind. He surveyed his world/his little world/from above.

He'd been here for years and the island – morphing from 'the island' to 'his island' – had become home. There were proprietorial feelings he felt for it. More proprietorial feelings than he'd ever felt for any of his English homes. And certainly more than for his ancestral home. And that/he assumed/would be where – if she was/as he assumed she was/still alive [two correct assumptions in a row] his mother still lived.

He wondered – a 'wonder' not a 'ponder' – about his mother [not often but occasionally] and about whether she was/or perhaps wasn't/still alive. He [see above] assumed the correct assumption that she would be. He knew – as far as it was possible for a man to know anything about hardnosed old Countesses – that hardnosed old Countesses like his mother didn't die/not in the same way mere mortals did. They [while 'chewing broken bottles & killing rats with their teeth'] went on-and-on slowly rusting/like decommissioned battleships/to the grave.

It was *his* island and how dare anyone else think to set foot on it? The decomposing corpses – he knew a bit about that from his fox-hunting days – weren't there before he'd landed on the island. That was [see above] years ago. If they were there before him they'd be skeletons by now and with none of the squishy bits he'd found.

So – somehow they'd [these four men] together with the metal chests/but separately [some months apart] come ashore/got themselves killed/presumably murdered – another correct assumption – and then got themselves buried. And all of it under-his-watch. And that – for the 6th Earl/as it would be for any of us – was a disconcerting thought to be thinking.

Mixed in/up with his thoughts of 'disconcert' were thoughts & feelings of indignation. How dare they – whoever 'they' was or were – defile the sanctity of his realm. He felt deflowered/despoiled/violated. He understood how a woman [a non-

129

consenting one] must feel when she was being 'all-of-the-aboved'.

But now it was about to happen again. If they/the people on the ship/were looking at a puny atoll they would – for sure/ wouldn't they – come here?

He climbed to the highest point and stood – like Hillary/or was it Tenzing [because no one seems to be sure] – on the highest rock. The ship was there/where it always was. His first instincts were to prepare his defences & fight for his island – to 'Fight on the beaches, fight in the fields, fight in the streets' – he would never surrender. But then – with his emotions cooling – he came rapidly to the realisation that there was little/if anything/ for him to defend his island with. He could lob coconuts and that was about it. The alternative – his only alternative – was/ once again/to hide. But where?

At that moment – as the Princes of Serendip rode into view – a rock moved beneath his foot. It was – like all the rocks around it – magma from the volcano he knew his island/a long time ago/ages ago/eons ago – so not recently – once was.

He could remember a bit about volcanoes from school. They did them the week after his 'are-chip-a-lay-go' debacle and – not wanting a repeat snigger from the swots – he'd paid attention.

The rock moved to one side. There was an empty hole in the once-upon-a-time cone. He pulled away more/much lighter than you might think. And/lo-and-behold/he was looking into the mouth of a cave.

He crawled through the opening. He scratched his dick on the way. He didn't care. He tried to stand up and he could... just. 'Oh frabjous day! Callooh! Callay! And he chortled in his joy.'

---
*

130

"Is that the Acme Trading Company of Jerusalem?"

"מה."

"This is Mitzi Johnson from New York. I want to speak to the boss."

"בבהש החנה." followed by clicking noises.

"Goodish mornings to you, I am the man calling himself Mr Ben," said a moderate-to-heavily accented man calling himself Mr Ben. "I am the man calling himself that man Mr Rubenstein's secretary."

"This is the woman, Mitzi Johnson from New York. I want to speak to the man calling himself the boss."

"Hello, Mitzi Johnson," said Mr Ben.

"Hello, Mr Ben."

"May I be telling Mr Rubenstein what Mitzi Johnson, is calling to him and for about?"

"Tell the old goat it's Mitzi from New York. He'll remember me. We had a summer of wild passion. Don't ask about it, you're too young."

"I will possibly and very shortly be putting you through to Mr Rubenstein." Clicking noises.

"Eli, you there? It's me." Silence. "You there Eli-honey?" More silence. "Cat-got-your-tongue honey?"

"Mitz?"

"That's what they call me, honey. Only ditched the end bit. Got rid of the asshole's name, then the asshole got rid of himself down the john. So now I'm back to li'l ol' me. Li'l ol' Mitzi Johnson."

"I heard about that."

"Good news travels fast."

"What do you want?"

"Still the same old romantic, eh?"

"You never complained."

"Nothing to complain about. You even got the choke right."

"I had a good teacher."

"It were a fun time, weren't it?"

"Sure was… What do you want, Mitz?"

"What makes you think I want somethin'?"

"You wouldn't call unless you did."

"Maybe I just want a phone screw."

"I doubt it. I'm sure you get all you need off-line. You want something else."

"Damn right I want something. Let's start with that big Jewish cock, how is he?"

"Fine thanks."

"Gettin' plenty?"

"Enough."

"You lit my fire for kosher cock, honey."

"Did I?"

"Sure did. Every time I suck a lychee, I think of you."

"Do you now?"

"Sure do."

"It was a fun time, Mitz."

"Sure was."

"Pity it didn't last."

"Sure was."

"But maybe best that it didn't."

"How so?"

"I'm not a good man to get tied up with."

"Maybe I'm the best judge of that."

"Maybe not."

"How so?"

"I do stuff you wouldn't approve of."

"Maybe I'm the best judge of that."

"Maybe not."

"I still miss your cock."

"You didn't ring to talk about my cock."

"No."

"What then?"

"Ever the businessman, eh?"

"Yup."

"Lighten up, hun."

"Light as a feather."

"Eli?"

"What?"

"Can you lend me an island?"

The silence told her everything she needed to know.

*

After all his boyhood travels Hai was happy never to leave Hong Kong. Victoria Island was his home.

He'd been happy [in an academic sort of way] to see the British leave. He'd been happy [in an academic sort of way] to watch the fatuous Prince mumble his script-written farewells in the rain.

He knew – like we all do & like they do – that the Russians got a heap of things wrong in the twentieth-century. But he believed – how could he not – that how they dealt with their royal family wasn't one of them.

He didn't – because he wasn't a stupid person – have much time for Communism. He knew about Communism and what it did to people. He'd seen it growing up. He knew it was where fat/ nasty & bossy people did nasty & bossy things to skinny/poor & frightened people/people too hungry & scared to fight back. He knew that 'Communism'…

◎ As opposed to 'communism' – the thing that seemed so right until I hit twenty.

…was the enemy of hope.

But that didn't mean he liked all the King & Queen stuff. He didn't have much time for that either.

He didn't dwell much on politics and was happy to keep out of its way. He wanted politics to keep out of his way too. His wants were simple.

He'd wanted – if it was possible – for 'the fat pansy cunt in a skirt' to pick up a drug-resistant strain of something unpleasant/something to rot his dick off/and then – if it was possible – maddened by his itching balls/to fall overboard on the ship home.

He wasn't – not by nature – a vindictive man and his years with his lover were enough to remove most of the vin– from the –dictive he was born with. But 'most' means 'not all' and 'not all' means that 'some' remained.

His time with Mr Woo – not the best time of his life – was enough to rekindle a natural predisposition – a thing we all have – for gratuitous & unexplained dislikes. He bore no love for the English and even less for their Scottish lackeys. He didn't – apart from the incident of the 'fat pansy cunt in a skirt' – know why. But he liked the Irish/who doesn't?

But the one thing he did like about the English was that – while they could be as rapacious as the most rapacious Chinaman – they believed in their own decency and always/as far as they were concerned/'acted-in-good-faith' – [i.e. were 'gentlemen of honour']. He admired the cognitive dissonance that went with all of that and had tried to be the same. And he'd succeeded.

He was unhappy [in more than an academic sort of way] to see as well as feel the increasing power of Beijing. With the Brits it was just a matter of finding out who had the authority to do what he wanted them to do and then working on them until they did what he wanted them to do – it was simple – but with the communists it wasn't as easy. There were whole tiers of bureaucracy and every tier needed bribing. It was driving honest-ish businessmen like himself potty. He missed the good – if philosophically questionable – old days.

He'd thought [more than once] about relocating. Taiwan perhaps/Singapore perhaps/Vancouver perhaps/even Australia. But he knew – when-push-came-to-shove – he never would. Hong Kong was his 'Beacon-on-the-Hill'. It was his 'Beacon-on-the-Hill' as he set out from Shanxi. It was still his 'Beacon-on-the-Hill' as he spent those years with his lover in Zhengzhou. It was still his 'Beacon-on-the-Hill' after reaching his 'Beacon-on-the-Hill'.

He knew – he'd read it somewhere – about the people of Trastevere. He knew – he'd read it somewhere – how they/some of them/had never – not in their whole lives – crossed the Tiber into Rome. He knew how they felt. He was comfortable in Hong Kong. He wore it like a favourite jacket.

Knowing that he would never leave – and putting all thoughts behind him that he might – there was time to ponder on other things. To 'ponder life's uncertain passage'/as most of us/at some time on our journey through life/do. And as he pondered on life/passages & uncertainty a phrase/a thought/a memory returned to him – 'It is the superior part of us that shall survive' – and/with that memory held before him/he burst into tears for the loneliness of lost love.

$$\overline{*}$$

With him being away from home so much/and in the knowledge of Noor's rampant infidelity/Tim [like Hai] felt lonely. But it wasn't the 'loneliness of lost love' because now/some-time before/he'd come to the realisation that he wasn't/never was/in love with her. He'd come to the ancillary realisation that what he'd mistaken for love was merely a full-on dose of lust.

But 'merely' – being a deprecatory diminutive – was far from correct/because a 'full-on dose of lust' is/after all/a 'full-on dose of lust'. And there's nothing wrong [and most of us know there's nothing wrong] as long as it doesn't get confused with love – with lust/'full-on dose' or otherwise.

But/lust to one side/he sought 'true love' – that 'very splendid thing' – for the first time.

But it eluded him.

He was – of course he was – invited to every legal shindig in whatever town he was in. He began to take enjoyment – why wouldn't he – in the simple act of returning his wife's infidelity. Every woman he lay with was a woman who wasn't his wife. What he did with/to & for the women who weren't his wife gave him pleasure from the simple knowledge of knowing that they weren't his wife. The pleasures of the lust – which we all [unless we're really unlucky/or fucked-in-the-head by religion] know to be legion – were a bonus.

It was in Bloemfontein on the last day/evening/night of a long-drawn-out case that he contracted what a doctor friend/a friend from school/said was gonorrhoea. He/the doctor friend/ the friend from school/gave him a prescription for antibiotics.

But he didn't take them – not until he got home and spent the night with Noor.

He felt no pangs of shame. Every time a pang panged he thought about where he'd last seen the eye wateringly large black thing.

He hoped she would pass it on. He couldn't think of a finer group of men to have pissing pus when they peed.

It was five days later. It was Saturday. His antibiotics were working just fine. He watched Noor walk a little more tentatively than usual down the stairs. She came into the breakfast room and/with unaccustomed care/sat down. He could tell the Neisserial incubation period was over.

He knew she wouldn't – because why would she – suspect him of being the donor. There were any number of 'colleagues' who could be responsible for that.

"Beautiful day, darling."

"Is it?"

"Great day for a cycle, darling."

He watched her as she almost – but not quite – winced.

"No thanks."

"How about spending the day in bed. We haven't had a marathon bonk session in ages." Her eyes flickered for a moment.

"Not today, my period's coming."

"Wasn't that last week?" He wasn't letting her off that lightly.

◎ 'Hell may have no fury like a woman scorned' – but – 'Heaven hath no vengeance like love turned to hate.'

—
*

In the large shed in Groblershoop the two men of country code 972 were finished. What they came to do was done. It was ready to go. So were they.

A small celebration followed the completion of each new Israeli bomb/but not here. The technicians were not in celebratory mood. No champagne was drunk. The men of the AWSB didn't drink champagne either. They drank gin out of a bottle/laughed unpleasant laughs & farted.

The truck backed into the shed and 'it' [the 'bit' that used to be a 'bit' but now wasn't] was placed with great – but illogical – care inside. The truck drove away.

◎ There's a funny thing about atomic bombs/not funny perhaps but unusual. We know – because we've been told – that you can crash a plane with an atomic bomb on board and it won't go off. But – be-that-as-it-may – we would [if we ever got the chance to] tip-toe-around an atomic bomb as though a loud noise will be followed by: A.) Our instant vaporisation: and B.) A mushroom cloud. That's just human nature.

And so-it-was that the truck – at a sedate pace/as well as avoiding pot-holes – left the shed and headed nor-nor-east.

Back in the shed/the men of the AWSB/while preferring to shoot the smart-arsed Yids [because Eichmann *et alii* were their heroes] were under instruction not to. Instead they drove them in a silence that was pregnant to the point of 'with menace' to Joburg International Airport – recently as well as disgustingly [that's what the men who drove thought] renamed for Oliver Tambo. They dumped – more threw – the Yids' suitcases into the gutter and left. They were told not to shoot them. But that didn't mean they should be/or needed to be/polite.

They drove off & away. They went not back to Groblershoop but to Ventersdorp. There was a meeting going on. All the big bosses were there. But not the biggest of the big bosses/not *il capo dei capi/die baas van base.*

Gene T Blanche 'The Biggest of all the Big Bosses' was in jail. He was there – or so they were told – because he'd killed some coon. So what – there were heaps of the *fokking doos.*

The woman/*Die vrou*/was there – all tits/all legs & all over von Grünge. *Fokking* typical of her – *fokking* her way to the *fokking* top.

They weren't nice men. They were big/fat/porcine & semi-literate men. They were men just like their fathers & their sons. They were men who 'daren't look up and see the stars, but belch instead'. They were perfect men for the AWSB.

The meeting broke up and von Grünge was 'The Biggest of all the Big Bosses' now. Noor – with a clearly unclouded [as opposed to 'clear & unclouded' – see above] idea in her head of where she was headed – waited for the others to leave. She went over to von Grünge. She shook his hand. She held onto it. She slid it inside her shirt. She let him play with what he found there.

"*Ma hart is vir ewig joune,*" – ["My heart is ever yours,"] – she said. Von Grünge – who had/in the not-too-distant-past/

enjoyed enjoying the fruits of this woman – knew he would be enjoying them again soon. Part of the reason he'd enjoyed enjoying her fruits was that she was just as disgusting & mean/nasty & horrible [etc. – but not as ugly] as he was.

He – even with/or possibly due to/the tiny morsel of decency that lay within him [it came from his mother who grew roses] enjoyed enjoying the fruits of this woman – because enjoying the fruits of someone as awful as her made him feel [just ever so slightly] a less repulsive person.

And so – after going to his room – she/he/they did what she/he/they did. But doing what she/he/they did – or only nearly did – was no great pleasure for Noor. That was because – like his recently incarcerated boss and a lot of the other fat/pre-diabetic men of the AWSB – he was a functional impotent. But then – after doing what she/he/they 'nearly' did – he said – "I have a mission for you *my liewe.*"

Noor now knew – because women can know things men can't – that she was about to find out the whys-&-wherefores of why [and wherefore] she was recruited/as well as the whys-and – wherefores of why she was steaming up through the ranks with such manifest ease.

"*Wat kan dit wees?*" – ["What might that be?"] – she asked.

"Do you have a passport?"

"No."

"Get one."

✳

"I'd like you to look at this, sir," said Ishmael. He always 'sir-ed' Boris when anyone else was about.

"What you got?"

"This."

"Where?"

"Here."

Boris took the sheet of paper and went slowly down the column of figures and names. "Now that's interesting," he said.

"Isn't it?"

"Why would John _____ be doing something like that, I wonder."

"And look when it started," said Ishmael. Boris did.

"How very, very interesting."

"Look where it's going."

"What's the 'Acme Trading Company of Jerusalem'?"

"Front company for some guy called Elijah Rubenstein."

"Who's Elijah Rubenstein?"

"I don't know yet."

"I think we'd better find out."

"Sure thing, boss."

Ishmael left the room. He took the lift down to Archives & Research.

◎ 'Archives & Research' is always in the basement and that's why archivists & researchers bear an uncanny resemblance to moles. I dated an archivist once. She had great boobs and liked humping to Schubert. But it didn't last.

Boris leant back in his chair. He stared at the ceiling. It's what he did when he needed inspiring.

He felt as though he was walking in custard – lots of output for no result. He was looking for a particular needle in a haystack that was now crammed full of them.

The 6th Earl was either flitting around the world with gay abandon or the sightings of him/and they were [or had been] legion/needed to be taken-with-a-pinch-of-salt.

He was in Miami with dyed red hair/in Melbourne with his moustache shaved off/in Glasgow with a limp & a squint and in any number of places in any number of manifestations. But – as the years had passed/as he'd ceased to be front page/then second page/then any page news – the sightings had dropped off. The last one was a year ago.

But he was still alive – somewhere. His mother told him that.

So – where the hell was he? Was there plastic surgery involved? He was a vain man – Boris knew that from what his wife said – so probably not. Was he working forecourt at some gas station in Wyoming? He knew/well enough by now/what made the 6th Earl tick and knew that he would rather share a cell in The Scrubs than do that.

So where-the-@#$% was he? Where do you go when you don't want to be found? Not somewhere where your ludicrous toff accent would give you away in seconds. So – somewhere where he didn't need to speak. To somewhere where there were no other people/guaranteeably no other people. Where were those places?

Then it came to him. "Islands," he said out loud.

He rang down to A & R – "Is Sergeant Taylor with you?"

"Yes sir."

"Put him on please."

"Yes sir."

"Ish?"

"Yes sir."

"See if this Rubenstein guy owns an island."

"Will do, sir."

———— * ————

It wasn't a big cave. There weren't bats flying around it. There weren't stalactites [or that other one with the 'g' in it] but it was reasonable/not claustrophobic. It was big enough for what he might and probably would [and as this is that sort of frivolous & predictable novel/almost certainly would/if not definitely would] need it for. There was room to lie down and there was room/just/to stand up.

What luck. His nickname wasn't 'Lucky' by chance – or was that just taking the piss? He wasn't used to luck in his life/never was. Women/horses/backgammon – you name it. And look where he was now?

But how was he going to manage it? He couldn't see the channel from his treehouse and neither could he from home-beach. How would he know if &/or when the men [he'd assumed – never being taught the dangers of assumption – they were men] from the ship were coming to his island? So if the men [which/as you know/not all of them were] decided to come to his island how was he to know? He didn't know. And because he didn't know – or could think of a way of getting to know – he sat on a rock and thought.

◎ And thinking thoughts – or so the philosophers thought/ and even Aristotle/who/together with Pliny the Elder [who shouldn't to be confused with Pliny the Younger] was an idiot [Ref. A WITNESS TO A LIFE p. 72] thought – is & was the precursor to knowing all the things that are & were to be known.

He was enjoying his life on the island much more than he ever thought he would. It was the first time he was able to enjoy much. There wasn't much he missed of home – the girl with the organ-stops [the ones that did the in intriguing things they did when he did the less than intriguing things he did to encourage them to do the intriguing things they did] perhaps/but not much else. He liked the new freedom to do whatever he wanted. There were no rules unless he made them – which he didn't/not much. Maybe the rule about going easy on the booze.

Too often – in his old Belgravia days – he would crawl into bed at two and wake with a blinder at ten [a mouth like the bottom of a parrot's cage] and no idea of what to do with the day/not until the club opened at six.

But now – with the coming of the dark – he would repair to his tree-top fastness. It was a nightly/a quotidian/ritual. It was a part of his life. And the life it was a part of was a good life. It was better than his old life. That was for sure.

He didn't want to go back to his old life – not to jail and what awaited him in the showers. He wasn't going to do a Ronnie Biggs. He wasn't going to give himself up after years of happy freedom. Things were too good now.

He wasn't sure that – even if he was able to go home/even if he was able to be free – he would decide to do that. He wasn't sure that/even if he was given a 'Get Out Of Jail' card/he would choose to play it. There was so much more to the life he was leading now – more than there ever was to his old life. He was fit/he was slim/he swam/he fished/he dived for clams/he picked green stuff from the stream/he cleaned & tidied his treehouse & his huts/he ran the beach – just for the fun of it.

So – he didn't want to lose this life. He didn't want these people – or any people – coming to his island/seeing who he was/going back to wherever it was they came from and telling people. The thought of that happening brought literal tears to his literal eyes. Why couldn't they just go away? Why couldn't they just leave him alone?

The thought of having strangers tramping all over his island – even in the knowledge that the men whose bodies he'd found/ and presumably the man-or-men who'd killed them/had been/ and not that long ago/doing just that – gave him a feeling of impending violation. And there was nothing he would be able [nothing he could think of] to do about it.

So – if/&/or when they came – all he could do was to hide. So – he needed to know if/&/or when they were coming. So – he needed a look-out. But there wasn't one. So – he needed to make one. So he did.

He was an old-hand at it now. Treetop carpentry was his forte.

The man appeared. He was as nondescript as ever. He was sitting on a park bench. Tim was jogging/pushing Perry around the 'Bot'. It was his Saturday morning exercise. They sat. They talked. Perry went chasing dragonflies. They discussed a number of things/one of which/not least of which – of course it was – was Noor. More specifically – Noor's application for a passport. More specifically still – what she'd written on the forms. Most specifically – the things she couldn't lie about [cf. all the things she'd previously lied about].

Tim – after reading what she'd written/the things she couldn't lie about [cf. all the things she'd previously lied about] – was perhaps a little/but certainly not a lot/surprised. There was – when he read what he read – no astound to be astounded by. He'd suspected – very nearly from the start – that the mumbo-jumbo about her past was [plain-&-simple] mumbo-jumbo about her past. Lies plain-&-simple. She sometimes muttered Afrikaans words in her sleep.

So – what did she need a passport for? There were no plans for an overseas trip. None she'd told *him* about. So it must be something with her 'new friends'. Was she planning to leave him? And – to a modicum of surprise/but no sort of astound – he wasn't that concerned that she might. There was never [not after Perry was born] any expectation of a golden anniversary.

And – if she was going to leave him – for which one of them? They all looked equally ghastly.

The thought of living without Noor – not something he'd thought much about before/just pondered on occasionally – didn't worry him a great deal. They were growing apart and had been from the start/right from before she got pregnant. The sex was OK/always was/but better at the start. Now/'it' – making 'love' to her – made him feel something he'd never felt at the start. Now/'it' – making 'love' to her/as well as doing the things she expected him to and got peevish & spiteful if he didn't – made him feel grubby. A grubbiness he couldn't wash off.

He didn't hate his wife/but he knew it mightn't be long before he did. He thought she might hate him already. The thought of that didn't affect him at all. Well – not as much as he expected it to.

Another of the things they discussed was the 'chatter' [radio chatter] between the men of the AWSB. Blanche was locked safely away but Hydras like the AWSB spawned new heads on request. The 'chatter' was encrypted now – a development they hadn't foreseen. No one knew what was coming up/other than that something was about-to-go-down.

The man asked Tim to help him/them/the Government/the country/his country and Tim said he would.

The man asked him to conceal/hide/clandestinely place a tracking device somewhere among his wife's possessions/ something she never moved without.

Tim thought about where that should be. But he didn't need to think the thought for long. He knew – as you probably do – exactly where he would put it.

$$\overline{\underset{*}{}}$$

First off – how did Mitzi know about the island? Second off – what was that phone call about – really about? It wasn't to talk about his cock.

He'd never thought of his time with Mitzi as being 'an affair'. It'd been something too fresh and too clean for it to be one of those. His thoughts of New York – when his thoughts turned to New York – were always mixed in with his thoughts/memories now/of that memorable & wonderful summer. He'd gone there to explore possibilities/all sorts of possibilities/of moving the operation to the States. Mitz was a plus and there was no doubt

145

about that. But there were minuses too – too many – the FBI/ DEA/ATF & IRS for a start.

But – like most unions of lust-&-affection – it didn't last long without love. There was [from his side of the equation] almost love/very nearly love/but not quite. That saddened him when he thought of New York.

So – what was the call about/really about? Sure – he was surprised when she asked about islands and he guessed his reply showed that he was. She was – because most women are/and few women aren't – a perceptive woman.

Was that what she rang to find out/that he & the island – that particular island – were in some way connected? Crafty dame – that's exactly what the call was about.

But what was her angle? What was it about the island that could possibly interest her? And why didn't she ask where it was? Did that mean she didn't care where it was? Or did it mean she already knew where it was? Was she only ringing to confirm it was his?

And – if it was to confirm it was his – what was it that made her interested? Did she have an angle? Did she want to use it? Did she have something to hide? Or did she know what was hidden there? How could she know? He didn't know.

They were too many questions for late at night. He would sleep on it. Let his subconscious work on it. That worked for him/when it worked.

He woke in the dark/it was two. He never woke in the dark/or at two. He was a sound sleeper. Only a bad conscience woke at two. He didn't *do* 'a bad conscience' – hadn't for years. He didn't wake at two/even when he had.

What was it? What woke him? He got out of bed. He wouldn't get back to sleep/not now. That didn't worry him. He could go without sleep. So why did he wake at two? What woke him? He didn't know. All he knew was that he was awake/it was dark/it was two.

He went downstairs. He went to the kitchen. He drank carrot juice. He was on a health kick. But that wasn't right. His 'wives'/ the women he lived with/all of them – in cahoots with his doctor – had him on a health kick. He wasn't used to losing but – being out-numbered eight-to-one – he knew when he couldn't win.

He could murder a hamburger/especially a goyim one/but the fridge was full of broccolini/spinach & almond milk. He made do with a handful of nuts.

He went through to his study. He sat at his desk and thought/ maybe pondered. Pondered like others pondered elsewhere.

So – Mitz was right – he owned an island. She knew that already. Maybe she wasn't sure she knew that already. Maybe she just wanted to make sure she knew that already. Maybe why she called. And now she knew for sure – for sure.

But so what? He couldn't give a damn. But that wasn't right. He could give a damn. He wasn't where he was/who he was/ because he couldn't give a damn. He could give a whole bucket full of damns.

Maybe she wanted to buy it. Maybe she wanted an out of the way island. Maybe a hide-away with this Rupert guy? Maybe she was doing a thing on private islands/something for *National Geographic*. Maybe she was just an inquisitive woman/a woman with too much money/a woman with too much time/a woman wanting to keep tabs on an old lover. But that was all bullshit – it was none of those things.

It was dawn/it was six/by the time he was halfway there.

It was – had to be – something to do with 'the thing'/'the things' on the island – 'the thing'/'the things' he'd put there. He knew *that* as sure as he knew that – or strongly suspected that – he had no soul. Eli wasn't a religious guy.

But – soul-or-no-soul – he didn't know and didn't know how he was going to get to know/not without taking steps/which one of the island's 'things' she was interested in.

He didn't – not until later/not for a long time – know that she wasn't interested in any of the 'things' on the island… but in something else entirely.

It was light/it was eight/before the 'whole bucket full of damns' was sorted.

By midday there were other things to occupy his mind.

*

The 6th Earl – now adept at treetop carpentry – took barely a morning to construct a not particularly comfortable/but comfortable enough/lookout. Now he could keep an eye on the ship and the boat that went – and would hopefully keep going – to the atoll.

He was left a pair of binoculars in his 'castaway-kit' but one of the lenses/the right one/was lost – it happened years ago – somewhere/probably in the sand. He was – like most of us – a right eye dominant guy and held his –nocular upside down.

He sat in his crow's-nest & watched. He could see the people better now. And they weren't all men.

It was/give-or-take/a decade since he'd spoken to a woman. And he only spoke to a man – an unbelievably black man – for an hour twice a year. He thought he would like to speak to these women. Maybe they spoke English. Maybe they would speak to him too. Maybe they could talk about all the mundane things in life/the weather/Ascot/how the Queen was doing & other stuff like that.

He wondered if any of them – there were a few of them – sported a set of organ-stops. It was a foolish thought for the 6th

Earl to think but/in mitigation/it was the sort of foolish thought any of us might think/or be more prone to think/after sitting in a crow's-nest for hours/and celibate for [give-or-take] a decade.

And then – after more hours of foolish wondering – he wondered a sensible wonder. What would happen – he sensibly wondered – if/but more probably when/they came to 'his' island? They would – wouldn't they – see his huts/his dam/his paths & his treehouse *extraordinaire*? And then [in the knowledge that there was a 'him' to be looked for] they would look for him. And/if they couldn't find him/they would keep on looking/and keep on looking/and keep on looking until they found him. They wouldn't leave the island until they had. That was human nature and the 6th Earl remembered a bit/quite a bit [but not an enormous amount] about human nature.

And when they found him – they would find out who he was – and when they'd found out who he was/they would tell other people who he was and those other people would tell more other people who he was/who would tell more other people who he was [*ad infer-fucking-nitum*]. That was human nature and the 6th Earl remembered a bit/quite a bit [but not an enormous amount] about human nature.

And the day would come when everyone knew who he was/ as well as where he was/when one of them would remember what he did/and that 'one of them' would talk to a policeman/ who would talk to other policemen. The policemen would talk about who he was and where he was and what he did/and those policemen would come and take him away from his island and take him back to a dark & cramped prison where nasty big men with tattoos – men who'd never even looked for the green flash of a tropical sunset/men who'd never heard the 'chimes of midnight'/ men with chips-on-their-shoulders about the English class system – would do unspeakable things to him in the showers/ and keep on doing them/on-&-on-&-on until the end of time.

Thoughts of those things – nasty men/tattoos/unspeakable things & 'the end of time' – made him think the other thoughts he was thinking. And think them as fast as any thoughts could be thought.

With the unpleasant thought of the thoughts he was so recently thinking held firmly in the front of his thoughts – and especially that 'last thought' he was thinking/the thought of nasty men/tattoos [etc.] he thought of how best to avoid all those dark/mean/nasty/ugly & horrible things.

And then – as he sat and thought – an unavoidable thought elbowed its way past his other thoughts. It elbowed its way into the front of his thinking.

They – if they came to his island/which he knew they would/ and it would be a stupid thought to think that they wouldn't – needed/if he was to avoid the above nastiness/to think he was dead.

That way they wouldn't—because they wouldn't need to/ because the *quaerebant corporis*/or what was left of it/would be right there in front of them – keep looking for him until they found him. So – he would need to be dead/but not to be dead/ and both at the same time?

And as he sat and thought that unpleasant – as well as unavoidable – thought [the one that had/not so long ago/ elbowed its way to the front of his thinking] he came to the realisation of what he must do.

And so – with spade in hand/head hung low [in both metaphor & reality] and in the manner of a lamb-to-the-slaughter – he walked/with neither-inward-nor-outward show of enthusiasm/back to the site of his previous digging.

He dug once more.

*

The assemblers of atomic bombs – just this one bomb – flew back to Tel Aviv. Disquiet and misgivings sat heavy [if not

150

heavily] in the bosom of but one of them. In the bosom of the other was the warm glow of a job well done. They both/their bosoms in varying states of contentment/returned to a seriously – I mean seriously – private/secret & undisclosed location in the Negev desert [but not far from Ramat Hovav and visible from the Be'er Sheva Highway – you can't miss it] and continued their previous work.

It was a month since they'd been seconded by their boss – a man who knew a man called Eli – to do what they'd just got back from doing. That was the thing the man with the disquieted bosom wasn't happy to have been asked to do and wasn't happy to have done/not even as he was doing it/but – as times must – had done it anyway. And – because of his unhappy & disquieted bosom – he went to talk to his boss.

The boss was a bossy man/as bosses sometimes are. He was short & fat/as bosses sometimes are. He smoked/as bosses sometimes do/a huge cigar.

◉ In the whole history of Western Civilisation there was never a short/fat & bossy boss – not one who smoked a huge cigar – who was able to/or was even inclined to/listen to criticism [polite/implied or otherwise] from those they bossed. Especially if the one they bossed was tall/thin & passably handsome.

And so it was that the atomic bomb assembler – the tall/thin & passably handsome one/the one with disquiet within his bosom – imparted to his boss [in a polite & implied manner] the nature of his disquiet.

He left the boss's office a short time later. He left with the certain knowledge [imparted in a neither polite nor implied/ but very much otherwise/manner] that he was to 'swallow-it-down'/'lick-it-up'/'harden-up'/'think of his career' & 'get the fuck out of my office before I fire you'. And all said in the best Aramaic form of Hebrew – of course.

It hadn't been quite the reception the man was hoping for.

But having done his stint – as all of his nation had – in that fine instrument of a benign(ish) government – the Israel Defence Forces – he knew not/following the example of Moshe Dayan/to give in & to fight on for what he believed in. So he did.

He went to see – of course he did – Mr Eli Rubenstein. It wasn't their first meeting because they'd met once before on his way to South Africa. Mr Eli Rubenstein received him politely. The man said what he wanted to say. He told Mr Eli Rubenstein what he wanted to tell him. And what he wanted to say and what he wanted to tell him was that he [together with his un-disquieted colleague] were responsible for placing a 20-kiloton atomic weapon into the hands of a far-right/swastika flagged/swastika tattooed/black hating/brown hating/Jew hating & by-and-large everybody hating pack of Afrikaner low lifes.

Mr Eli Rubenstein – after the man left – sat and thought about a 20-kiloton atomic weapon being in the hands of a far-right/swastika flagged/swastika tattooed/black hating/brown hating/Jew hating & by-and-large-everybody hating pack of Afrikaner low lifes. It wasn't the first time he'd thought about it. It didn't worry him the first time and it didn't worry him now – in just the same way it was unlikely to worry him in the future. That was because he knew something no one else did.

*

Sometime before this – a young lady/no longer a girl/but continuing to sport a fine pair of organ-stops – went to see the oldest-&-closest-friend of a man she once knew.

He – not the oldest-&-closest – but the man he was the oldest-&-closest of [the man she once knew & had once/many

152

times more than once/'known'] was the only man she'd ever 'known' who'd looked upon her organ-stops with prurience & affection but not humour.

She/the same young lady/liked watching him as he looked upon them with prurience & affection but not humour. She liked – even more – the things he did to get them to do the things they did. She liked – even more than the things she liked 'even more' – when/after doing the things she liked 'even more' [i.e. the less than intriguing things he did to encourage them to do the intriguing things they did] he did things [other things] that threw her into the throes of what he threw her into the throes of.

It was fun and she knew – even when she was naked/pissed & drugged-to-the-eyeballs – that it would be fun even if she wasn't.

She liked throes of any sort/all sorts/and being thrown into throes of all sorts – with a belly full of booze & a schnoz full of coke – was/up until later/the only way she knew to be thrown. But she knew [see above] because she was a woman and [see above] because women know all sorts of things men have no idea about/that she didn't need to be either of those things [things with her belly & her schnoz] to be thrown into throes of all sorts.

It was years since and – as 'absence makes the heart grow fonder' – she was missing him more. All the things they said he did/ the one big thing they said he did/which he probably did/didn't matter to her/not one bit. So what? It was a mistake/wasn't it? Everyone's allowed the occasional mistake/now-and-again/ once-in-a-while/aren't they?

She felt sorry for Nanny [in an academic sort of way] 'but' [she mused] 'that's life'/'bad stuff happens'/no point getting-your-knickers-in-a-twist-about-it. We all have to die sometime/ don't we?

Without the mistake [without the metal pipe & the bludgeoning] they might have made a go of it together. They were kindred spirits. She knew he wasn't/just like she wasn't/ happy with the life he was living.

She knew he didn't love/not even like/his wife – why would he? She was a bitch. She knew he didn't love/not even like/his children – why would he? They were ghastly Sloane-Clones and everything she was brought up to despise.

She was a grammar school girl and was once [by her parents anyway] thought to be smart. She may not have been as smart as they thought she was but she was still pretty smart. She was certainly 'smart enough'/although 'smart enough for what' was uncertain.

Her father was an unreconstructed Commo-Leftie of the Attlee/Bevin era – a fatuous old soap-box bore who/somehow-or-other/had made it to being Shadow Minister of Something-or-other and everything *le fin du siècle* zeitgeist of her generation was telling her to despise.

Her mother – more at home in the mind-boggling ordinariness of Yorkshire [and that goes for anywhere/ everywhere north of St Albans] than in London – was never/ rarely-if-ever/seen without curlers in her hair. She was everything the man – the one who threw her into throes of all sorts – was leading her to despise.

So it came as no surprise to her large family – devoutly Catholic as well as devoutly Communist/and of which she was happy to be the black-sheep – when she told them she was leaving.

She was happy to be leaving the drab/dirty & futureless streets of Bradford. She was happy to be leaving the drab/dirty & futureless oiks who made fun of her organ-stops.

She was happy – when she got to London – to find a job as cocktail waitress in a Mayfair club.

She was happy to be – as a nightly occurrence – naked/ pissed & drugged-to-the-eyeballs in the arms of a man who/as well as not laughing at the intriguing things her organ stops did/ knew how to throw her into throes of all sorts and who said he was [but she didn't believe him at first and only did later] the 6th Earl of Somewhere-or-other.

She liked being pissed & drugged-to-the-eyeballs because she wasn't [because devout Catholics frown on the pleasures of the flesh & devout Communists on pleasures of any kind] used to being either of those things. She liked being naked because being naked/pissed & drugged-to-the-eyeballs – together with having 'her Earl' [possessiveness is human nature] comfortably ensconced where she liked him to be comfortably ensconced – made her happy.

'Happy in Bradford' was an oxymoron.

But what she liked almost most of all – and the thing that made her almost the happiest she could remember – was when she could see how much he enjoyed watching what was about to happen as it was about to happen and then happened. But what she liked most of all and the thing that made her the happiest she could remember was when he did all the clever things to make the thing that was about to happen/happen.

She knew the man wasn't a clever man – not in the way clever men were clever – but when it came to doing the things [even though they were less than intriguing things] that were the things she liked him to do/the things to encourage her organ-stpops to do the [even to her] intriguing things they did [as well as all the things he did to throw her into throes] he was as clever as any clever man/or even a cleverer man/or even the cleverest of cleverer men/needed to be.

So – with all the booze & all the drugs & all the throes she was thrown to – she was happy.

So – she went to see the oldest-&-closest friend. She was no longer a cocktail waitress and no longer spent her time naked/pissed or drugged-to-the-eyeballs. She was now a diesel mechanic in Luton. And [let me assure you] being a diesel mechanic in Luton is a long way from being a cocktail waitress in Mayfair.

The reason she went to see the oldest-&-closest-friend was that she was sure – and always had been/right from the start/ right from 'the night'/'that night'/'the last night'/'their last night' and onwards – that 'her Earl'/the 6th Earl/the 6th Earl of Somewhere-or-other/was still alive and that her previous boss – purveyor of all things/things to keep young cocktail waitresses [because there were others just like her] naked/pissed & drugged-to-the-eyeballs – would know where he was/and might even be the reason for him being where he was.

So – when she went to see him/and he remembered her – she laid her [in metaphor] cards on his [in metaphor] table. She told him what she wanted. She said nothing of what she might do/say/tell if she didn't get what she wanted. She alluded/not at all/to the things she knew about the things she alluded/not at all/to. She didn't need to. She knew he knew the things she might do/say/tell if she didn't get what she wanted. She knew he knew the things she alluded/not at all/to.

It may be said – and probably has been – that a life in Luton [a fair way north of St Albans] as well as a life spent buried in the depths of a Mack truck [finely engineered though one of those may be] are not conducive to 'the contemplative life'. But for this young lady – now hovering towards her thirties – the contemplative life was the only life she knew.

She'd contemplated/when young – hovering her way through those ghastly mid-teen years – on the rightness/or otherwise/of the anarcho-syndicalism of her parents and on how that could possibly fit with her father's eagerness to accept the position of Shadow Minister of Something-or-other *and* the [five times the average wage] salary that went with it.

She knew – by contemplating her way to the knowledge of it – that the things her parents believed in weren't believed in isolation and that the wherewithals of life – the new fridge/ better car & holidays in Spain [where they lay prostrate on beaches] – didn't impinge on what they believed. And that was because what they believed were beliefs about how *everyone else* should be living their lives.

She'd never heard the term 'cognitive dissonance' but she sure knew what it meant.

She'd contemplated/when young – hovering her way through those ghastly mid-teen years – on the rightness or otherwise of the Catholic faith and – while she was at it – of any faith. She wondered how her parents were able – seemingly without problem – to juggle the schizoid personalities of a God-the-Father [a jealous & petty/an unjust & unforgiving/a vindictive & bloodthirsty/a misogynistic & homophobic/a racist & infanticidal/a genocidal & megalomaniacal as well as a capriciously malevolent bully] with that of 'the loving and caring' Jesus/God-the-Son and all that stuff in the Gospels.

She didn't have much time for the mumbo-jumbo of any variety of god.

What she did have time for were the books of Wollstonecraft/ de Beauvoir & Greer/the music of Bikini Kill & Sleater-Kinney. She was a feminist's feminist. But only most of the time. But 'only most of the time' = 'not all of the time'. And 'not all of the time' = for 'some of the time she wasn't'. And 'for some of the time she wasn't' = 'for some of the time she was the opposite'.

So – while not Catholic in her beliefs/she was catholic in her tastes.

None of the girls she'd gone to bed with had ever laughed at the way her organ-stops looked or at the intriguing things they did when not particularly intriguing things were done to encourage them to do the intriguing things they did – only the guys – and 'only the guys' had one guy – one particular guy – as an exception.

So – 'some of the time' she liked guys/a guy – one particular guy – to do the things [even though they were not particularly intriguing things] he did to encourage her organ-stops to do the intriguing things they did.

So – to have an arch feminist/and especially one well read in feminist literature/prostrating herself/naked/pissed & drugged-to the-eyeballs at the feet of a 6th Earl – as well as having her beg him to do the things outlined above – was about as cognitively dissonant as 'cognitive dissonance' can get.

So – when she went to see the oldest-&-closest-friend/and when she didn't allude/other than in a deflective & non-alluding sort of way/to the things she knew/she knew – she could tell – that he knew that she knew them.

She was confident that – in the knowledge that he knew what she knew/but wasn't alluding to – he would see things her way/which he didn't but needed [because there was little choice in the matter] to hear her out.

So – after laying her cards on his table – she said – "Well, what about it," to which he said – "But he's dead," to which she said – "No, he's not," to which he said – "Yes, he is," to which she said – "No, he's not," to which he said what you know she said.

Having got nowhere for quite some time – because repetitive affirmation & denial are for the young/and the young get nowhere useful but older – the oldest-&-closest changed tack by saying, "How do you know," to which she said – "I'm a woman, I know," to which he said – "Bollocks," to which she said – "Bollocks, yourself," to which he said – "Get out," to which she said – "Make me," to which he said – "Get the fuck out," to which she said nothing.

But – as she was an ocean-going/24 carat/weapons-grade/ Chateau bottled feminist and because the opportunity presented itself and because Luton's a tough town and because she knew the importance of getting her retaliation in first – she kneed him/*avec toute la force d'une femme enragée*/in the groin.

◎ Now – being 'kneed in the groin' has/over time/received greater accolade from the feminist lobby than it 'mostly' deserves: A.) Because most of the time it's not that bad/ although sometimes it is: and B.) Because there's a significant [but not long] lag-time between the kneeing & the what comes after it.

And so it was that the oldest-&-closest – knowing that the kneeing was of the more professionally performed type/and that the *avec toute la force* was indeed *avec toute la force* – knew what to expect.

In the knowledge of what was coming he returned the favour by head butting her [Mayfair isn't all pink-gin & roses] in the face/breaking her nose & causing her to say [with a somewhat nasal intonation] "Fuck."

They sagged to the floor together/he holding his adnexa & she her face. It wasn't the best introduction/but things would improve. They would – in the fullness of time – become friends.

$$\overline{\ast}$$

Noor was in the bathroom. She was taking a shower. Never being reared with a shower and performing her ablutions as-needs-be/which was probably not as often as it needed to be/ with a hose & cold water out the back of the kitchen/she was taken by the amenities of the modern bathroom. She took to them as a-duck-does-to-water. She showered/she lay in baths/ she sat on loos with seats and then showered & bathed again. It rarely took less than an hour.

This – of course it was – was the time Tim chose for his debut into the world of electronic surveillance.

He went to his wife's handbag/a shoulder-bag/a big one – she carried a lot of things/none of them feminine. He opened it. He rummaged around inside it. He came up with – you guessed it – the eye wateringly large black thing. He unscrewed the unscrewable bit. He inserted what the nondescript man had asked him to. He rescrewed the rescrewable bit and returned it to her bag. He then [remembering where he'd last seen it] visited the ground floor bathroom/washed his hands thoroughly/and went through to the conservatory for breakfast.

He was finishing his second cup of coffee by the time his wife appeared. He was playing 'snap' with Perry.

"How are you darling, nice bath?" A grunt.

"There's a trial starts in Durban tomorrow. I'm leaving tonight. I'll be away a couple of days."

"I'm going to Holland." He feigned surprise.

"What for?"

"Sick aunt."

"I thought you didn't have any."

"I do now."

"When are you off?"

"Now."

"Oh," he said and then thought how good it was that he hadn't delayed doing the thing he'd just done.

*

The stench from the pit was no better the second time around – maybe worse. He was expecting it this time and thought that might make it better – but it didn't. He jammed cone-shells up his nose to finish the digging. Then there was a choice – of course there was. Which one?

Both were [he'd chosen the less recent pit] well past the bloating & gut rupture stage/but they were still a gruesome sight.

He looked down at them. He looked with a contemplative air. Which one? But the choice wasn't hard. He decided/because he was a tall guy/on the taller guy. But it wasn't a perfect choice because the taller guy sported [with the 44 Magnum being/ as Clint Eastwood so memorably informed us all/the most

160

powerful handgun in the world/and with this poor 'punk' being clean out of luck] a little less head than the other. He wanted the taller guy's body but with the shorter guy's head/and for one fleeting moment thought an unthinkable thought. But with moral rectitude – never his long suit – improving with his years and not what it was as he battered Nanny's brains out – he unthought the thought of thinking an unthinkable thought.

So he decided to go with what there was – the tall guy – *sans une partie de sa tête.*

◎ Life's full of compromises. We all know that. It's just the way life is.

He tied a plaited vine – he thought of them as his 'Tarzan ropes' – around the guy's ankles. He hauled him out of the pit. But – just before he got him there – the feet came off and the rest of the guy slithered back in.

But he got it done. He dragged the body – minus feet/he would need to go back for them – along the path to home. He didn't want some clever-dick counting bones and coming up short.

By evening it was finished. The body – complete with trotters plus the squishy bits of whatever they were that detached themselves along the path – was in the reluctantly/but by necessity/sacrificial hut. It/he/the body/the tall guy was laid out on the bed in anatomical(ish) position.

Up on the hill the cave was as full of stores as he could make it. Rocks and vines were ready to cover the entrance. He was ready to go.

He went up to the crow's-nest and looked out at the channel. The ship was where it always was and the boat trailed behind. He went to his treehouse. He lay down. He slept. It wasn't the sleep of the weary – even though he was – but the in-&-out sleep of the uncertain.

And the thing he was uncertain about/most uncertain about/was when to set fire to the hut.

Should he do it first thing in the morning? Or not?

If the people on the ship weren't intending to come then the smoke would alert them. Then they would come. Just what he didn't want.

Should he wait-and-watch? Should he only set fire if he saw them coming? That seemed more reasonable but he wasn't sure. If he wasn't quick enough – or if the fire didn't get going fast enough – they might get to the hut before the fire could destroy it. Then they would – discovering a half burned/long dead and decomposing corpse [*sans une partie de sa tête*] – come to the conclusion that mischief was afoot and/in coming to that conclusion/do things he didn't want them to do – like look for him.

He knew there were reasons – if they were going to come at all – why they wouldn't come at night. Reason 1.) Why would they? Reason 2.) They would only come at night if they wanted to surprise him – which meant they knew he was there – which they didn't. Reason 3.) Finding the gap in the reef was hard enough by daylight.

With the first of first-light he went down to the huts and into 'the hut'. He packed everything combustible/every frond & twig/every empty crate & cardboard carton/around the stinking – now fly-covered corpse. He made sure the *Bic* lighters were working. Then he headed back to the crow's-nest.

He sat & he watched. He watched the ship. He watched the boat. He watched the boat boarded. He watched the boat motor to the atoll. It was one of the most boring days he could remember.

He could remember boring days at home. Belgravian society was all about the appearance of boredom. Not to appear bored

162

– to show interest in things & have things to be-getting-on-with
– was to show the highest degree of *non-chic*.

But he was often legitimately bored too. There wasn't much
to do/not until the club opened. Life didn't equip men like him
for a life of being anything but bored.

But his time on the island had changed all that. Now he was
a man who *needed* to do things. Now he was a man *having* things
to do. One of the things he needed to do was think up ways – the
best way possible – of doing the things he needed to do. He was
used to full days of walking & swimming/of diving & collecting/
of fishing/repairing & building. He went to bed happily tired.
Sleep – until now – had come easily to him. He was never bored.

But now – by necessity – he was back in the drawing room
at home. Lounging around in the crow's-nest/just as he did on
the old Chesterfield sofa.

He wasn't enjoying the atavistic feeling this day – a day of
enforced inactivity – was producing within him. He was now –
without realising it/perhaps realising it – a different man from
the snivelling/self-pitying/blame transferring arsehole he was
when he first arrived. His 'road to Damascus' had been a decade
long – give-or-take – event.

He slept 'OK' that night but only just 'OK'. The fullness of his
everyday day wasn't there to lull him to the sleep of the weary.
Only to the sleep-awake-sleep-awake sleep of living an empty day.

The next day was no better/nor the one after. As he climbed
back up to the crow's-nest – lack of enthusiasm oozing from
every pore – for his fourth bout of chained Promethean misery/
he expected this day to be like the others… but it wasn't.

$$\overset{*}{=}$$

A year before that – [How are you managing with the timeline?]
– the oldest-&-closest lay on the floor. He fondly fondled his
fondleable parts. Beside him/propped up against the leg of his

desk/sat a young(ish) lady. She sported a broken nose. Her name was Lucy. There was blood. It was hers.

And so – as it transpired with regards 'sterner stuff' [the stuff we all admire] Lucy's stern stuff was sterner stuff than the oldest-&-closest's stern stuff. She stood up first. And being from Luton and mixing with diesel mechanics on a daily basis [and wishing once again to get her retaliation in first] she started kicking him.

But then – after a few kicks to the exposed & available parts [which weren't many because he was rolled up like a hedgehog] she came to the appreciation that this was not the best way to go about getting what she wanted.

She leant over him/dripped a little blood onto his Gieves & Hawkes silk smoking-jacket/prodded him with a toe and said – "You OK?" to which he replied – "Fuck off." Which/because it seemed a reasonable suggestion/she did.

But not before: A.) Sitting at his desk/dripping a little more blood onto his bespoke Quill stationery and writing him a letter: and B.) Pulling the Armando Caruso handkerchief from his breast pocket and holding it to her nose.

Friendship seemed as far away as ever. But not quite – because/when he was sufficiently recovered to stand/he stood/ he limped to the desk/he sat/he read/he pondered.

$$\overline{\underset{*}{}}$$

Hai now knew everything – everything it was possible to know – about Eli Rubenstein. But not everything there was to know – obviously/because there are some things we can never know about other people. Things like [for example] whether listening to the William Tell Overture brings back memories of the Lone Ranger & Tonto. Things like [for example] whether the smell of cigars/yesterday's food & stale wine brings back [like Proust's madeleine did for him] memories of early mornings in Leicester Square when you were seventeen. Things like that.

So – he didn't know everything/because there was a lot about Eli Rubenstein that no one knew – but he did know a lot.

He knew/for example/that Mr Rubenstein was – in some way that was some significant way – tied up with the presence/ then absence/then presence again/then absence again of half-of-half-a-ton of Afghan-best.

Hai was never an avaricious man – not in the way Mr Woo was – and he wasn't worried about any 'reputation' that might accrue to him after the removal of said Woo.

As major drug traffickers go Hai was about as laid-back as it was possible to be. He was to the drug trade what David Gower was to cricket.

But – with the removal of said Woo and his nights of Padmasanical communion with his lover – things were changing. She spoke to him on those nights. She spoke to him in a way she never did before. And because of the way she spoke to him and the things she said to him Hai was a changed-&-changing-man. But he wasn't changed-&-changing into a new man because he was a changed-&-changing-man into the man he used to be. So – he wasn't so much 'changing into' as 'changing back into'.

The man he was/now was/once again was/was the man he used to be. He was now the man who'd changed back into being the man he was before. And the man he was now – the one he'd changed back into – was a nicer/in every way/man than the man he was before. So it was a good thing that he was changing [or had already changed] back into the man he was now – as well as the man he was before. If you-follow-my-drift.

One of the things that the new-new Hai was changing into [back into] was a man with a moral compass pointing north. And not a moral compass that – thanks to the malign Gaussian influences of an uncouth Cantonese arsehole [a *hūn dàn* who/up until recently/got his jollies from strangling monkeys] – pointed all-over-the-place & anywhere but north.

◎ I guess moral compasses need nurture [just like the other parts of us do] so as to keep us from the sin of hubris/the errant stupidity of confusing religion with morality/& the socially frowned upon habit of strangling monkeys.

So – in what practical ways and significant ways [because/as-we-by-and-large know/only the 'practical' can/whatever the navel-gazing philosophers might say/be 'significant'] were the changes in Hai manifesting themselves? Just one really. Apparently lots/but just one.

He was determined to be a 'good' man and – in that determination – to cease being the man he was before. Not the man he was a long time before/when he was a good man [although not in the opinion of 'a fat pansy cunt in a skirt'] but the man he was not too long ago/before when he wasn't a good man at all/not to anyone/not even to himself.

'Exceptional times call for exceptional men to do exceptional things.'

Having completed his journey to Damascus he talked to his best-of-the-best-of-the-best – to each of them... and separately. He sowed seeds of doubt & division within them. The seeds grew. They bore the fruit of enmity & violence. With the 'enmity & violence' came the disappearance – as Hai was hoping it would – of them both.

He was thankfully – & at last & as planned – devoid of the best-of-the bests of any variety. He could relax in the absence of their presence and the existence of their lack of it. They were gone. He was ready for the next step. The next step needed them gone.

It was – what he did – [the 'doubt & division'] a Machiavellian thing to do and he knew it. But 'exceptional times call for exceptional men to do exceptional things.'

He didn't think of himself as exceptional – however much his lover told him he was. He saw himself as an ordinary man with out-of-the-ordinary things to achieve.

His thoughts could now/as they did/return to Mr Eli Rubenstein. He pondered upon a man he knew/or thought he knew/to be worse than Mr Woo. He assumed – although wrongly – that Mr Eli Rubenstein would have his own best-of-the-best-of-the-best and wondered [in an academic sort of way] whether he hadn't got rid of his own a little too soon.

In consequence of him having [since his arrival there] no desire to ever leave Hong Kong and/in consequence of that 'no desire'/ no intention of ever doing so – he needed to be spoken to/most seriously/by his lover that night.

She'd never spoken to him like that/not before. She spoke not of things that 'were' & 'why' but of things that 'were not' & 'why not'. By morning his quest for the Holy Grail of righteousness was clear before him.

He applied for a passport.

＊

By the time Bert *et alli* [Mac & Jimmy] arrived in Newcastle there were silences. By the time they got to Coffs the silences were palpable. By the time they got to Murwillumbah they were anything but golden. They were stony & pregnant with menace. And neither the menace nor the pregnancy were coming from Bert.

Mac & Jimmy were doing what men like Mac & Jimmy always did/always have. Probably since Cane got pissed off with

Abel. They were doing what people in confined spaces do. Places like prison cells/places like a 70-ish foot luxury cruiser which/by the day/was getting smaller & smaller.

Mac & Jimmy weren't big men and with anyone – other than the other one – the space would have been fine. But the thing Bert didn't realise – quite as well as he might – was that Mac hated Jimmy/& Jimmy hated Mac/with a hatred that – just like God's mercy [but remember what happened to you if your family wasn't Noah's] 'surpasseth all understanding'.

A trip to an island in the Calvados Chain – an island off the tail of New Guinea [and back] – was never going to work. So – somewhere off/about fifty miles off/because he went further out to sea for the occasion/the beaches of Surfers Paradise – and after getting them both horrendously & vomitingly drunk – Bert heaved them overboard. It seemed – under the circumstances – the only reasonable thing to do.

He arrived in Brisbane alone but happy. He rang his defrocked navy Commander. He offered him a disgusting sum of money. The navy Commander – having continued the activities that resulted in the defrocking [tampering/and more than 'tampering'/with under-age girls] and in the awareness that policemen were starting to ask questions/accepted the offer with alacrity.

They motored north and by the time they got to Cairns/ days spent looking at nothing but the sea & navigation screens – screens that Captain Cook/greatest navigator in history [if he wasn't already dead] would die for – and not/as he did/end up high [if not completely dry] on Endeavour Reef.

Their little bit of friendship – spawned/like a rock-oyster/ in Sydney Harbour – became 'a little bit more' and – going up through/along/beside & over the only animate object visible from the moon – their 'little bit more' grew to be 'a little bit more still'.

Their sharing of a Thursday Island girl in Townsville – Bert hoping she wasn't underage & the defrocked Commander hoping she was – made their 'little bit more still' into 'quite a lot more'. More than either of them – if they were to think about it which/given the sorts of men they were/or let themselves become/...

◎ Because we become/don't we/the sorts of people we let ourselves become?

...they didn't – would ever have thought possible.

They – neither of them – were intrinsically 'bad men'. They just became that way out of laziness. It takes – as we all know – effort to follow a moral compass and especially one that insists on pointing north. North – by-its-very-nature – is an-up-hill-battle and sliding south is the easy way to go.

They stayed for a week in Cairns. There was no imperative reason to/just a relative one. They were refuelled & revictualled within a day. They were happy in one another's company and didn't need a rest from it. They cruised the bars. They picked up women and took them back on board. They cruised the ocean. They took turns at the helm/as well as other things/until the early hours.

There is no accounting for the aphrodisiacal effect of a third Aperol Spritz on the supratentorial inhibitions of a party-girl. Especially one who finds herself undressing [because she wants to/because her friends say she wants to/because everyone else says she wants to/because everyone else seems to want to/because she just snorted the same stuff her friends did & everyone else did] on the fantail of a luxury yacht that's ploughing the high seas. And – what's more – with the guy at the helm wearing nothing but a Nelson hat & a pair of unbelievably young-looking Chinese girls [twins by the look of it] that he'd picked up on the dock.

Hai's knowledge was vast/his intel vaster & his reach vaster than vast. The unbelievably young-looking Chinese girls were daughters of parents who owed him. They/the parents/came/just as he did/from the poor province of Shanxi. There were adventures – of course there were – on their road to Hong Kong but none of them/not from what Hai could gather/as memorable as his own.

Hong Kong – while better than Shanxi – had not been as good to the parents as it had been to Hai. They'd prospered/after-a-fashion/but not really. Hai was paying for the girls' 'round-eye' schooling and the wife's fourth round of chemo.

They – the unbelievably young-looking Chinese girls – were/just as appearances suggested/twins. They – because they were good daughters of good parents – were/as well as well-educated/obliged to help. They were happy to. Even without their mother's endless chemo [and the endless obligation that went with it] they would still be happy to help. They were asked to – and were happy to – take on board what they were given to. They were happy to hide it where they were asked to. And that was somewhere where it wouldn't be found.

*

By day four – with the chick-magnet status of the *Trixie* well established – nights were nights of partying & boozing/snorting & stripping and all that [by human procreational nature] happens after that. The nightclubs of Cairns were starting to feel the pinch.

The cops didn't mind at all. It was all being done in Federal waters. They referred to the *Trixie* as 'Cirrhosis On The Sea'. The ghost of Errol Flynn was delighted.

But there came a time – as there does in-the-affairs-of-men – to say their *au revoirs*.

The last night – as they are at *The Proms* – was the best night of all and it was standing/lying room only. The foredeck and the fantail were a snake-pit of writhing bodies. Cabins were four to a bed. A Bolivian copper miner would work for a century to pay for the sniffables.

But there were casualties – there always are.

One 'face-down/washed-up/party girl' was one 'face-down/washed-up/party-girl' too many/even for the State Police. "Fuck the Feds," – this was on their turf now.

Sadly – the 'face-down/washed-up/party girl' was the daughter of the Presbyterian Moderator of Queensland and that was why/given her Somerville House education & impending honours degree [probably a 1st] in Fine Arts/it was all so hard – or was it – to understand.

And because it was all so hard for her parents to understand – even though for anyone with a scintilla of insight it wasn't – it must be someone else's fault/because it couldn't [even though she was the one doing the boozing/snorting/fornicating & falling-overboard-ing and doing it as voluntarily as any boozer/sniffer/fornicator & falling-overboarder has ever boozed/sniffed/fornicated & fallen-overboard] be their dear daughter's fault.

They couldn't believe that their daughter had been boozing & sniffing [let alone fornicating] her way to freedom & revenge. Revenge & pay-back for the claustrophobic upbringing they – an 'Old Testament-up-the-bum' father and an 'incapable-of-love' mother [but both 'good Christians'] – were giving her.

And – even though she was so obviously the author of her own demise – it must be 'someone else's fault'.

So – screamed *The Cairns Post* & *Courier-Mail* – 'WHOSE FAULT WAS IT?'

Well – it must be the *Trixie*'s and whatever depraved scum owned/operated/skippered & crewed it.

Luckily – for both Bert & his closer-than-ever friend – they were well beyond even the Fed's jurisdiction by the time whatever it is that hits metaphorical fans hit the metaphorical fan.

But unbeknown to Bert – but well known to the defrocked Commander – two unbelievably young-looking Chinese girls [twins by the look of it] and as they intended to be all along [because that was Hai's plan all along] were still aboard and happily sleeping off/in the defrocked Commander's cabin – where else – the excesses of last night. It was where they intended to be all along [because that was Hai's plan all along].

When they woke they checked the thing to be checked. It was emitting nicely.

*

Noor – some considerable time before all of the above – arrived/ by a circuitous route [because the 'circuitous' was important] in Tel Aviv.

There were lots of Jews around – of course there were – she was told to expect that. She did her best not to show what she was thinking. It wasn't a good 'best'/but it was adequate.

She didn't like Jews/in the same way she didn't like most people. There was only one Jew family in her local dorp and the only one she knew before making it to Cape Town.

Old Man Guttman ran the dry-goods store in town and his daughter Ziggy was the only Jew girl at school. Noor – as both expected & with pride – had led her band of likewise minded girls on the all too expected campaign of abuse/invective & obloquy ['Piggy Sluttman', etc.] until poor Ziggy/a sensitive child/an unwise thing to be in a place like the Great Karoo/ walked down to the river and drowned herself.

Now she was surrounded by them. But she had her instructions. She had a job to do. So now/for as long as it

172

took/for as long as she needed to be/she was on her best behaviour.

There was an appointment with a Mr Rubenstein and she kept it. He'd done/she knew/business with the AWSB before.

*

For Eli/the AWSB – because they were prompt & reliable payers – were/in a purely business sense/perfect clients. Even his recent interview with the atomic-bomb assembler [the one with the disquieted bosom] did little to dampen a desire to deal with them further.

The reason for that – the 'desire to deal with them further' – was because of what no one other than Eli Rubenstein knew anything about.

*

Noor's instructions were explicit and – given the simple nature of the men who gave them – simple. She was to confirm the deal. She was to accompany Rubenstein & 'the bit-that-was-no-longer-the-bit'/see it taken to its agreed safe-haven/see it deposited there/record exactly where 'there' was and then/once secure in the knowledge that no one else knew where 'there' was – kill him.

She was looking forward to that bit. It was years since she'd killed anything.

But she was looking forward to the seduction too. She was going to seduce him. She was going to beguile & tantalise him. She was going to enchant/bewitch & enslave him and then – with him as putty in her hands – she would degrade/demean & humiliate him and then [she was still thinking of how best to do it] kill him.

What – she mused – would give her most pleasure? Something slow & painful/something she could sit & watch. Stringing him up by the neck with one toe on the ground would be good. She'd watched her father do that to a kaffir. Something good to get her juices hot. Something good like being with Billy. Anyway – he was just a fucking *Joodse doos* – and any way of killing him would be fun.

◎   But life doesn't always work out the way we plan… does it?

*

Oldest-&-closest-friend – largely recovered but with a residual ache in the groin – sat at his desk. He read the letter. It was clear and to the point. The writer's stated beliefs/together with the implied [but not stated] threats and the express assertion that she wasn't going/not until she got what she wanted/away/made a further meeting sadly imperative.

With the realisation of the reality of the real world and not the non-reality of the concocted and un-real world he lived in he [we'll call him John from now on] took the rest of the day to decide on what to do next.

Arriving early at the club – barmen preparing to bar/ croupiers preparing to croup – he instructed his secretary to ring the number/slightly obscured by a blood spot [was it a 6 or an 8] written at the bottom of yesterday's letter.

Arrangements were made for a meeting on neutral turf. And – of all the meetings to occur on the surface of our oblate-spheroid that day – it was not/for the earth/to be counted among the more earth-shattering. But for them – for the two of them/for Lucy and John/not yet Lucy & John – it was.

It was to affect another person too – but he was far away/ sound asleep & a better man than once he was.

Boris – realising that this matter was going/at some time or other/to extend beyond the jurisdiction of the Met – had arranged a meeting with a colourless man. The colourless man sat in a colourless office. The colourless office was in an anything but colourless building. It was on the South Bank of Mother Thames.

"*Only the English*," mused Boris.

'Only the English,' he mused/could/would/would even think to house their most secret-of-secret departments in the most flamboyantly obvious building in the middle of their capital city. It was – he mused further – typical of his nation. A nation whose national pastime was understatement & self-deprecation/but couched in the certain knowledge that they were/always were/would always be/superior to the Frogs/Krauts/Yanks [etc.] and were/after all/the chosen of God.

God was – without a shadow of doubt – an Englishman. He played-cricket-with-a-straight-bat/rowed stroke for Cambridge/regretted all that earlier stuff in Palestine and would/because that was his *raison d'être* for creating the universe in the first place/look after his chosen people. So why bother too much about security when God was on your side?

The colourless man – as colourless as Tim's man in Pretoria was nondescript – was understanding but/sadly/non-committal. He said he would see what he could do and get back to him. Boris – having experienced assurances from men like the colourless man – never expected he would. But he was wrong.

The colourless man rang that afternoon and asked him to return to the anything but colourless building the following morning. There was someone who wanted 'a chat'.

The man Boris met was not a colourless man at all. He/more than anything/took after the building outside and it was quite possible that the colourlessness of the colourless man made this man's colourfulness more colourful.

◎ We sometimes underrate the relativities of life.

The colourless man introduced the colourful man as Sir William Ponsonby-Smythe. "Call me Bill, old chap, everyone does," – which Boris knew he never would and doubted if anyone/even Lady Ponsonby-Smythe/did.

They sat for an hour. They talked of many things – not of 'shoes and ships and sealing-wax' – of course not – but of other things.

Boris left the meeting with a spring in his always sprightly step. He knew he should – although he knew he wouldn't because 'Bill' told him he couldn't – keep his Ass Comm up-to-speed/in-the-loop & informed of events.

Part of – if not all of – the reason for the spring in his always sprightly step was that he [together with Det Sgt Titus Ishmael Taylor] were now co-opted agents in the service of Her Majesty's Secret Service/MI 6.

$$\overline{\underset{*}{}}$$

Hai – anything but happy about it/but having no say in the matter [because his lover's instructions were quite specific and left no wiggle-room to modify or ignore them] – flew to Singapore.

It was the first time he was ever in/on/or anywhere close to an aeroplane and/given the choice/he never would be in/on/ or anywhere close to one ever again/but [see above] he had no choice in the matter.

After a sleep-disturbed night – disturbed at the prospect of repeating the experience the next day – he repeated the experience the next day. He flew to Port Moresby.

"@#$% *what a dump*," was the thought he thought. An understandable thought to think and a thought thought by many.

He was met by a man/'his man'/colourless by nature/smart by nature & dressed in a most colourful way.

◎ As we know – camouflage isn't always about *not* being seen. Sometimes [which means 'not always'] the best way to be covert is to be overt. Sometimes [which means not always] 'hidden in plain sight' is the best way to be hidden.

And so it was that Hai – both 'shaken & stirred' after his second white-knuckle flight in two days [and with the prospect of the same on return] – and after saying *au revoir* to his colourfully colourless man – boarded a motor yacht of some 70-ish feet. He then headed off/with a crew of one [the blackest man Hai had ever seen] to an island in the Calvados Chain off the tail of New Guinea.

The blackest man said he knew where to go. He showed Hai charts [because there were no roads on them] of where they were going. He said he was there some years before and – as you may remember – he was.

⁎

For Eli – helped by being-around-the-traps more than once – there was a better than good idea of what was going on. He didn't come-down-in-the-last-shower. He knew-how-many-beans-made-five. He wasn't-born-yesterday. He was a-big-boy-in-a-big-boy's-world. He knew exactly what was going on – almost.

So – the one question – the reason for the 'almost' – was why were a pack of swastika waving/swastika tattooed/black hating/brown hating/Jew hating/by-and-large everybody hating/pack of Afrikaner low-lives – with misogyny ranked high on their tablet of Commandments – sending a woman/this woman/to do their bidding? Why not more of the pig-boys they sent last time?

But after thinking about it – as well as not-being-born-yesterday [etc.] it didn't take him long to work out why. This woman – with all the right stuff in all the right places – was a Trojan Horse/a Trojan Mare. She was Mata Hari with bigger tits.

He felt flattered – in one way – that the swastika waving low-lives thought he could be swayed by the lures of the flesh. In another way he felt insulted that they could possibly think that a man of his race [the smartest race ever to walk the planet] would fall for such an obvious ploy.

Without the knowledge making its way to the surface of his thoughts he knew how patently obvious it was that this woman – built & dressed but not overly dressed/*déshabillé* of both chest & thigh – was sent to wriggle her way/via the weakness of his/ Eli's/Eli Rubenstein's/Rubenstein-the-Great's libidinous id/into a position of intimacy & trust.

And – what's more – in anticipation of a lamentable lack of judgement on his part – she would mesmerise him/become inseparable from him/accompany him to the resting place of the aforementioned WOMD/and once sure of its whereabouts/kill him. How stupid did they think he was? 'Very' – obviously.

Then – as she sat across the desk from him – he decided on how he was going to play the game. Outflanking stupid people was what he'd spent his life doing. It was what he was good at. It was why he was where he was in the world. It was what made him 'Rubenstein-the-Great'. It was going to be fun.

$$\overline{\underset{*}{}}$$

Boris & Ishmael weren't to visit the-not-uncolourful-building again. A house in Cornwall Street – Pinner was supplied for them. A colourless man and an equally colourless woman supplied them with everything they needed/as well as a lot of things they didn't think they needed [not until they were given them] and some things they didn't have a clue they needed [not until they were given them]. There were things/electronic & non/laid out on tables. They were things that would make the nerdiest of nerdy nerds wet their knickers.

Both of them assumed – and it wasn't an unreasonable assumption to assume – that The Yard would have everything open-and-shuttable when it came to gathering intel. But their assumption [as assumptions so often are] was wrong. It was wrong/wide-of-the-mark/by a long way/a-country-mile.

At the end of the first day they travelled home by tube. Both of them were feeling a feeling/and it was the same feeling each of them felt. And the feeling they were feeling was a feeling from somewhere deep within the interstices of their brains/from somewhere deeper than the *nucleus platitudinus*.

It was a warm feeling. It would be/and was/hard for either of them to say exactly what the feeling was. But/in an inexact sort of way/they were feeling the feeling that – with men & women like the colourless man & woman – the 'Safety of the Realm' was in good hands.

They didn't – like most of us don't [except in a 'not much'/ occasional & academic sort of way] – think about the 'Safety of the Realm'. But now/when they did [because they did] they thought about it in a warmer & happier way than they ever did before.

As a bonus to those warmer & happier thoughts – they/by the end of a week/knew everything there was to know about Eli Rubenstein – absolutely everything. Almost absolutely everything. But not *everything*... obviously.

As mentioned [see above] – and as I am sure you will agree – there are some things not possible to know about any of us – the William Tell/Leicester Square stuff for sure/but maybe stuff about what we *really* think/not just *appear* to think/not just *say* we think.

So what was Eli Rubenstein *really* thinking? Neither of them knew.

But they didn't need – did they – to know what Eli Rubenstein was thinking/not even what he was *really* thinking rather than what he *appeared* to be thinking? The questions they needed the answers to were A.) If he was – then B.) Where [if he was] was he hiding the 6th Earl of Somewhere-or-other?

They knew pretty well the answer to the 'if he was' bit of the question – which was an almost/nearly/just about certain-ish – 'yes he was'. And the answer to the 'where' bit was – given the 6th Earl's oldest-&-closest-friend's bi-annual payments to The Acme Trading Company of Jerusalem/and The Acme Trading Company of Jerusalem's synchronous & bi-annual payments [they'd needed a second Court Order – given-the-thumbs-up by a lady judge whose only daughter was/since the previous week/ shacked up with an older woman called Something-or-other Kosminski – to get that info] to a barge skipper in Port Moresby/ together with the testimony of said barge skipper/given – with only a moderate degree of duress & coercion – to Detective Sergeant Willy Poma of the Royal PNG Constabulary – together with their A & R generated knowledge that Mr Rubenstein owned an island in the Calvados Chain off the tail of New Guinea – somewhere in the Calvados Chain off the tail of New Guinea.

'Call me Bill' visited Cornwall Street. It was time to put boots-on-the-ground – their boots/not MI6-for-real boots/ Boris & Ishmael's boots. "Accountability, old chap. We're trying to avoid any more cock-ups this year, know what I mean?" Boris was given no choice. He complied.

His Ass Comm now partially – because that couldn't be avoided – in-the-loop was happy(ish) as long as 'Call me Bill' – who said he would – picked up the tab.

⁻
*

Eli knew a thing or two about women. Apart from his time in Ktz'iot there were always women in his life. He liked women around him and he liked the women around him to be happy. Having an unhappy woman around wasn't a happy thing to have. If the woman he was with was an unhappy sort of woman – because some women can be...

◎ And/at this juncture/the author is obliged to [if not frightened not to] say that men can be just the same.

...he was happy to trade-her-in.

He liked the feeling he got when he made women happy. He liked it when the woman he was making happy fell in love with him. He liked the feeling of 'closeness' it gave him. He liked it even though he knew the feeling of 'closeness' he was feeling wasn't love. There were eight women who'd fallen in love with him. It gave him a good feeling to know he was loved. He wondered [sometimes/occasionally/but not often] why it was that he wasn't able to love them in return.

But – even without the love – he 'liked' the women who loved him. He liked them a lot/more than just a bit. He liked them for sex – of course he did – but he liked them for more than that. He liked them for their companionship.

He didn't *do* male friends. He wasn't sure why. He suspected it might be something to do with the male ego. About having to be the one at the top of the tree. It was lonely at the top of the tree. But it was better than looking up at some other guy's arse.

With women there were no ego problems. He wined-them-and-dined-them and bought them beautiful things. In return they did an array of wonderful things to him and were company.

His view of women – in his early days – was somewhat two dimensional. But he'd gotten better as time passed. It was out beyond the third dimension that was the most fun.

With the passing of the years he took real pleasure – more than in just wining-and-dining and buying beautiful things – in making women happy. He became a thoughtful & always gentle lover. He learned the knack of making a woman's body feel the things the women wanted their bodies to feel. He learned the knack – partly/but not completely/from his knack of making a woman's body feel the things the women wanted their bodies to feel – of caressing their brains as well.

For a woman – for anyone – to have his/her brain caressed is the greatest caress of all. And – because of all the caressing of bodies & brains he did – women 'fell-in-love' with him. There were [see above] eight of them – and while he never loved any of them in return he still cared for them and enjoyed the feeling of being loved. He repaid them with as much 'almost love' as he could.

None of the women who fell-in-love with him ever fell-out-of-love with him and they were like a family. They lived together in a big house overlooking the sea.

They were smart women & Jewish women/all of them/and those were the women he liked. Dumb women & goy women were put on earth – or so the Talmud says & The Old Testament infers [Genesis 2:21-22] – to satisfy the needs of dumb men & goy men. Eli was neither of those.

While they knew he didn't love them in return/they knew he cared for them.

And he cared for each of them and 'almost loved' each of them in a way that was special to each of them. He spent time with each of them. He made each of them feel special. That made them love him more. The life he gave them and the care he gave them was enough for them. They could live without his love.

Being intelligent women as well as Jewish women they – as since Abraham's time – got on well together. They were friends. They were a sisterhood. They were in love with the same man. They were happy.

And-so-it-was that the not-so-nice Eli of his youth – under the influence of eight intelligent Jewish women [almost a tautology] – became the much better/but not perfect [because he still killed people from-time-to-time] person of his middle years.

And now before him sat this tallish/lopsidedly coiffured & handsomely featured woman. The sunrise of her nipples threatened/at any moment/to appear over the horizon of her purposefully visible/purposefully diminutive & purposefully scarlet bra. He was amused.

Being all the things previously mentioned – counting beans up to five [etc.] – Eli knew there was more/quite a bit more/on the woman's agenda than just the things they were talking about. And [because of all the things mentioned previously] he knew she was here to seduce him/bewitch him/beguile him & – when she knew the things she wanted to know – kill him. It wasn't the first time. He knew the script.

What she said she wanted/which was a large part of what she wanted/but not all of what she wanted [because she didn't mention the killing bit] was to have the thing that used to be 'The Bit'/but was now no longer 'The Bit'/shipped to somewhere safe.

He said that could be arranged. They talked preliminaries/generalities/specifics & money. A price was agreed. Business was concluded. She uncrossed & recrossed her legs. The diminutive triangle of her scarlet knickers was – as he expected it would be – flashed. He invited her to lunch. She accepted. They went. After lunch he invited her to the Presidential Suite of a hotel he owned. She accepted. They went. It was on the top floor. Presidential Suites are usually/mostly/more-often-than-not/on the top floor.

By evening Eli thought he might go home. By evening Noor thought/suspected/knew she was in love. She was confused. She – until now – knew nothing of love.

It was more than the Scales of Saul/Road to Damascus/ blockbuster & eye opener of an afternoon for Noor. Gentle things were done to her – such gentle/caring & crafted things that no man had ever come close to/not-within-eight-rural-furlongs of/ doing to her before. All the men she'd known – with the exception of her weak *Engels* husband/and maybe the maths teacher/who just did what she told them to – treated her as nothing more than a collection of easily accessible vents. She'd never imagined that something like this could-or-would happen to her.

All she could think of doing was to keep on doing all the things they were doing and to keep on doing them until the end of time. Thoughts of killing him left her. They were never to return.

Eli thought that might be the case.

The last thing he did – a thing he came back from the door to do/as though it was an afterthought/which it wasn't/because it was a thing he often did – was to come back to the bed and kiss her gently/ever so gently/on her nose. She purred out loud.

◎   The aphrodisiacal effect of being kissed on the nose has
    been largely overlooked by the poets. Trust me.

He left/he went/he was gone. All Noor – poor love sick Noor – could think to do was remove the eye wateringly large black thing from her bag and throw it in the trash. Her life was turning/ had turned/a corner.

$$\overline{}_{*}$$

John and Lucy [not yet John & Lucy] met on neutral ground. It was the no-man's-land of a Burger King on the M1. It wasn't a million miles from Luton/just ten. It wasn't a million miles from Mayfair either/just ten socio-demographic light-years.

The conversation was – as you might imagine – slow to get started.

Lucy – because her recently damaged turbinates were still swollen – sounded rather/more than just a bit/adenoidal.

She knew: A.) By instinct: B.) By being told it by her Aunty Agnes who'd been [just as Lucy was to hers] the black sheep of her family and was once described by Lucy's mother [who was always in bed by nine] as being a 'woman of the night': and C.) By experience – that it's harder for a man – a weaker vessel and doomed/like Sisyphus/to carry his boulder-like ego for life – to apologise for his actions. And [because of that] she said – "Sorry for the knee in the goolies, mate."

John – arriving at the meeting abristle with righteous indignation – was surprised to hear her do so.

He had been reared in an age – and of a class – and of a 'set' – where the sanctity of 'the idea' of a woman was chapter-&-verse in every 'gentleman's' internal bibliography. He would no more walk through a door ahead of a woman than he would cheat at golf/although he did.

But he'd been reared in an age – and of a class – and of a 'set' – where the 'reality' of a woman was that she was [see above – Genesis [etc.] 'Adam's rib' and 'a thing' given to man by God. 'A thing'/a being/weaker & dumber and off-the-planet a week once a month.

He – like many of his class – despised women. He despised them/incorrectly [because men look in mirrors just as much as women do] for their perceived vanity. He despised them/incorrectly [because men are just as fickle/frivolous & inconstant as women are] for their perceived fickle & frivolous inconstancy. He – like many of his age and class – didn't actually 'like' women. He – like many of his age and class – sported his own collection of smutty 'blonde-jokes'.

Just as Lucy was a feminist's feminist – John was a misogynist's misogynist.

So – you may be surprised to read that/after talking in a downwardly spiralling and thus decreasingly contentious manner/they found themselves [having driven back to Mayfair and being neither pissed nor drugged to the eyeballs/but certainly naked] going-at-it liked crazed weasels.

It was at the time of his Second Coming that John came to fully appreciate her. She intrigued him. She was like no other woman he'd met. On paper she was all he found least attractive in women. But it's not on paper that weasels/crazed or otherwise/ go-at-things – is it?

He'd assumed/up until then – incorrectly he now realised – that women didn't grow/not like men did/hair in their armpits. He'd assumed/up until then – again incorrectly – that women didn't grow hair/not like men did/anywhere but on their heads. He was/up until then/exposed only to women who'd corroborated that incorrect notion. He now realised – for the first time – how much time the women he knew must spend doing the things the women he knew must.

He remembered Lucy from her waitressing days. She was different then – *manicuré partout son corps* – just like the other girls he employed – and *manicuré* to the point of *très*. But all of that/the 15-denier sheerness of her body/armpits [etc.]*was* all some years ago/quite a few.

People/he mused/change… and how?

This – if he remembered rightly – previously pliable young woman was no longer the docile beast she once was. She – if he remembered rightly – had never/not at all/demurred to cavort naked/pissed & drugged-to-the-eye-balls with his friend the 6th Earl. And – if he remembered rightly [which he knew he did because no one forgets a thing like that] she'd never/not at all/demurred at having her employer watch their cavort as they cavorted it.

Lucy's arms were tattooed – quite a lot/more than just a bit.

That would normally – for a man-like-John who/under

186

the influence of Lucy Mk II/was becoming less of 'a-man-like-John' than the-man-called-John ever thought he could possibly become – be a major turn-off. But it wasn't.

He'd lived – until the advent of Lucy Mk II – in a world where tattoos were things to despise. They were/he thought [until he was shown the wonders of going-at-it-like-crazed-weasels] for those of a lower & unpalatable demographic. But – finding the palatable parts of her body to be more palatable than he ever thought palatable parts of any woman/tattooed or un-[as well as *manicuré* or un-] could possibly be – he revised that opinion.

The bull-dog and '*Mack*' on one side & '*Happy Harry*' in his straw boater on the other lent an air of excitement and sleazy sophistication to events.

John came from a demographic where there was grudging acceptance that the lower orders were: A.) More inventively carnal: B.) More uninhibitedly venereous: C.) Just happier to go about screwing one another than they/his demographic/were: and D.) Not 'giving a toss' about any of it. And so it was that [thanks to Lucy Mk II] A.)-thru-D.) were confirmed.

He was getting-his-rocks-off in ways he never thought possible.

Lucy's hands were calloused and roughened from the things she did. That would normally be a major turn-off. But it wasn't. She could do things with those hands that other hands/softer & less dextrous hands [not hands used to finding their way through the interstices of a/more compact than most/Scania engine] either couldn't or wouldn't do. It was her lubriciously imaginative id that boosted the calloused & roughened hands into doing the things they did.

John never expected – not at his age/somewhere beyond forty – to experience the things that he did. It was all good/better than good/and he knew it.

But for Lucy that was all-very-well. Because now there was this man/another man/a second-man/a second man who didn't/just as the 6th Earl didn't/laugh at her *en repose et/ou en rampant* parts.

But – be-that-as-it-may – he was the-second-man and not the-first-man and however much she was enjoying this-second-man bringing her to the point where her *signature parts* did their signature things [as well as the cascade of things to happen soon after] he wasn't the first man. And it was the-first-man she needed to find.

She was a woman obsessed.

◎   And – as we all know – obsessions are rarely understandable. Neither understandable nor quenched by indulgence.

So – they [now Lucy & John] conjoined the weekend away. Until/ at last/it was time for her to return to Luton – to the wonders of Selective Catalytic Reduction.

With her gone – deep ennui overcame him. He lost interest in doing the things he did. He could do nothing but sit & remember.

He could remember the 6th Earl's infatuation and could remember wondering why that was. But now there was an inkling/more than an inkling/of why that was. It wasn't her anatomy alone that intrigued him [intriguing to watch though watching it was] but more the realisation that the way the intriguing parts morphed to the-more-so was Lucy's overture to lyric events.

They were often in D minor/but never loud. She would start out *adagio* and progress through *andante* towards *allegro*. She was more oboe than French horn.

But there was more than just the sight of her & the sound of her. It was the freedom of her.

It wasn't what she did/or even the key she did it in/but the way she did it. There was a freedom of expression-ish-ness/a dare-devil-ish-ness/a far out-ish-ness/an I-couldn't-give-a-toss-what-anyone-thinks-ish-ness about the things she did and the things that happened to her as they did the things they did.

It isn't often that a man knows [for certain] that what he's doing is doing what it's supposed to do.

He couldn't remember – because he was [or had been up until recently] a self-centred and uninspiring lover – taking time/or expended effort/to give someone else that sort of pleasure. But that was all different now. The Golan Heights were behind him. The lights of an ancient city shone in the distance.

And so – the oldest-&-closest-friend was as mesmered as he was never mesmered before. But it wasn't just the things already mentioned that were doing it – because what the things already mentioned were the-crowning-glory of were as good a looking pair to have crowning-glories be the-crowning-glory of as any of us are ever likely to come across in a-long-day's-march

But it was/he realised/the whole package/tattoos included. There was a better than passable body and her face wasn't too bad either. It wouldn't 'launch a thousand ships' or 'burn the topless towers of Ilium' but it was better than 'OK'.

There were – of course there were [this being a racy & ribald novel] other things as well. And the 'other things as well' were all the things she did to/with & for him.

He couldn't remember having some of the things she did to/with & for him done to/with & for him before and that was because they never had been. His id-of-old was being dragged [but not/that's for sure/kicking-&-screaming] into unknown/uncharted & unheard-of territory.

And what's more – the one-or-two things he could remember being done to/with & for him before – he couldn't remember being done so well.

And – after getting the hang of all the things she liked him to do to/for & with her – it became a two-way-street. It was biblical [2 Corinthians 9:7]. They 'gave & they received'. It was synergism. It was synchronism. It was symbiosis.

By Tuesday the weekend seemed so far behind him. The weekend ahead/an eon away. He was *un homme perdu*. He was *un homme seul et triste*.

That's why he drove to Luton.

---

*

Luton is known for the Luton Girls' Choir – not a lot else – trust me.

---

*

A nondescript man from Pretoria – another one/not the man Tim knew but a different one – sat in the foyer of the hotel. He watched Eli leave. There was a van parked outside. It wasn't full/only partly full/of electronic gear. There was another nondescript man/and he was from Pretoria too.

---

*

Eli ate dinner with his 'wives'. He told them about Noor – her request/her unspoken/her lethal intentions/his morning/their lunch/their afternoon. They talked about things to be done. About whether there *were* things to be done. One of the 'wives' had an interesting idea.

---

*

The nondescript man nodded to a nondescript woman. She was from/or looked to be from/house-keeping. She left the foyer. She entered a lift. The lift rose to the highest floor.

She knocked on the door/the door she was told to.

"House-keeping!" There was no answer.

She let himself in. She could hear ablutions being loudly abluted.

She – because women like her/as well as men like her/were trained to do just that – checked the trash-can. She looked – with some watering of her eyes – at the eye wateringly large black thing discarded there. And knowing what it was/because she was told what it was/as well as what was in it/she picked it up. And – because she was cognisant of its provenance – with a paper handkerchief. Thinking-on-her-feet [as women like her have the capacity to do] she opened it/removed what she found there/closed it and returned it to the trash.

Just as 'shower being got out of' sounds sounded/she placed what she'd removed from the eye wateringly large black thing into the lining of Noor's handbag – a shoulder-bag/a big one/she carried a lot of things/none of them [as yet] feminine.

⁕

Eli returned during the night just as Noor hoped he would. He came with a 'wife' – the one with the 'interesting idea'. The 'interesting idea' became an 'interesting night'/then an interesting day/just as Eli & Wife thought it might/would. Noor's life was never to be the same.

⁕

The boat – it was a Zodiac – left the ship. The 6th Earl expected it to/as usual/head off towards the atoll. But it didn't. It headed towards him. It kept heading towards him.

He didn't scamper [because Earls/whatever their number & whatever their age/don't scamper] but very nearly scampered down from his crow's-nest and ran – Earls are allowed to trot but only when absolutely necessary. But this one ran/and ran in such a way to suggest [as we know he was] an Earl on a mission.

He [in a figurative-cum-Road Runner sense] skidded to a halt by the door of his sacrificial hut. He would be sad to see it go but – like Bentham & the 'greater good' – sacrifice was demanded & unavoidable.

'Sacrifice' was a newcomer to the widening pantheon of the 6th Earl's moral compass. It went unmentioned on his Coat of Arms. There was no *alios sacrificare* in the family motto.

To the 1st Earl [the 6th Earl's G^3 grandfather] – sacrifice of any sort – certainly his own – was an alien concept/although that of others was not. He thought little about it – I have little doubt about it – as he ordered light English guys on light English horses to 'do their duty'/'not reason why'/'do and die' as history [so poetically] records they did.

"*Thank God for the Frogs*" – thought the 1st Earl's G^3 grandson/ but only in an abstract sort of way/as the *Bic* lighter [75p at Woolies] lit first flick/which his gold-plated Dunhill [£250 at Harrods] never did/and the kindling caught fire under the *ignis funus*.

Putting abstract & benevolent thoughts of *le bon Baron* behind him he ran to the top of the island. He could see the Zodiac through the palms. It was nosing its way through the opening in the reef. He looked back. He could see smoke. He ran on to his 'Alamo'.

⁎

John wasn't overly impressed by Luton. There was no reason why he should be. It was a town conceived in soullessness/planned with the frigid catatonia of austerity & built with an insensate avoidance of humanity. It was the pits. But that didn't matter. A woman/the woman/the only woman/lived there. He didn't know *where* she lived but that didn't matter – he knew where she worked. And where she worked/the place he planned to visit and did/was like no other place he'd ever visited before.

◎ Without the diesel truck 'the world-as-we-know-it' would be a different place – bordering on 'very'. There are lots of them. We all know that. And without them moving all sorts of stuff to all sorts of places/'life-as-we-know-it' [as well as 'the world-as-we-know-it'] would be in all sorts of bad places. We rely on them for near-enough everything? So – who would the world miss most – the Pope/the Archbishop of Canterbury/the Grand Mufti or Lucy from Luton? You guessed right.

Because John's trip to Luton came not from a desire to kneel at the feet of someone more important than the Pope – but an understandable desire for more earthly & earthy things – he'd left the chauffeur at home.

He found the LDSC [the Luton Diesel Servicing Centre] with little difficulty. It was a large affair just north of the town – which means he'd driven through it to get there – which/ while depressing/was not depressing enough to dampen his expectatory ardour.

As he drove into the forecourt and as he applied the hand-brake he became aware of a mounting erection.

＊

One dark/but not particularly stormy/night – some months after the first of Noor's glittering Tel Aviv moments/but quite a while before the recent runnings of 6th Earls – a motor yacht of some 70-ish-feet pulled in & anchored in the channel between the island & the atoll. The channel was empty – not because the ship you were expecting to be there was gone/because it wasn't/ but because it wouldn't arrive for some time.

In the first light of dawn – as the 6th Earl slept the sleep of the not totally innocent/not totally many things/but definitely the bludgeoner of Nannies/but generally on the improve – a boat containing a metal chest left the 70-ish-footer. It came with neither check nor hesitation [because the man at the helm/ having done it before/knew where to go] through the gap in the reef. It landed on the beach. A hole was dug [beneath two quite distinctively bent palms] next to where a previous hole was dug. The metal chest was dragged to & placed into the hole. As were the bodies of the two draggers & diggers – their heads being Dirty Harry-ed by a Dirty Harry Thing/the noise of which/but for a fleeting moment only/caused the 6th Earl to stir from his dreams.

The person at the other end of the Dirty Harry Thing was Noor. She – though a much-changed person from the one you know/and having her nose so regularly and so gently kissed by the man she loved/as well as by a number of smart Jewish women – still got pleasure from killing things.

The Jewish women – in the knowledge of the thing that must soon & unavoidably happen to the diggers & draggers/and with a preference for ignoring such things – were staying on board.

Killing the islanders – not the same as the kaffirs at home but still kaffirs-of-sorts – gave Noor [because she was only part way along the road to moral realignment] unexpected & unlooked for pleasure/but pleasure [not inconsiderable pleasure] none-the-less. It was up there with [but not as good as] axing her father. The intensity of the pleasure and the knowledge that she/ together with the man she loved/were alone on a deserted beach/

poured industrial quantities of serotonin/moderate amounts of dopamine/together with a smidgeon of oxytocin all over her joyously expectant *anima*.

And because of that – as the first light of dawn lit the eastern sky [thus heralding the start of another magnificent day] and after removing her clothes – she lay on the sand/assumed an unladylike pose and suggested that he might/asked him if he would/begged him that he should/perform a number of vulgar acts upon her person.

Eli – being a man who knew when and/more importantly/ when not to give a woman what she suggests/asks & begs for – took her by the hair/dragged her down the beach to the boat and told her to get in – which/without demur/she did.

Noor didn't think it was possible to love the man she loved more than she did – but now she did.

Halfway across the lagoon he remembered her clothes. They were still on the beach. That wouldn't do. So – in the knowledge that 'that wouldn't do' – he pushed her overboard and told her to swim back for them – which/without demur/she did.

Noor didn't think it was possible to love the man she loved more than she did – but now she did.

Returning to the boat and being pulled aboard by her hair she didn't think it was possible to love the man she loved more than she did but now/once again/she did.

Back aboard the 70-ish footer 'the wives' awaited their return. Knowing the workings of their 'husband's' mind/they took Noor down to his [the big one] cabin. They showered her/they anointed her/they lay her *in flagrante delicto* upon the bed.

Noor's *prosencephalon* & *supra-optic ganglia* – even though she didn't know what those were – might never/although they did/ recover. The wait/the pulling of hair/the pushing overboard/the pulling of hair/the anointing/the being lain *in flagrante delicto* [and all the things she hoped would happen after that] were the key.

Eli knew – because he knew a lot of things about women – that/for a woman like Noor/they would be.

They steamed out of the channel and back to where/whence they came from. Months passed.

*

With 'Call me Bill' being generous-ish/but far from profligate/ and with his departmental budget running no further than a 50-ish-footer – Boris & Ishmael/together with an unbelievably black-skipper-with-charts/set out from Moresby.

They thought it appropriate – their boat being green – to take [but only in something between metaphor & allegory] 'some honey and plenty of money, wrapped up in a five-pound note' – and in doing so they/and once again in [see above] 'sailed away for a year and a day to the land where the Bong-Tree grows'/ and when they got there they found [not 'a Piggy-wig with a ring at the end of its nose'] but a ship anchored in the channel between the island [the island their unbelievably black-skipper-with-charts assured them was the one they were looking for] and a not too distant atoll. And – in addition to the ship – they found 70-ish footed versions/a number of them/of their 50-ish footed one.

*

Hai – no longer capable of being surprised by much – was not surprised to find the channel choc-a-block with shipping.

He knew – in advance – that another 70-ish footer would be there before him. He knew that – not because of some mysterious oriental wisdom/foresight or *feng shui* – but because of the unbelievably young Chinese girls [twins by the look of it] and the electronic gear they'd smuggled on board in Cairns.

They anchored a cable's length – 200 yards for the Brits/240 for the Yanks – off the port bow [off the left side of the pointy bit]. Other 70-ish-footers lay at anchor nearby. It was all very chummy – and then a 50-ish-footer arrived.

✳

Tim was happy with his life *sans* Noor. And his son barely seemed to notice the absence of a mother. His practice was flourishing and he was in demand. There was talk of a judicial appointment.

But Tim desired – at that point in his life – no changes to his life. He was content with his life as it was.

He wasn't surprised to not hear from his wife. He was surprised – however – not to hear from her lawyers.

◎ Lawyers – as we all know – were created late on the sixth day. That was when God [knackered from creating the-universe-&-everything/and with his further oversight of not providing – not until quite a bit later – Adam with an Eve] can be forgiven for being less than divine.

Tim was surprised to the point of 'very' at the lack of demand upon the-coin-of-his-purse.

It seemed – given what he was shown in Pretoria – that she was 'moving on'/but certainly not 'up'. And/in his imagination/ he saw her as some kind of gangster's moll. A 'comfort-woman' for the men of the AWSB/or worse – although he couldn't imagine what 'worse' could possibly be. She would be at home in the company of men like that. Probably 'the-worse-the-better' would be [Freud] right-up-her-alley.

On occasions – but rarely/increasingly rarely – when 'right-up-her-alley' crossed his mind – he wondered how the eye wateringly large black thing was bearing up under the strains-

and-stresses of its new life. He wondered [when he was bothered to wonder that wonder] whether his clever little addition was still bleeping out its whereabouts. Little [nothing at all] did he know of its new home.

"*How long do these modern batteries last?*" he – but only rarely – wondered. And being of a nature that held unanswered wonders [even rarely wondered wonders] to be the thin-end-of-wedges in the fall of Western Civilisation/he decided to find out. And the answer to his rarely wondered wonder was – 'for ages'. "*How wonderful,*" he thought.

In general/as well as in specifics/he realised how lucky he was and what a lucky escape it had been. He hoped-against-hope [whatever that's meant to mean] that she wouldn't come back.

While a gregarious man he was happy with his own company. He liked nothing better – when time allowed – than to take Perry for weekends in the Drakensberg and share father-son adventures. But there were the calls of his body too – of course there were.

There were girlfriends – of course there were. His status as deserted husband & solo parent was common knowledge – of course it was – and his boyish charm/professional prestige & philosophical acceptance of his lot brought women to him in numbers – of course it did.

He – like many before him – had come to the belief that a deserted husband secretes some sort of hormone that attracts women like catnip does cats. He wasn't beating them off with sticks – but nearly.

There were favourites – of course there were – but he was wary of things going further than friendship & the occasional night of shared lust.

His functional bachelorhood was – of course it was – a not uncommon topic of conversation whenever & wherever women of a certain type got together.

His nondescript man – he thought of him as 'my George Smiley' – kept in touch. It was a regular thing/a once-a-month thing/and Tim suspected his name was somewhere in the electronic calendar of things for the man to do. It was usually a phone call but when work took him to the nation's capital he was asked to pop in for a chat/which – why wouldn't he be – he was happy to do.

He wasn't sure why 'George' kept in touch. He was never asked to do anything – not since the business of putting what he was given to put into the place where he put it. They didn't seem to be [although he thought they should be] interested in the disappearance of his wife. 'George' was just keen to chat.

Tim – being a smart & insightful man [and you didn't get to being what he was without being both of those things] knew he was being 'kept on the books' and that one day the 'polite chats' might become more than that – not 'impolite chats' but more than just 'chats'. He suspected the man of seeing him – and he wasn't unhappy [perhaps just a bit] to be seen – as a 'potential asset'.

The ['perhaps just a bit]' was with the word 'potential'.

Perhaps – he pondered/when he pondered about it at all – he was holding on to some deep-down schoolboy desire to be a kind of 'Reilly, Ace of Spies'? He wasn't sure – but the thought of it wasn't an unpleasant one.

And so/when the monthly chat happened only a week after the last one/he knew something more was about to be asked of him. And it was.

And what it was/was this.

Tim knew – because he was told some months before – that his wife hadn't [after her fictional visit to her fictional aunt] returned to South Africa. He knew also [because he was told some months before] that she was now living in Israel.

And that – in the knowledge of her irradicable anti-nearly-everybody but especially blacks/browns/yellows & the Sons of Abraham – he'd found surprising.

He didn't know until now [because he wasn't told some months before/or at any time] that she was 'shacked up' in a house by the sea [fully visible & heavily photographed by certain boats passing by] with 'one of the worst men on the planet'.

◉ But you – knowing more about 'one of the worst men on the planet' than the nondescript man did – may not be quite so hasty in your subjective judgement of the man – Eli of course – who/while being a knave in many ways/was not a knave in every way. And/as far as being 'one of the worst men on the planet' goes/that has yet to be seen – as/in the fullness of time/it will be.

Being asked [because Tim did just that] about the whys-and-the-wherefores of the matter – the man agreed to tell him/and supposedly told him/'everything'.

But in the being told 'everything'/Tim – being a smart & insightful man [see above] – doubted that the word 'everything' meant quite the same to the man as it did to him.

He was told about the AWSB and about their contacting of [as well as their contract with] 'one of the worst men on the planet'. He was told about the/how-&-from-where/acquisition of the 10 kilos of Pu-239. He was told about its arrival [town drunks sometimes remember things no one expects them to and harbour-masters/even those who rise late/can put-two-and-two-together-to-make-four] in Lambert's Bay. He was told about the shed/quite a large shed/in Groblershoop [a place in Griqualand in the Langberg & not far from Bechuanaland]. He was told about the men from somewhere in the Negev as well as what they came to Groblershoop to do… and did.

Then – the man was forced to admit – they'd lost track of what they were keen/to the point of 'very'/not to lose track of. But there was a lead.

Thanks to what Tim had concealed in the eye wateringly large black thing [a constant source of ribald & smutty conjecture between the man & his assistant] they were able/and continued to be able/even after its relocation to the lining of a handbag/to know of Tim's wife's – the word 'Noor' was never uttered – whereabouts.

Tim was interested in – and why wouldn't he be [but only in an academic way and certainly not in any emotional way] – the goings on of his no-longer-in-any practical-sense wife. But he was unsure why all this information was being given to him/or why now. Smart & insightful though he was/he couldn't see how he could possibly help. This was spook territory – no doubt about it.

The man stopped talking. He peered into Tim's eyes. Tim didn't do 'disconcerted' – but if he did do 'disconcerted' he would do 'disconcerted' right then. There was something in the peer that peered deeper than any peer he'd ever had peered at him before. That – or so it appeared to Tim/the man being peered at – was how the man's peering appeared.

"Would you consider helping us again?" Tim swallowed.

"How, after all you've just told me, could I possibly do that?"

"Good question, we can't think of anything either. We thought you might."

It was at about that time that Tim started to lose [not a lot/ but more than 'just a bit'] confidence in the Intelligence Services of his native land.

He slept poorly – but by morning he was more awake & alert than he ever was prior to coffee. He went into Perry's room. He was playing with Lego. He trod – as all parents have – on a shard concealed in the rug.

"Fuck," he said.

"Daddy!" said Perry and giggled in the universal way children giggle when their parents tread on a shard of Lego and say "Fuck."

"Do you want to go and see Mummy?" The giggling stopped. Perry looked seriously serious – which for a boy of his age wasn't easy.

"Do *you* want to, Daddy?" …Out of the mouths of babes.

Tim knew the answer to Perry's question but couldn't burden him with the truth of the true answer. He sat & stared at his son. He looked seriously serious – which for a man of Tim's age wasn't hard.

Tim rang the nondescript man. He told him about the thought he was thinking. The man/while about to fly back to Pretoria/ came straight round.

⁻ₓ⁻

Lucy – her head buried deep in the wonders of a Kenworth – wasn't aware of his arrival. Not until the boss kicked her leg and said – "Some toff's 'ere to see ya."

There is no doubt that/for Lucy/last weekend had been up there with the best weekends she could remember. She'd enjoyed [as was her habit] remembering her more memorable memories when sitting on the loo. She liked sitting on the loo. It was a quiet & contemplative time. She did her best thinking & remembering when she was sitting on the loo.

She'd turned on the telly once – it was years before – and there was a programme about some French sculpture guy called 'Robin'/ or something like that/and before she could change channels [because all that culture stuff got right up her nose] up popped a picture of a guy who looked like he was thinking real hard and – as sure as hell – he was sitting on the loo/just like she did.

Before coming to work that morning she'd tarried longer on the loo than usual. She was remembering the high points [more

Freud] of the weekend just past. She was looking forward to seeing him again and was wondering if she should wait for him to call or/perhaps/call him first.

And then/at work/where she didn't think about those things – except when she went to the loo – there was her boss kicking her leg and saying – "Some toff's 'ere to see ya."

She extricated herself/climbed out from under and stood in front of the 'toff' who was ''ere to see 'er'. Her hair was tied in a makeshift bun and her cheek was smeared with grease.

"*How lovely,*" he thought without saying it.

"*I must look a wreck,*" she thought without saying it.

"I need to talk to you," he said.

"Do you?" she said.

"I do."

"What about?"

"Not here."

"Where?"

"Let's go for a drive."

"I'm busy."

"It's important."

"How important?"

"Very."

"Very about what?"

"Our mutual friend."

"I'll talk to the boss." Which she did.

⁎

Inspector Fang of the HKPD was not a man to be diverted by difficulties/perceived/real/or otherwise. He knew how-many-beans-made-five and a whole lot more besides. He was an old-fashioned copper's copper and – because of that – both admired & missed the British.

The British – he was certain – made the world's best

policemen/in the same way the Germans didn't. And in the same way the French made the best chefs/the Italians the best lovers and his kinsmen [teeming around on the sad & sorry mainland] made the best nothings-whatsoever – perhaps liars/ cheats & cheap shirts.

He was reared in the finest traditions of Hong Kong Crown Colony policing. He knew right-from-wrong and possessed a nose for sniffing out evil equal to none. His moral compass never veered – not even by a degree/not until later [as you will see] from true north.

The disappearance of Mr Woo – when it came – came as no surprise to him. He was expecting it. And the reason he was expecting it was his knowledge [because he'd made a point of acolyte watching] of the sort of man Woo's *numero due* was gradually/then rapidly & increasingly/showing himself to be.

He'd taken an interest in Hai Chang and researched him. His interest & research went all the way back to the mainland – to a small village outside a small town in the small/poor province of Shanxi. It went back to a disgraced commissar. It went back to Zhengzhou and to the wife-become-widow of a 'Hero of the Republic' and to the years he'd spent with her. It went back not – obviously not – because his intel wasn't [and no intel can be] quite that good – to a 'fat pansy cunt in a skirt'.

But it did go back to the tunnel beneath the wire they kept an eye on. It went back to the sharks of the South China Sea & to the state of their diet.

His given name was Xin/but his mother – still alive at ninety-three – called him 'Xi-xi' but [because 'Xi-xi' was & is inconsistent with his gravitas/and out of respect for his many respect-provoking properties & talents] we will continue to call him 'Inspector Fang'.

And Inspector Fang [as you know] knew a lot – even an awful lot – about Hai Chang and the more he got to know the more he was intrigued by what he knew. And the more he was intrigued by what he knew/the more he was intrigued by what he didn't. He was determined to find out more. It was an upward spiral of knowledge/intrigue & determination.

He knew – for example – about the half-of-half-a-ton-of-Afghan-best. He knew where it came from. He knew who it was meant to go to. He knew who it went to. But he didn't know where it was right now. And he suspected – even though he didn't know about the unbelievably young-looking Chinese girls [twins by the look of it] or what they were given to put where they put it/but wouldn't/if he had known/been surprised – that Hai Chang might know more than he [Inspector Fang] did about the whereabouts of the half-of-half-a-ton.

He [Inspector Fang] knew that there was something going-on/coming-up & about-to-go-down. He knew – not being a stupid man/*mais au contraire* – not what was going-on/coming-up & about-to-go-down but that something was. He knew – not being a stupid man/*mais au contraire*—that it [the 'something'] would have something to do with the half-of-half-a-ton – where it was/who had it & who wanted it.

So – in the knowledge of that knowledge – Inspector Fang laid his plans.

But – and life is/isn't it/so full of 'buts' – Inspector Fang was not to know [because he was not in the knowledge of/because no one was in the knowledge of/other than Hai Chang & his lover who *were* in the knowledge of] what plans they [Hai Chang & his lover] were making for the half-of-half-a-ton-of-Afghan-best.

Should – as he later did – Inspector Fang have known the plans being made for the half-of-half-a-ton-of-Afghan-best he would have been surprised to the point of 'very'.

But – even with all of his wonderful contacts and the truly intricate nature of his intel web – he knew nothing of 6th Earls …or of 20-kiloton bombs.

Exit Chorus.

I watched, in my one-eyed way, as the men went off in the Zodiac. Macaulay wanted to show them what he called 'my island', even though we all, Macaulay included, knew it was really more of an atoll.

There was time to sit and talk. I wanted to talk to Mitzi.

I knew, because we all did, that Mitzi's friend Rubenstein owned the island we needed for what we were planning. I knew, because we all knew, because Macaulay told us long ago, that Kawanak had cisterns and clever ways for collecting the wet-season rains, but that it wouldn't be enough. We knew Matorina had none at all. So, we needed this Rubenstein character on board.

None of us wanted to fuck the planet further by setting up a desalination plant. Maybe Rubenstein could give us what we needed.

When Mitzi talked about him, and there was never a reluctance to, I could tell, because I know how women talk about ex-lovers, and I've had my fair share of those, that he'd been more than just 'a friend', and more than just a run-of-the-mill lover.

I don't know whether I do, but I assume I do, like other women do, get a certain look when I talk about ex-lovers. Especially the few who were special ones, before the ex came along and turned something special into something sad.

She got that look when she talked about Rubenstein, and from what she told me about him and about the time they'd spent together, I knew the end was sad.

He was a pre-Prousian lover, her last pre-Prousian lover. He was her bridge from the happy times of now, back across the unhappy times of Prouse, to the happy times of before. There were only happy memories of him and her regret was the pain she'd caused him.

After our ship anchored in the channel Mitzi thought she should go ring Rubenstein. She wanted to tell him we were here to explore his island.

She came back from the radio room with a strange look on her face. It was part perplexed, part smile.

"He said we're not allowed, not until he gets here. He's flying out. Here in two days." Then she paused and the smile won over the perplexed. "Fuck that. What's he hiding? Fuck all, I bet, just being a mysterious little Yid. Let's go take a look."

And that, the next day, was exactly what we did. And that, the next day, was exactly what we wished we hadn't.

$$\overline{\ast}$$

Enter Chorus.

Inspector Fang knew – because he knew almost everything else about him – that Hai Chang never/ever left Hong Kong and rarely/almost never left Victoria Island. So it came as something of a surprise to be informed that Hai's application for a passport was in the process of being processed.

He – because he could – because he knew people in the right places who could ask/instruct/order other people in other right places to place a small/tiny/ludicrously small-and-tiny transmitting device into the back cover of the aforementioned [and in the process of being processed] passport.

Never being the owner of a passport before [and only having experience in crossing borders underground] Hai was unaware/ as you or I possibly would be/of the thickening in the back cover of the aforementioned [now fully processed & issued] passport.

Inspector Fang/hoping that/almost convinced that/this – Hai's not noticing the thickness of the back cover – might be the case was happy in the knowledge that what was about to-come-down was about to-come-down overseas – and thus outside his jurisdiction.

But for Inspector Fang – a copper's copper with his moral compass pointing/at that time/true north and not/like many others in the department and increasingly since the British left/ varying by a single degree – skulduggery was skulduggery. And because of his unwavering moral compass [which some in the department considered to be excessive] he knew skulduggery to be skulduggery wherever in the world it might be being skulduggered. And so – in the certain knowledge of that – and in the certain knowledge that the skulduggery was partly/if not largely/home grown – he bypassed his superior and approached his superior's superior.

Chief Inspector Chou – the one he by-passed – was a numb-skull plant from Beijing and his parrot impersonations would take him far in the party. He was a man with none of the beliefs & values that Inspector Fang believed in & valued.

Superintendent Chin/however/was the opposite. He was a man for whom Inspector Fang felt both liking & respect. Both these feelings [because of their convergent view on Chief Inspector Chou and their wives being sisters] were reciprocated. So – when it was suggested to Superintendent Chin that he/ his brother-in-law/might be given *carte blanche* to pursue 'the bad guy' to wherever he might go – he had no hesitation in complying.

Inspector Fang checked his own passport and waited.

He didn't – he didn't expect to – need to wait long. Things were hotting-up/coming-down/in just the way he'd hoped & expected.

---
*

Eli – not having visited the island since burying the second metal chest [etc.] – which was now some months ago – had not/not until the call from Mitzi/intended visiting it again. But now he knew he must go there again/and *avec tout vitesse*. Which he did.

Leaving his 'wives' – but taking his abjectly compliant play-thing with him – he/once again/set out for far flung [with some believing them 'not flung far enough'] parts of the globe.

It – 'the now some months' – had been a turbulent time for the abjectly compliant play-thing. All sorts of strange & wonderful – as well as some not quite so wonderful – things had happened to her. The rough edges of the Great Karoo had been smoothed off and not [except for now-&-again when the stubborn streak of her Boer ancestry made it necessary] knocked off.

Much of the time – if not most of the time – it was a matter of massaging the unpalatable bits away. It was a-work-in-progress and [because of the volume/weight & size of the unpalatable bits she'd arrived with] was going to be a-work-in-progress for some considerable time to come. But they were getting there... slowly.

No one who knew her in her previous manifestation [as a goat fucking/anything fucking/baby elephant killing/father killing/daughter of a hard people/a hard time & a hard place] would have recognised her now. Perhaps by appearance – although the incipient prickle & pout/sneer & smirk of her visage had softened to a more benevolent countenance. The thing most striking among all the other striking things was her demeanour. She was no longer *Freyja*/goddess of venery & death/but of *Snotra*/goddess of courtesy. It was a profound change and – as with the taming of shrews – so it was with Noor.

Eli [Noor's Petruchio] was happy with how things were going.

---

*

The 6th Earl watched the Zodiac nose its way through the opening in the reef. He watched it land on the beach below him. He was feeling – although he didn't know it – the same way a young German soldier was feeling/sometime in June/

somewhere in Normandy/some years ago/as a landing craft [chockers with angry & 'here-to-get-their-own-back' Brits] landed right in front of him.

The 6th Earl's only uncle – his father's younger brother – was killed that day. "Serves him bloody right for volunteering," was all the 5th Earl said/reportedly/when he heard.

It – the "Serves him bloody right for volunteering" [together with the cock-up in the Crimea/together with the inadvertent bludgeoning of nannies/together with a whole lot more] was a family failing. One of many.

The 5th Earl had been – not unexpectedly – a supporter of Oswald Moseley and thus a not-so-closet fascist [anything to keep the lower orders under-the-thumb]. He was – without knowing it/but possibly suspecting it – high on Churchill's list of nobs-to-be-interned if/&/or when the first *sturmtruppen* landed in Kent.

The 6th Earl hadn't & never had – and there was scant reason why he should – liked or respected his father. It wasn't because of the fascism because he – in his pre-exile years – leant that way himself/and why wouldn't he? He'd always warmed to the idea of keeping all available lower orders under all available thumbs.

He hadn't liked or respected his father. The 5th Earl had been – even compared to himself – a useless drone who should &/after losing a bundle on 'futures'/eventually/as well as thankfully/did/do the world a favour by shooting himself in his asinine head.

But it was a long time since the 6th Earl had last thought those contra-filial thoughts. He was now – it had taken years – a more understanding & forgiving man.

He crawled down into his cave. He pulled the vines forward and arranged the rocks to hide its entrance. He sat in the dark and felt an exhilaration quite unknown to his former self.

His pre-exile exhilarations had been few. Winning sixty-thou from friend John was up there – but he'd lost it all the next week so that didn't do it. The pair of things that did the things they did when he did the things he did to encourage them to do the things they did were up there too. Maybe his first snort of coke/but not a whole lot else. Maybe killing Nanny had done it for him [he could remember getting a hard-on as he was doing it] but that was when he thought it was his wife's head he was smashing in. This was different. This was 'life' ['101' & beyond] he was living.

It was him – just him – against a mean & hostile world. He was on a high.

⁕

They left Luton and drove to London. They didn't talk much.

They got back to Mayfair. They drank a dry-martini/then another one. They still didn't talk. They drank & they stared. Then they showered.

He washed the grease from her cheek. Then he dried her with the hair-dryer. All of her.

No one had ever done that to-or-for her before. She liked it. Some of it she liked more. Some of it she liked most of all. She wasn't used to having warm air blown where he blew it.

◉ If you are a man who has never dried a woman with a hair dryer and blown warm air where he blew it/or if you are a woman who has never been dried with a hair dryer and had warm air blown where he blew it/then you have a pleasure in store. Trust me.

Then they – of course they did – went to bed. When they got there they – of course they did – spent time in the guise of ferrets-demented. It was a good night for both of them. But by the morning things were significantly & quite a lot [more than just a bit] different.

'Different' – together with 'significantly & quite a lot' – was because something had happened to them/to each of them/to both of them during the early hours. It continued to happen the next day. They couldn't/neither of them/*say* what it was that had happened. But they/both of them/each of them/had felt it happen. And in the feeling of it as it happened they/both of them/knew [in a 'not quite knowing what it was that had happened' sort of way] what it was. And in the 'feeling of it' [as well as in the 'not quite knowing what it was that had happened' sort of way] they knew the other 'felt it' and 'not quite knew what it was that had happened' too/either.

It wasn't love – of course it wasn't.

◎ That sort of stuff only happens in shallow/racy & ribald novels and not in deep/serious & cerebral tomes like this one.

It was something more subtle than the crushing awareness of love. There was no 'scrape me off the ceiling' moment. It started – they both supposed – when he got up for a pee and found her there before him. It was how he leant back against the sink and watched her pee and how she liked it that he did. It was how they spoke about mundane things while she tinkled away. It was how they talked about where they would go for breakfast. It was how she watched him and how he liked it that she did. It was how they talked about what they would do for the weekend as he tinkled away. It was how they went back to bed/how they rolled over and how they went back to sleep. It wasn't love. It was the nascent domesticity of friendship.

---
*

Inspector Fang wished to follow and followed Hai Chang. He wished to be/but wasn't/on the same flight.

Not being a stupid man/*mais au contraire*/he knew/strongly suspected that Hai – being a man he knew not to be a stupid man/mais *au contraire* – would know what he [Inspector Fang] looked like.

It was tempting to assume a disguise. But problems [should he do so] would inevitably ensue. He would need – of course he would – for customs/security & getting on board/to look pretty much like he did in his passport. He took a later plane.

He learned/on his arrival in Singapore [because the HKPD had & has tentacles extending well beyond home] that Hai Chang was booked to fly to Port Moresby the next afternoon and that a sizable motor yacht/one of 70-ish-feet/awaited him there.

Acting on that intel he boarded an earlier flight.

Detective Sergeant Wang Lei [meanwhile & in Hong Kong] having been instructed to do so/rang Inspector Jerry Poma of the Royal PNG Constabulary in Port Moresby.

Being met by Detective Sergeant Willy Poma – the inspector's nephew – Inspector Fang was driven straight to Police headquarters where a full-&-frank discussion [with all cards-on-all-tables] took place between himself/Inspector Poma & Chief Superintendent Poma – an older brother.

Having 'fullied-&-franklied' for almost an hour the Chief Superintendent dialled a number on his brand-new & proudly displayed Nokia cell-phone. He asked for Captain Poma – an uncle & the PNG Navy's only Captain.

They drove to the harbour and boarded the pride of the navy/an ex-RAN [Attack Class] patrol boat. Inspector Fang & the gathered Pomas 'fullied-&-franklied' once more.

The next day – after watching a tall & thin [remarkable of both] Chinaman climb aboard the 70-ish footer in question – they/after watching it leave the harbour and giving it a good hour's start – 'weighed anchor' [which means they 'cast-off from the wharf'] and headed out to sea in safely distanced pursuit.

Captain Poma & his crew – in wonder at the wonders of the modern world – followed-the-bouncing-ball ['the beep' from Hai's passport] on Inspector Fang's IBM [no longer available] laptop.

*

Tim met with & talked with the nondescript man. What they talked about was this:

There was a bomb. It was a big bomb. Big enough to blow up a city. It was made from the bit-of-a-bomb that was that bit of a bomb what was almost/but not quite/the bomb that was/or would have been/'Bomb No. 7'. It was – they now knew – made in Groblershoop. It wasn't – they now knew – in Groblershoop anymore. So – where was it?

The man was – together with other men – uncertain where it was/and it was the uncertainty of where it was that was worrying the man [together with the other men] and because it was worrying the man [together with the other men] it was worrying Tim too.

Was it still in the hands of the AWSB? Probably but not certainly.

It was the 'but not certainly' that was worrying the man [together with the other men] and because it was worrying the man [together with the other men] it was worrying Tim too.

And why was Noor – he couldn't bring himself/not anymore/ to think of her as his wife – in Israel? The bomb wouldn't be in Israel. That would be 'bringing-coals-to-Newcastle'. The Mossad *et al* wouldn't let an atomic bomb [not someone else's atomic bomb/not an atomic bomb owned by the AWSB/a black hating/ brown hating/Jew hating & by-and-large everybody hating/ pack of Afrikaner low lives] into the country – now would they?

So – they didn't know where it was. So – who did? Did Noor know where it was? Maybe. Did this man/this Eli Rubenstein/

this man she was living with/know where it was? More than 'maybe'.

So – if he did know where it was/and they decided to assume [even though they knew the dangers of assuming things] that he did – how were they going to get him to tell them where it was?

Tim suggested a visit [by him] to see Noor. He explained why. He suggested other things/things that other men might do.

The man flew back to Pretoria. He talked to his boss. His boss talked to his boss [etc.]. The wheels of state [the deep-&-hidden ones] turned.

Tim went home. He waited. He didn't wait long.

—
*

Lucy couldn't say – not even when asked/which/by John/she was – what it was that made her feel the way she did about the 6th Earl. It was nothing to do with love or even with liking/because when he'd been doing the things to encourage things to do what they did/she'd usually/if not always/been pissed & drugged-to-the-eyeballs.

She'd thought/but not often/about what it was. She'd asked herself/but not often/what it was. But she'd never got an answer. So – instead of knowing what it was or telling herself what it was – she took a guess at what it was. And what she guessed it was/ was that the 6th Earl was the first man who'd ever – but because she was smart [wasn't stupid] she knew she could [might well be] wrong about it – cared for her.

She could remember the feeling she felt [it was a good feeling to feel] when she'd got the feeling he cared for her. It was a good feeling to feel because it was the feeling that there was another human being out there [another person in the 'wild and wasteful ocean' of life/among the myriad people who didn't] who cared for her. The feeling the feeling gave her was the feeling of not feeling [not anymore] alone. It was – of course it was – a good/ bordering on fantastic/feeling to feel.

215

And the feeling had/over the years/grown within her. Seeing him again – so that she could feel the feeling again/after so long of not having seen him/and ∴ not having felt it – was the only thing she wanted.

Like all obsessions [and it was an obsession] it cried out to be quenched. And/like all obsessions/it never – although 'never' only rarely means *never* – could be. And so/like all obsessions/it was never – not in the way she expected it to be – to be quenched.

She tried to explain it [this feeling she was feeling] to John. But she got the feeling – an incorrect feeling – that he didn't understand. And the reason for it being an 'incorrect feeling' was that it was the exact same/give-or-take/feeling John was feeling for her.

So – in the belief that he didn't understand – she tried harder/ even as hard as she could/to help him/to make him/understand.

John – who already understood but pretended not to – liked the sights & sounds of her as she tried to help him/to make him/ understand the thing he already understood. He didn't know it yet but he was well on the way to being in that thing songs get written about.

John – even if the allure of her alluring parts hadn't been as alluring as they were – was fully aware of how much he enjoyed watching & listening to her as she tried to help him/ to make him/understand the thing he already understood. He enjoyed the simple presence of her. He enjoyed being with her & talking to her & listening to her laugh when she laughed about the things they laughed about. He enjoyed watching the simple things she did and watching the things that happened behind her eyes as she did them. And in watching the simple things she did and in watching the things that happened behind her eyes as she did them/he came to see more clearly the person she was. And in seeing more clearly the person she was/he came to care for her. He never knew – not before & not until later/not until it dawned on him – that he was capable of feeling that way.

He knew he lived a trivial life and knew the life of his oldest-&-closest was a trivial life too. He knew – because of what he knew about himself/together with what he knew about the 6th Earl & others of their 'set' – that the triviality of their lives was a fragile thing. They were/he knew/nothing more than crystal marionettes – and doomed to trundle their way through 'the vile blows and buffets of the world' along the same rough & rutted pathway.

And then/all of a sudden/there was this woman. A woman who'd walked back [unexpected & uninvited] into his life. No longer a young girl – no longer happy to be naked & pissed & drugged-to-the-eyeballs & taken to the room upstairs. This woman wasn't that woman. This woman was an omni-dimensional woman/an up-&-down woman/a side-to-side woman/a front-to-back woman/a then-&-now woman/but always a-something-extra woman. He wasn't certain what the 'a-something-extra' was but he knew it was there.

What John didn't know – but came to know later when it was too late for him to do anything about it – was that the 'nascent domesticity of friendship' [the thing he'd once read about but never thought he would know about] was turning/was already turned/into that thing Donne wrote all those soppy verses about.

John was never in whatever it was he *was* in before. It was a strange feeling. It made him feel more precious/more valuable than he ever had before.

He knew Lucy wasn't feeling the same feeling [whatever it was] that he was feeling for her/for him. And/for some reason/that didn't worry him. He didn't care. All he wanted was to go on feeling the feeling he was feeling and feel precious.

But that wasn't quite right/because he was feeling another feeling too. He was feeling jealous of his oldest-&-closest-friend.

He knew the thing Lucy wanted and he knew that no man [not a man feeling the feelings he was feeling] would feel it reasonable to deny her. For that reason/after taking her for an afternoon at the Tate/to dinner at Simpson's [where the waiters looked/ because that's the way they are trained to look/askance at her C & A clothing] he took her home for a night [among other things/like peeing & talking] of rutting like unhinged stoats.

As the sun rose behind St Paul's he told her everything she wanted to know.

Lucy – after being told everything she wanted to know/and more than she expected to be told – said – "Let's go see 'im."

To which John – never thinking that he would – said – "OK."

Exit Chorus.

*

I saw the smoke. We were coming through the reef. I pointed to it. Annie saw it. Annie pointed to it. Zola saw it. Everyone saw it.

We didn't know what it was. It was a desert island. It was a deserted desert island. What could it be? We didn't know. We needed to find out. We knew that. So we did.

We landed on the beach. We walked across the island. We walked to where the smoke was. There were huts. One of them was burning. We watched it burn. There was nothing else we could do. There was no choice. That's why we watched it burn.

When the burning was burned we went and looked. There was a body. It was burned. Of course it was. Who was it? Who once was it? Who was it once? It was no one now. Not anymore. There was nothing to say who it was. Nothing we could find. I assumed it was 'he'. There was no way to tell. There wasn't much left. Whoever it was he was here a long time. There were cans & bottles. There were piles of them. There was a stream. There was a dam. It was the water we needed. We didn't think about that. Not then. We thought about other things. About who the person was. Why the fire started. Why it started when it started. Why did it start then? Why as we were landing on the island?

Did it start *because* we were landing on the island? We didn't know.

We found other things. We found a house in the trees. Was there just one person? Just the burnt person? Was there someone else? We didn't know. We looked around. We couldn't find 'someone else'.

We climbed the hill. We climbed to the top of the island. We couldn't see the whole channel. We couldn't see our ship. We walked to where we could. There was a lookout in a tree. I climbed up. I could see everything from there.

I climbed down. We looked around again. There was no one. We sat on the beach. There was something to do. Andy said he'd do it. Andy was a doctor. Death didn't do to him what it did to us. I said I'd help. Annie said the women should go back. So they did. Macaulay went with them.

Macaulay was a doctor. But of long dead things. Dead four thousand years. He looked green. I never saw a person look green before. Not as green as Macaulay.

It was good they went back. It wasn't good what we did. It was good that we did it. We got it done.

We buried him. What was left of him. Andy said it was a 'him'. Something about the hips. We buried him on the beach. Some bits were come-apart-bits. We buried the come-apart-bits too. It was good we did that. I wouldn't care if it was me. Maybe this man would. Andy made a cross from sticks. We didn't know his religion. Or if he had one. I found a bottle in the other hut. It was whisky. We sat on the beach. We stared at the sea. We passed the bottle. I tried not to think of the thing we just did.

Andy looked at me. It was an unusual look. "There's something wrong."

"What?"

"You didn't notice?"

"Notice what?"

"The feet?"

"What?"

"The corpse's feet."

"What?"

"They were at the end of the wrong legs."

"What?"

*

We talked as we went back to the ship, of course we did, we were a boat-full of women. A boat-full of women will talk at any time, but after finding a burning hut with a burning body, a boat-full of women will talk more than any other boat-full of women.

I didn't know why, but Mitzi, the biggest talker of us all, wasn't talking as much as she did when there wasn't much to talk about. So, why wasn't she talking to-the-max right now, like the rest of us? I wondered why, and then I understood why. It was something to do with Rubenstein, and I could see she was worried. Was it something to do with why he told us not to go to the island, not until he got here? I didn't know if it was, but I could see Mitzi was worried it was.

We got back to the ship and she went to her cabin. I knew, because I'm a woman who knows stuff like that, that she wanted me to follow, and that's why I did. I didn't have much choice. Not to follow her when I knew she wanted me to follow her would be a bad thing not to do. I knew she wanted to tell me something important.

As well as knowing more-often-than-not what other people are thinking, I'm, always was, someone people are happy to tell things to. You know, those things they wouldn't be happy to tell most people. I don't know what it is about me. I don't know how people can tell, just by looking at me, that I'm someone who'll keep their secrets. I've always been good at keeping secrets – other people's as well as my own. Back-in-the-day there were a lot of my own secrets to keep so I'm good at it, and with the practice at keeping my own I got good at keeping other people's.

220

We got to her cabin and she locked the door.

We sat on the bed and the hard-boiled New York widow evaporated. She told me everything there was to tell me about young Mitzi Johnson and young Eli Rubenstein. She told me how her father brought her up from Mississippi, and how he parked her in an apartment on 5th, and how she met Rubenstein who lived next door. How he charmed her and dined her and showed her the treasures of the Met. How they spent a wonderful summer of fun together. How she fell in love with him without knowing she had, because there was no way of knowing she had, because she was never in love before. She told me how deep down she knew she was in love because the feeling she was feeling couldn't be anything else.

But he was Jewish and she knew an Israeli Jew, not one whose father ended up in a gas-oven, wasn't what her father parked her on 5th to find. She was there to find some Old-World toff with some Old-World title. There were plenty of Old-World toffs and titles wafting around New York back then. Wafting around and looking for girls just like Mitzi, girls with fathers just like Mitzi's, loaded plus-plus with what they came to New York to get their hands on.

But, never-the-less, she fell in love with Rubenstein and they were lovers. Then her father found Prouse – or more likely, because I knew how the bastard worked, Prouse found her father. Then her father heard about Rubenstein, was probably told by Prouse about Rubenstein. There was a scene. She wouldn't give him up, but then she did. It was the worst thing she ever did. Even worse than marrying Prouse and even worse than spawning his son.

She cried as she told me. Then she stopped and told me other things. She told me how Rubenstein was honourable. How he didn't try to undo what she'd done.

She didn't know anything, not much, about the things he did for a living. She knew they were maybe shady things, maybe things on the edge of the law, maybe things on the other side of the law. But that didn't matter to her and it didn't make her love him any less.

She told me that, until she fell for Rupert, she'd 'held-a-candle' for Rubenstein through all her wretched years with Prouse. And now, even though she loved Rupert, Rubenstein would always have a special place in her heart.

But that wasn't what she wanted to tell me, because what she did was about her worries. She knew there was something strange about the island and about what was going on there. She knew it from the way he told us not to go there. She knew it was something he didn't want us to know about, and because of that it was something that would cause him trouble, maybe lots of trouble, if it was found out what it was. That's what she was worrying about.

He must, because of how he spoke on the phone, know about the man on the island.

And why, what's more, *was* it his island? Why would an Israeli businessman want an island at the other end of the world?

Maybe he knew about the man in the hut. Maybe he knew who he was. Maybe he'd arranged for him to be there. Maybe that's why it was his island. Maybe that's what he was trying to hide. So, who was the man in the burning hut? And why did it start burning just as we arrived? Did the man set fire to himself? And if he did, why? If he didn't set fire to himself, who did, and why?

There were lots of 'maybes' and lots of 'whys'. None with an answer that made any sense. Not then, not until later.

I left her in her cabin and went up top. I waited for Tommy to get back. I wanted to talk to him.

*

We sat on the sand. We stared at the grave. The six feet of raised sand and the cross. The Judaeo-Christian way of doing the thing we just did.

"Are you sure?"

"Tom, I'm a fucking doctor, of course I'm sure."

"He might have crossed his legs."

"Crossing your legs doesn't put a right foot at the end of a left leg."

"No… suppose not… You're certain?"

"Absolutely."

"Fuck." I didn't often swear but this seemed an appropriate time.

"Yup, fuck… what's going on?"

"Something funny."

"Not too funny for that poor sod."

"No."

"We'd better not tell the others… not yet."

"No… agreed."

What the fuck was going on?

I wanted to talk to Annie. Of course I did. I wanted to tell her something, the thing Andy just told me. But I knew I shouldn't. So I knew I wouldn't. It was a hard secret to keep.

I wasn't good at keeping secrets, not about good things. There were no good things in my childhood. Only later were there good things. I told everyone those. The whole of Darwin knew when Brosie got pregnant.

The secrets of my childhood were secrets about bad things. I could keep those until death. No one knew how I hated Father – maybe Mother. Then I told Annie. So, not until death, until rebirth maybe.

We got back to the ship. Annie took me to our cabin. She talked to me. The 'maybes' in her head were the ones in my head too. What was going on? Something strange was going on. It wasn't a hard thing to know.

And I knew one more thing than Annie knew about the things that were going on.

We'd stumbled on something. We'd discovered something. We'd disturbed something. Something that was going on for years. Something that needed a man to be dead. Why? What could it be that needed a man to be dead? And how did the man die? People didn't set fire to themselves – not with wrong feet on wrong legs. And even if they do set fire to themselves, they don't lie in a bed and burn away – not with wrong feet on wrong legs. I didn't buy 'lying down and burning'. Neither did Annie. And she didn't even know about wrong feet on wrong legs.

Was he asleep when the fire started? Perhaps he was. He'd be awake pretty soon, wouldn't he? I didn't buy 'deep-sleeper'. Neither did Annie. And she didn't even know about wrong feet on wrong legs.

What would she think if she did?

So, if he didn't lie in bed and burn away – then what? There was only one answer to that. *He was already dead*. And then, after thinking the 'only one answer to that', we thought another 'thought worth thinking'. '*Already dead*' people don't light fires …do they?

Ergo, if he didn't light the fire – because he was already dead – then someone else did. *Ergo*, there was someone else on the island. *Ergo*, because we didn't find the 'someone else on the island', we didn't look hard enough. *Ergo*, we needed to look again. *Ergo*, we needed to go back. So, that's what we needed to do. So that's what we did.

But, before we did what we did, another thing happened. A boat appeared. It came up the channel. It looked about 70 feet long.

*

Enter Chorus.

Tim & Perry flew to Israel. Eli was expecting them. A man

who was 'his man' met them at the airport. He took them to the hotel/which was a hotel Eli owned. They were taken to the Presidential Suite. It was on the top floor. Presidential Suites are usually/mostly/more-often-than-not/on the top floor.

⁎

Two nondescript men and a nondescript woman flew from Pretoria. They flew to Israel. Eli wasn't expecting them but/ if told they were flying to Israel/as well as from Pretoria/he wouldn't have been surprised. They were met/not by Eli's men/ but by two nondescript men. They were nondescript men who'd arrived in Israel some/quite a few/weeks before. They went to an apartment in Nofei Yam. They could see the sea.

⁎

Eli met Tim the next morning. He went to the Presidential Suite. He rang the doorbell. There was a pass-key – of course there was – but he was a wealthy/powerful and sophisticated Yehudi/so he rang the doorbell. What else would he do? Perry ran and opened it.

"Daddy, there's a funny looking man at the door."

"Ask the funny looking man to come in."

"You can come in," said Perry to the funny looking man. "My name's Peregrine, but you can call me Perry. My daddy's name is Tim, so you can call him Tim."

"Thank you for your kind invitation, Peregrine called Perry," said Eli who knew quite well that Peregrine was called Perry. He wasn't where he was without knowing easily knowable things like that. He knew a lot of other things besides.

He talked to Tim for some considerable time. He learned a number of things. Some of the things were things he already knew so he didn't really learn them but it was good to have them confirmed.

The things Tim confirmed for him were that: A.) He – Eli [short for Elijah] Rubenstein – kept many fingers in many pies/ and *that*/because they were his fingers/was something not in need of confirmation: B.) That one of those fingers & one of those pies was of interest – extreme interest – to the Security Services of the Republic of South Africa/which Eli [never being a naïve man] already suspected it might: C.) That the SS of the R of SA knew about 'a thing' arriving [as well as what 'the thing' was] in Lambert's Bay: D.) That they knew where 'the thing' went [to a shed in Groblershoop] as well as what was done to it there: E.) They knew who the men were [the men who did things to 'the thing' to make 'the thing' into 'the thing' it was now]: F.) They knew who it was [him/Eli] who'd supplied the men who did the things to 'the thing' to make 'the thing' into 'the thing' it was now: G.) That Tim's wife had come to Tel Aviv some months ago: H.) That she had come to see him [Eli] on behalf of the AWSB: I.) That the AWSB wanted somewhere 'safe' to hide 'the thing': J.) That the AWSB wanted him [Eli] to supply the 'safe' place to hide 'the thing'.

Eli didn't know that the SS of the R of SA knew about that last thing/but being who he was/he wasn't surprised when he was told that they did. Eli was a pretty hard man to surprise. But wait…

Tim continued: The second last thing was: K.) That his wife [Tim's wife] was shacked up with him [Eli] together with a number of other women/and had been for some months past/in a villa overlooking the sea.

Many men of lesser stature than Eli would inwardly/& perhaps outwardly/smirk at the knowledge of being 'shacked up' with the wife of the man he was talking to – but Eli did neither.
Being a perceptive man he perceived no fumes of acrimony

wafting around Tim's mention of his wife. Now – after the 'some months past' – he felt he knew her well. Now – after the 'some months past' of delving into her psyche – he felt he knew her as well as it was possible to know her. And – in the knowledge of knowing her well – he was not surprised at Tim's lack of acrimony. His only surprise – and Eli [see above] wasn't an easy man to surprise – was that they'd ever got together in the first place.

He suspected – given the way she was when he found her – that Tim would be happy to be rid of her/and that his presence in Tel Aviv had nothing to do with wanting her back.

Tim went on to say things – and the things he went on to say were entirely conjectural – but like much that is conjectural/ entirely or not/was entirely [depending on your definition of 'truth'] true. Tim was good at turning conjecture into 'truth' and it was why he was so good at what he did.

The things Tim conjectured about were the AWSB's intentions. Not their 'general' intentions [which were to do nasty things to anyone who wasn't one of them] but their more immediate & specific intention – which was to have Tim's wife confirm the location of 'the thing' and then/when that was done/ to leave the world with one Eli [short for Elijah] Rubenstein less than before.

Eli – of course he was [it being the main/but not sole/reason for the seduction/pacification & emotional zombification of Tim's wife] was fully aware of that.

But: L.) A thing that made even a man of Eli's famed *sang-froid* swallow [& twice] was that/at that very moment/ nondescript men from the SS of the R of SA were arriving in Tel Aviv with the express intention – given their firmly held/though entirely conjectural/but like much that is conjectural/entirely or not/was almost/very nearly/but not entirely/true – that he/ Eli alone would know the whereabouts of the 20 kilotons and that by 'rubbing him out'/'knocking him off' & 'sending him to his maker' they would ensure that what was hidden – and they knew/by conjecture/that it would be well hidden – would never/ not ever/not this side of Armageddon/The Final Reckoning/The Second Coming [etc.] ever be found again.

"That," said Tim – "is what I've come to talk to you about."

"I see," said Eli – who/feeling a feeling that was alien to him/ felt how others in similar circumstances must have felt since Moses climbed Mount Sinai for the second time.

"But there may be another way. That's what I've come to talk to you about too."

"I see," said Eli – who didn't like the way he was feeling/even though he'd never felt that feeling before.

Perry crawled out from behind the sofa. "Is Daddy going to kill you now?"

"No," laughed Eli. "Your daddy's not going to kill me now. Not yet anyway."

"Are you, Daddy?"

"No, not yet," said Tim. He smiled. Eli smiled. They were genuine smiles.

Tim – as you know [and if we overlook the dose of 'clap' he'd passed on] – was a good man. He was as good as any man could be expected to be/and as good as any man could be expected to be right then & right there. And/because he was good/he was good at smiling genuine smiles. Even his not-so-genuine smiles [he was a lawyer remember] looked genuine. But this one was.

"Do we go and see Mummy now?"

"Do you want to?" asked Tim.

"Not really."

"OK."

"But I think you should," said Eli. "You may be surprised."

So – they did and they were.

228

Oldest-&-closest-friend John/together with Lucy/after a drive to Peterborough [the down-side of decentralisation] to pick up Lucy's passport/flew to Singapore. It was Lucy's first time on foreign soil. She liked it. It was different to Bradford & Luton by-a-country-mile. It was different to Mayfair by less than that but still by a lot. Everything was so clean & organised. Everyone looked so neat & tidy and no one – absolutely no one – was chewing gum.

They stayed – of course they did – at Raffles. They drank – of course they did – Singapore Slings. They threw – of course they did – their peanut shells onto the floor of the Cad's Bar. Lucy decided she liked 'foreign'.

They stayed for a week. They – taking the advice [apropos 'temptation and how to deal with it'] of Oscar Wilde – yielded – of course they did – to the temptations of the flesh. But they weren't to stay forever. They weren't even to stay for long – just [see above] for a week. But a week at Raffles – doing all the things they did & yielding to all the things they yielded to – seemed longer than that.

But there were other things – other than yielding to things – that they needed to do. And because of that they did them. They flew from Singapore to Brisbane. They flew from Brisbane to Thursday Island. Thursday Island wasn't – of course it wasn't – at all like Singapore. They were met by a man with a sea plane and after loading it with all sorts of things [including a case of Chivas Regal] flew east.

*

Macaulay – no longer green but still owner/through inheritance/ of Kawanak Island [more of an atoll really] wondered/being English/'what the devil's going on?' His wife/Jess/wondered/ being American/'what the fuck's going on?'

229

They had once [as you may remember] spent months-and-months on the island/atoll and never seen a soul – not until the day they saw a foot-print/more of a boot-print/in the sand and were woken at dawn next morning by polite but resolute men who'd asked them to stand up and then [without asking them if they might] went on to change the rest of their lives/mostly/but not completely – especially for Jess who went on to spend time in Oxford/some of it spent tied to a chair with electrodes attached to the only part of a woman's chest that a man versed in torture [which he was] but with singularly limited originality of thought would attach them – for the better.

And so – what the 'devil/fuck' was going on?

Their own ship/fine/obviously/the 70-ish-footer a coincidence/a second 70-ish-footer/more of a coincidence/then another 70-ish-footer/way beyond the coincidence of coincidence. And then a 50-ish-footer and then some sort of navy ship. Way/way beyond the coincidence of coincidental concurrence. And now a chopper circling overhead. And all of that with a body burning in a hut on an island where no one lived.

They knew no one lived there because Mitzi told them no one lived there because a man called Eli told her no one lived there. And so – in the knowledge that no one was *supposed* to live there – what the 'devil/fuck' was going on? It was all so confusing.

And – because it was all so confusing – they went to talk to Tom who – because it was all so confusing – was talking to Annie & Mitzi & Zola & Prue & Andy & Ambrosia and the skipper.

The skipper said – "I never seed nuttin' like dis befo. I t'ink we should be getting' de 'ell out of 'ere." But because he looked about twenty [and ageism works both ways] they took no notice of him.

Macaulay & – but to a lesser degree – Jess felt proprietorial feelings – of course they did – towards Kawanak Island/Atoll because it was theirs. It was in the same way that Mitzi felt proprietorial feelings towards Matorina Island/Atoll because it was hers. But they/all of them/assumed [a safe-to-safe-ish assumption to assume/they thought/but were wrong] that Mr Eli [short for Elijah] Rubenstein would not feel/because he owned so many other things around the world/such feelings towards this/his island.

There were plans – Macaulay & Jess's plans – for what they were going to do with *their* islands and – with Mr Rubenstein's consent – *his* island.

Macaulay & Jess knew Kawanak like the back of their hands. It was where they'd once spent [see above] months-&-months. And now they knew Matorina. They knew what they wanted and where they wanted it to be.

Then came the time to look at the other island – the real island – the one with the hill/cone/whichever it was/in the middle of it – and water.

And now there was this – a burning hut & a burning body/ where a burning hut & a burning body – [any burning hut or any burning body] weren't expected to be.

And so it was that Macaulay spoke to his wife – the love of his life – and then to Tom and then to Annie.

＊

Noor knew – because Eli told her – that he would [there was a better-than-evens chance] be coming home with her husband & son. The 'wives' were gathered to support her.

Motherhood – as we know/or should – suits some women – and in the knowledge of that comes the equal knowledge that for some women – as we know/or should – it doesn't. Noor – as we know for sure & certain [and as Tim & Perry knew better than anyone/and better than 'for sure & certain'] – fell into the latter category. Motherhood to Noor was what child-care was to King Herod/empathy was to Joe Stalin & seeing the other guy's point-of-view was to Attila-the-Hun – but that was before/that was the old Noor/that was the Noor of yesteryear.

A seismic fault was riven deep through Noor's life and – as a consequence of that – there was 'a before' & 'an after'. The seismic fault was – as you may have guessed – riven deep the day she met Eli. It was the day gentleness/caringness & thinking-of-others-first [but not all at once because it *had* taken some months] entered into it. She was no longer a recognisable person to a person who only recognised – as Tim & Perry only recognised/because that was all they had ever seen – the person she was 'before'. She was a changed & changing woman and all the changes [how could they not be] were for the better.

The 'now' Noor/the 'New Noor' was feeling apprehensive and 'feeling apprehensive' was a feeling she'd never felt before.

The closest the 'Old Noor' had ever got to 'feeling apprehensive' was when she saw the tattooist's needle hovering over the first nipple.

"*Fuck, does that hurt?*" she'd thought as it entered her tenderest of tender skin but – being a daughter of the veldt and daughters of the veldt were tough – she'd said nothing.

With the apprehension of impending pain – and the pain that was no longer 'impending' because it was now 'fucking painful' – she'd come to the realisation that the tattoos were a mistake [as well as a waste of good goat-fucking money].

While aware of the mistake – but not wishing to show her feelings of apprehension or pain [because she was a daughter of the veldt & daughters of the veldt were tough] to the girls gathered to watch – she'd gritted her teeth and soldiered on. She'd felt [for the sake of her reputation as the toughest-of-the-tough] that she should grit & persevere/which she – as you know – did. The second nipple – for sure – took guts.

'The Now Noor'/'The New Noor' – being fully aware of what 'The Old Noor' once was – mused upon the altered circumstances of her life. She mused that – if the person she was now was the person she was back then – then things might/now/be different and she might be happy to live her *Engels*/Gatting & Cape Town life.

She was happy with her new life. She was happy to be a better person. She was happy – or whatever it is that's more than that [if there is anything that's more than that] to be in love. She was happy to be as much in love with this man as it was possible for any woman to be in love with any man. She was unhappy/however/but not equally [because her happiness was so happy] when she remembered the woman she once was. And in the knowledge of that unhappiness she felt remorse.

'Remorse' – being a stranger to the veldt – was – of course it was – a stranger to Noor's primal bosom/but no longer. 'Stranger' though it had been/it was a welcome stranger now.

With the passing of the months – with the gentleness & caringness [with the eroticogenic kissing of noses] – something was opened within her.

And so it was that/and as you may have guessed – if there is such a thing as a 'whatever-it-is' that's the opposite of a 'Pandora's Box' – Noor released nothing but goodness into the world.

With – of course – the exception of the two kaffirs she'd Dirty Harry-ed [see above]. But that may be/even should be/ forgiven [or almost] because that was in the early days of her moral resurrection.

233

Noor was no longer a witch's brew of discord & contumely. She was an angel's draught of unity & politeness. It was a pleasure to be in her company.

And running in tandem with the transmogrification of her soul [if there is such a thing/and if there is such a thing Noor now owned one] ran the transubstantiation of the 'bread & wine' of a *meisie van die veldt* [not a good thing to have been] into what she was now [which *was* 'a good thing to be'].

And what she was now [in relative terms & to anyone who knew her in the old days] was [in addition to 'a good thing to be'] a wonder to behold.

And so it was that – as 'remorse' entered through the front door – 'lack of it' departed through the back. She regretted being the person she once was and tried – as much as she could – to put out of her mind all the things she'd done in the past. She tried not to remember the baby elephant killing/goat fucking/ father axing [etc.].

So now – for this comely & caring as well as kindly & decent woman – there was no way out. All ways out were closed to her and the holder of the key was – or course it was – the man she loved. And the man she loved was the man she would do anything for – even commit murder for – which [as you know] she already had.

She wanted only to do good/to do *only* good/but would do bad if-and-or-when she was told to – which – as you will possibly see [because this is only 'Part One' and the author doesn't want to tell you the rest of the story yet] she might possibly do.

And it was the same with Eli too. He was a man conceived into/born into & reared into a world of violence/theft & all the things our mothers told us were naughty. But he didn't only/ just do naughty – only/just mostly. He wasn't all bad – only/just mostly.

234

So – somewhere between laying Solomon to rest under the car park in Tel Aviv and the salvation – in part but not *in toto* – of Noor's chances [previously nil but now a little better than that] of sitting with Yahweh &/or Jesus – Eli was changed & changing too.

◉ My mother [wisest person to ever grace the planet] hoped there was no 'life-hereafter'. "Can you imagine spending eternity with all those *good* people?"

She lived a Rabelaisian life and wanted [I imagine] somewhere she could Rabelais forever. I hope she found it.

It's hard to say what it was that precipitated the change in Eli/ because the change was not precipitate. It was more 'continental-drift' than 'Road to Damascus'.

But – slow as the change was – it was change none-the-less and/with the Gondwana-ish passage of time/the changes were substantial to the point of being lots/heaps & more than just a bit. It seemed ages since he'd murdered/eliminated/eradicated or bumped-off [he preferred 'bumped-off' because there was a more homely sound to it] anyone.

The business with the islanders/both lots/was simply a matter of business and as the world knows/or should/the business of the world/the whole world/but especially the Jewish world/is/ was & always has been/will be – business.

◉ How come that guy Coolidge got so much press for 'stating-the-fucking-obvious'?

And so it was that – all things considered – the 'business with the islanders' didn't [not really/not in anything but an academic sort of way] count against either of them.

Eli was good at making money and had made a lot of it. He was wealthy to the point of 'very'. And – because he was not totally devoid [as the author is] of belief in a benevolent God – he...

◎ How can anyone [and keep a straight face] make a nexus between the Christian God/the Jewish God/the Muslim God [etc.] and the word 'benevolent'?

...wanted/before it was too late/to do things that might ameliorate what a God [Jewish or otherwise/benevolent or otherwise] might think of [even though He/God had done a lot of worse things Himself] as pretty bad things. He wanted – on Yahweh's celestial clipboard – to rub out some of the crosses and replace them with ticks.

There were a lot of crosses/he knew/and he knew that he needed to work on the ticks – as long as it didn't interfere with business... of course.

But even with the terrible/nasty/bad & not very nice things he once did [and still on occasions did] 'there was always something good inside Eli'.

That proposition – 'there was always something good inside Eli' – would almost certainly be contested by his mother/but now [because she was pushing up daisies in the Nahalat Yitzhak cemetery] that didn't really matter [other than in an academic sort of way].

It – the 'something good' – was what made him a more-than-half-decent & caring lover and why the 'eight-before-they-became-nine' women in his life adored him. They could – because women can/some women can/all Jewish women [or-so-I'm-told] can/and better than goyim women can/and especially women from the veldt can – see through the harsh outer man to the sweet soft centre within.

They – all eight-before-they-became-nine of them – knew/and even the cook & housekeeper knew/that there was something special inside Eli. They knew it better than he knew it himself because [believe me guys] that's what women can do. They may be lousy at map-reading/at knowing which way's north [except in a moral sense] knowing which way to undo a nut/inverting the wheel/sending guys into space/invading & conquering places – but they're good at quite a few other things.

They knew – for example – eight of them knew [because it was before the eight/with Noor as their Shamash-candle/became nine] that when the men from the AWSB of the R of SA – men who/they were certain/would have swastika tattoos under their jackets/if not on their dicks – visited Eli/he would both accommodate them & thwart them. These men/they knew & were certain/needed to be accommodated but [when viewed through the prism of anything decent] were crying out to be thwarted.

Ruth – number three in the chronological hierarchy of Eli's hanukkiah – was both a seer & a doer. She could see the future and [when the muse was upon her] could do things to change it. Not change the physical things of it – not move bricks around or bend cutlery – but change the ways people [people she knew well enough to know how they thought] thought.

The 'muse' was upon her that day. And 'that day' was the day the men from the AWSB of the R of SA – fat & mean/nasty & ugly/as well as horrible men – came to the house to talk to Eli. She read the inside of her lover's head/his mind. She could see the thoughts being thought there. She could see the thoughts he was hiding there. Not thoughts he was hiding from her – of course not – because when the 'muse' was upon her he could hide nothing from her.

And now – the thoughts she saw hidden there [Eli's thoughts] she knew were there to be hidden from the fat & mean/nasty & ugly/as well as horrible men.

So when Eli went to his study and talked to the fat & mean [etc.] men/Ruth sent things/a number of things/to him through the aether.

Somewhere between the *paraventricular* & *supra-thalamic nuclei* of Eli's ever receptive brain a bright light appeared on a hill. It was a light to illuminate but not follow.

This light/Eli's light [which was really Ruth's light/because she was the one who lit it] was a light to throw light into the dark & unlit places of the fat & mean [etc.] men. And then a thought [which was Ruth's thought/because she was the one who thought it] appeared beside the light.

It wasn't – he thought – his own thought he was thinking/ or even a thought he would think of thinking if he was only thinking his own thoughts. So – he realised – the thought he was thinking was a thought sent [in ways aethereal] as a thought being thought by Ruth.

By the light of the light he saw the thoughts being thought by the fat & mean [etc.] men. They weren't nice thoughts to see being thought. They were thoughts wound around with the runes & incantations of malign alchemy.

He knew what the men wanted. He would provide what the men wanted. Almost.

Eli's continents were drifting slowly apart.

And then – with Lambert's Bay & Groblershoop behind him – but still with 20 kilotons to secrete somewhere [and he was already decided on where] Noor/the agent of the ASWB/had appeared in Tel Aviv.

But that – and everything to cascade from that day – was/as they say [and as you know] 'history'.

$$\overline{\underset{*}{}}$$

Noor waited with mild/bordering on moderate – swinging occasionally into the red – apprehension. It was a year/give-or-take/since she'd last seen her husband & son – and while that didn't worry her at all/not in the early months [not even in an academic sort of way] her transformation from what she used to be into what she was now came with the remorse of knowing the sort of person she once was. Knowing/by remembering/the things she [as the person she once was] did/as well as didn't/she knew – how could she not – that she was a lousy wife & lousier mother.

She wondered why they were in Tel Aviv. And/in the wondering of that wonder/she knew [because she wasn't stupid] that they didn't come to Tel Aviv to see her/just/only/ or at all.

She suspected – correctly as it turned out – that it might be something to do with why *she* came to Tel Aviv. And – when she thought about that – the needle of apprehension swung far into the red – to the borders of trepidation.

*

Tim & Perry met her on the terrace. Eli introduced them to [littered around the pool] his 'wives'. There was a view of the Med.

Tim looked at Noor. She looked different. "Hi," he said.

Noor looked at Tim. He looked just the same. "Hi," she said.

Perry looked at his mother. He couldn't remember what she looked like before. He didn't say anything. He just held his father's hand tighter.

"Hello, Perry," his mother said.

"Hi," he said and turned to look at the sea.

The meeting was not a success – not on a 'deep-&-meaningful' level. It was an 'OK' one on an 'on-the-surface' sort of way. They sat in the sun and drank lemonade. The conversation was polite & trivial. Noor smiled a lot. Not something Tim had seen her do before.

Eli took his guests to the study. There was a full-&-frank. Tim left satisfied. They left without saying 'goodbye'. They returned to their hotel & the nondescript man. They waited.

They didn't wait long. Noor's handbag was on the move.

*

Fat & mean/nasty & ugly/as well as horrible men are thought of and [more-often-than-not] correctly thought of as being stupid men. But while that may [more-often-than-not] be the case/it isn't always. And it wasn't the case with the men who came to do business with the Acme Trading Company of Jerusalem – [Head Office in Tel Aviv – it's the name that counts].

They knew – because they'd taken the time to find out/not an easy thing for them to find out – that a Mr Elijah Rubenstein owned an island in the Calvados Chain off the tail of New Guinea. They knew – as close to knowing as 'knew' could be/or assumed – as close to assuming as 'assumed' could be – that the island in the Calvados Chain off the tail of New Guinea would be where Mr Rubenstein would hide 'the thing' they wanted hidden.

But that didn't help them a whole lot. Did it? It wasn't an 'enormous' or even 'big' – but bigger than 'small' – island. So – knowing it/'the thing'/the thing to be hidden 'thing'/would be somewhere – almost certainly buried – on the island/but knowing nothing more – would be like knowing there was a star in the sky with your name on it and then guessing [because it could only be guessing] which one it was.

An 'infinite number of monkeys' and-so-on.

So – what they needed to know/and what Mr Rubenstein [because he was keen on remaining alive] was unprepared to tell them/was the spot – the exact spot – where what they wanted hidden was to be hidden.

So – aware of this dilemma – they'd sent Noor/their Trojan Horse/Mare/mole/mixed metaphor/to keep tabs on 'the thing' [the as yet to be hidden thing] most dear to their blackened hearts. And when the 'as yet to be hidden thing' became 'the now hidden thing'/to blow [or in any other way she wished to do it] Mr Elijah Rubenstein's metaphorical brains out.

But not trusting her either – because they didn't trust anyone/not even one another – they'd inserted a small bleeping thing into the lining of her never/rarely away from her sight – baby elephant skin handbag/shoulder-bag/a big one/she carried a lot of things/now/some of them/feminine.

And so – as you know – in the depths of the bag/in the depths of the lining/two bleeping things bleeped their separate bleeps.

*

The 6th Earl sat in the dark. He ate baked beans from a can. He heard people pass by. He heard talking. They were speaking English and he wasn't sure if that was a good/a not so good/ or a bad thing. He and his exploits with the metal pipe would probably/almost certainly/be unknown to the non-Anglophonic world. It was those of his mother-tongue he needed to be wary of.

He didn't know – because there was no way he could possibly know it – that at home/in the-land-of-his-fathers/ he was an iconic figure in the pantheon of 'things ridiculous'. He was [without having an inkling that he was] up there with George Best's liver(s) & Mick Jagger's parsimony/with Prince Charles' tampon moment & Freddy Mercury's teeth.

It wasn't so much for 'the metal piping' that he was remembered but for the 'disappearing without trace'. It was part of the zeitgeist of the time that any out-of-the-way person seen in any out-of-the-way place would [with a modicum of humour] be referred to as – 'That must be the 6th Earl of Somewhere-or-other'. But the 6th Earl didn't know that.

He suspected that 'the metal piping' & the 'disappearing without trace' – even after all these years – would linger in the folklore of the folk of his native land. He thus knew to be wary of those speaking the King's.

So he stayed put/ate baked beans from a can & passed wind as quietly as he could.

*

Boris & Ishmael – with a touch [if they were honest] of whatever it is that's the same as penis-envy – looked at the longer/quite a lot longer/20-ish feet longer/boats in the channel. They knew James Bond would be sporting a 70-ish – if not longer. But they – being aware of tight times in Whitehall as well as good servants of The Crown – complained inwardly but little & outwardly not at all.

Then they watched a third 70-ish come into view and anchor not far away.

"*Like Shepherd's Market on a fucking Friday,*" thought Ishmael – a Lambeth lad.

"*Like Cowes Week,*" thought Boris – who came from somewhere higher up the convoluted chain of English society.

"What now, boss?" asked the Lambeth lad.

"Not sure, let's just wait."

"OK. Sounds good," said Ishmael. "*Not much fucking choice,*" he thought.

"*Not much choice,*" thought Boris. "Not much choice," he said.

*

Bert & the defrocked Commander – with the unbelievably young-looking Chinese girls instructed to stay below – went up-top and surveyed the increasingly chock-a-block channel.

"Like fucking Pitt Street," said Bert – a Sydney boy.

242

"Yeah. Like fucking Bourke Street," said the defrocked Commander – a Melbourne boy.

"*Like Victoria Harbour*," thought the elder – by sixteen minutes – of the twins as she peered through the port-hole.

"What the fuck do we do now?" asked Bert.

"Your choice. Not a lot we can do."

"That's for fucking sure. What these cunts want?"

"Dunno. Maybe they want what you want." Which was exactly the thought/fear/apprehension [as well as perturbation] that was on Bert's mind too.

"Fuck," he said.

The unbelievably-young-looking – being fluent in English and now being cognizant of the seemingly habituo-perennial use [in 'the-land-down-under'] of the words 'fuck' & 'cunt'– were *au fait*/because of open port-holes/with the conversation occurring above. And having come to expect & accept the deviance of the defrocked Commander/and because of their instructions from Mr Hai/they lay on the bed & awaited whatever fate [the Yin & Yang of life's uncertain passage] had in store for them. And because the defrocked Commander/two days before/had pitched their clothes overboard/they held onto one another for warmth as well as solace.

*

Hai – happy/relaxed & with neither apprehension nor perturbation – took a turn on deck. He was enjoying [because he frequently enjoyed/because his lover frequently enjoyed] a glass of ice-cold water.

But it wasn't 'simply' a glass of ice-cold water such as his lover enjoyed. It was a glass of ice-cold water with the addition of two nips of Black Label – an addition unavailable to his lover or anyone else outside the ruling elite of the People's Republic of China.

It was the glass of ice-cold water that he – since arriving in Hong Kong – partook of whenever the slightest possibility of apprehension &/or perturbation loomed. Which wasn't that often – but more so given the recent traumas of air-travel & other events.

Because he was a thin man [and because the swarming spawn of The Middle Kingdom lack the hepatic enzyme *alcohol dehydrogenase*] and because it was his third such glass of 'ice-cold water'/Hai was – to use epithets from a more derisive world – about as 'Brahms & Liszt': pissed, 'elephant's trunk': drunk – 'Yanked': tanked – 'piddly-diddly': tiddly – and as 'under-the-weather'/ 'skunked' & 'rat's arsed' as it was possible to be without falling over or – in Hai's case – falling overboard.

Hai's state of being 'all-of-the-above' – and in addition to him not falling overboard – was in-no-small-way responsible for him being happy/relaxed & free of either apprehension or perturbation.

But it did [somewhat] – however – slow his usually razor-sharp thought processes.

"*What the @#$% should I do now?*" he thought to himself/ in Mandarin of course/and in a not overly-thoughtful way. 'But answer came there none' because – sitting out on the fantail – he'd fallen fast asleep.

---
*

Noor – returning somewhat reluctantly to the other side of the world – not her favourite side of the world [least favourite because of what she did there last time around] and now no longer being the sort of person who took pleasure in Dirty Harrying things/even kaffirs [and with the memories of 'last time around' disturbing her] wished she was back home in Tel Aviv and in the arms of her lover & sisters-in-arms.

Arriving there with the only person she would ever love she was – to a degree/which was quite a degree – discombobulated by the turns & twists of recent events.

All-things-considered she would rather be somewhere else/ anywhere else/even Philadelphia.

A significant part of her discombobulation came not from her recent meeting with her husband/but from that with her son. Gatting had been a stepping stone and a lot of women/she knew they did/married men as stepping stones to get what & to where they wanted.

Cape Town – she knew: California – she suspected: Sydney – she was told – were full of them. So – not loving her husband didn't worry her in the slightest. She didn't give a hoot [not even the tiniest of hoots] about what Gatting might/and probably did/think of her.

But with her son it was different. No woman could rationalise – to themselves or anyone else – the 'not loving' of a perfectly lovable son. She knew – and she didn't need to go deep down to know – that her lack of love for Perry was 'a character flaw' and one of more than minimal significance. She knew she was the product of an awful place & of awful people. She wasn't stupid.

And while her time in Cape Town had done little to change what she was back then [that all happened in the Holy Land] she did know/she wasn't stupid/that she was being exposed to a different world & different people. A 'different world & different people' where what was best for 'you-&-you-alone' wasn't the only way to think.

And once in the Holy Land – with the Christ-oid miracle that was worked upon her – she was steadily/with the tuition of her sisters and encouragement of her lover/coming to appreciate what made normal people 'tick' – or in her case/but no longer/'tock'.

*

Eli – on the other hand – could 'tick' &/or 'tock' as the whim took him. He was able – because he was a fast learner – to know the difference between them [between right-&-wrong/good-&-bad, etc.] He was inclining more towards a life [and was for several years past] where possible/which wasn't [given the business he was in] always possible/where the heavenly 'ticks' outweighed the satanic 'tocks'.

He knew – because he wasn't stupid – that x1 'tock' = x1 'cross' on Yahweh's all-seeing-all-recording broadsheet.

He wanted – for no discernible reason/certainly not one he could fathom – to do 'good'/'less bad'/in the world.

As you will know – from remembering his past – Eli was not cast as 'the good guy' in life's uncertain drama. He was by nature a Tybalt/a Fagin/a Dolokhov. So – why all this need to be what he wasn't? Was it just the fear of eternal damnation? He wasn't devout/never was. He was a 'chancer' and had been all his life. A player-of-odds. A man who took the opportunities that came his way. And the ones that didn't come his way he took from other men.

But there was always something. Something not quite right with his performance of Richard III. What was it? He wasn't 'cheated of feature by dissembling nature' – he was moderately/if you didn't mind a sizable conk/handsome. Nor was he 'deformed, unfinished, sent before his time'. He wasn't Michelangelo's David but his body was fine. So – why was he 'determined to prove the villain'? Well – was he? Or was it [like 'greatness' is for some men] thrust upon him? Maybe hard to tell. So – who's to know?

But – be-that-as-it-may – he wasn't all bad/not even mostly/ although [as you know] that can be a matter of perspective and the prior owners of the bodies [the ones buried under car parks/ enshrined in concrete or Dirty Harry-ed at the far end of the world] might not agree.

But/agree or not – while there was much about Eli that smouldered-in-the-dark – there was something that sparkled-in-the-sunlight.

Now – at the height of his powers & the leader of one of the world's more skulduggerous enterprises – he was humble. And the humility [increasing as the cocky young man became the more worldly-wise & older one] was genuine. He saw men of his own race doing things he could only admire. Barenboim & Wiesel were his friends. He wished to emulate them.

He & Noor flew to Dubai and/by necessity rather than choice/ spent the night there.

"*My-oh-my* [אוי ואבוי] *boy-oh-boy* [ילד או ילד] *what-a-dump* [איזה חור]," thought Eli. An ostentatious dump & a glitzy dump/ but a dump nonetheless. You may know [if you've been stuck there and don't play golf] how he felt.

They flew on to Singapore the next day – "*A city with style*," he thought – "*No bull-shit-towel-head-vulgarity*," he thought.

Then they flew to Moresby.

And Eli – being a man of definite/if not definitive/tastes [as well as having been in Moresby a number of times before] – thought thoughts in accordance with that. Most of the thoughts he thought/he'd thought a number of times before/and most of them were thoughts [see above] thought in Hebrew.

Hebrew is a good language for thinking the sort of thoughts Eli was thinking right then. There was a lot of מזכל הצדה – and other thoughts going on in his head. They were all good kosher – as well as somewhat ribald – thoughts to think... and accurate.

They hired a chopper and – of course – a man to fly it. Eli was a pluri-talented man but he didn't do 'menial'. And flying things [just like driving things] fell firmly into the category of 'menial'.

They flew – refuelling on the way [because I/like you/have no idea how far a chopper can fly without needing to] – and hovered over/in the middle of a channel between an island and an atoll/the fantail of a ship with a crane.

247

The recently arrived – at the island they already knew quite a lot about – cohort from the AWSB surveyed the scene. Two other 70-ish footers rode anchored…

◎ Why do ships 'ride anchored' while people 'stand anchored'?

…nearby. A 50-ish footer rode-at-anchor…

◎ Why the '-at-'?

…not far away. One ship/plus crane/rode [rather than stood/but definitely-at-] likewise.

What the *fok* to make of it all?

And – of course – 'what the *fok* to make of it all' was for them to assume or suppose that everyone was there for the same thing they were.

And – of course – 'the same thing they were' was/for them/ an understandable assumption to suppose. But being an *understandable* assumption to suppose didn't make it a correct one.

Being the sort of men they were – probably because there were no adequate role-models to teach them otherwise – they were not the sort of men any of us would be happy for our daughters to bring home. They thought only dark & unpleasant thoughts. They thought only dark & unpleasant thoughts – of course they did – about [near enough] everyone.

But [right then] the dark & unpleasant thoughts were exclusively reserved for the occupants of the other vessels in the channel.

They knew also – because of the 'bleeping things in handbags 101' they were given before they left home – that Trojan Horse/ Mare/mole/mixed metaphor/Noor Coetzee/né Gatting was their ace-up-the-sleeve.

They knew nothing of her altered [& very much for the better] state. But – even if they had known – who among them/ the *broederskap*/would have given a *fok* about it?

They – like too many men before them – thought they 'had-all-bases-covered'. They knew [or thought they knew] that their wonderful SOTA hardware [the new 6.8 mm ones ordered from & received from the Yid Rubenstein] would give them a supremacy-of-might.

But they were men [just as Hai was before he fell asleep] uncertain of what to do next. And like all uncertain men – throughout [possibly] all of knowable history – they sat on the fantail of their 70-ish footer and/after opening bottles/several bottles/a few more than several bottles/got as Brahms & Liszt/ *gedrink* [etc.] as it was possible for three fat & mean [etc.] men to get on cheap South African brandy.

—
*

The ship-with-the-crane's seldom used chopper took off to make way for Eli & Noor's incoming. It flew to a beach on the atoll. The Zodiac went in to bring the pilot back.

It was on their way back – the Zodiac coming close to the 70-ish footer of the AWSB – that the fat-thru-horrible men/being [by now & as you know] as-pissed-as-parrots & armed-to-the-nines/as well as noting the dusky hue of the occupants/and not having killed anything for what seemed like ages/opened fire. They/being as pissed as parrots/missed their primary targets but did hit – a number of times – [how could they miss] the Zodiac. And the Zodiac/being full of nothing but air/started quite rapidly to deflate and sink.

Aboard their 50-ish-footer/Boris & Ishmael took note.

Hai/woken by the gunfire/and seeing [in double] as well as hearing what was going on/took note.

Bert/seeing as well as hearing what was going on/took note.

The defrocked Commander/even though he was down below and performing deeds worthy of a five-year prison term/ took note.

Inspector Fang & Captain Poma/arriving in the channel as they so recently had/took note.

The channel was awash with people taking note.

Even the 6th Earl – overcome with curiosity at the sound of gunfire – shinned up to the crow's-nest and took note.

⁎

Tim/Perry & two nondescript men from Pretoria/seeing & hearing nothing because they were on an incoming chopper/ took note only of the channel & its shipping.

They prepared to land.

⁎

Boris & Ishmael – being the fine men they were [and luckily white] launched their own [downmarket] version of a Zodiac to pick up the swimmers/now *sans*-Zodiac of any version/which they did. They took them back to the ship with the crane.

They went aboard. They were met by a woman with one eye/a man of Semitic appearance & the blackest of all black women. The blackest of all black women clung to a tall man's back. Boris/ having studied the research of the researchers/recognised the 'man of Semitic appearance'.

⁎

Tim/Perry & the nondescript men/uncertain of where to land/ but knowing that Noor's handbag was now stationary somewhere below/decided – the least descript of the nondescript men decided/because he was [even though a shadow of the man Tim was] the boss – to zip across the channel – noting/as they went/ the upturned faces on the vessels below – and land on the beach of the island – the real one.

And to say that that discombobulated the 6th Earl would be up there with 'Houston'.

They climbed out. Perry saw little crabs scuttling down the beach and/as little boys have been doing since before Jesus bonked Mary Magdalene [of course he did/or at least I hope he did] he chased them.

Tim/happy for his son to chase crabs/said – "Now what?"

To which the less-descript said – "Not sure."

To which Tim said – "Me neither."

To which the more-nondescript said – "We need a boat."

To which Tim said – "Yes."

To which the less-descript said – "Is the island inhabited?"

To which the not-so said – "Doesn't look like it."

To which Tim said – "Let's fly around and see. We might get a boat."

To which the less-so – wishing to confirm his status as boss – said to the not-so – "Stay here with the boy," and/with Tim following/climbed back in the chopper & took off.

It wasn't [as you know] a large island/although [as you also know] it was larger than the 6th Earl first thought it might be.

It didn't – once they were up to a thousand-or-so feet – look like much of an island at all. But at the far end of it something caught their eyes – both eyes of both men.

There were huts by a beach. There were fish traps on a beach. There was a boat pulled up on a beach. So – it being a reasonable/if not the obvious/if not the only thing to do – they landed nearby.

There was/they noted after climbing out [and as you already know] a burned-out hut/but there were [as you also already know] huts that weren't. There was a treehouse and signs of recent [not too distant] habitation by an inhabitant/inhabitants neither of them could see.

They looked around & called out around – of course they did. They – of course they did – talked about what to do. They decided – because there was really no choice in the matter – to 'borrow' the boat. It looked sound/which it was/which was good. There were oars/which was good. There were only oars/which wasn't so good.

Tim – 'stroking' the 1st Eight – of course he did – the year Bishops won – of course they did – at Henley – said he'd row it round to the channel. The less-nondescript [never having rowed a boat in his life/and being slightly/bordering on moderately/afraid of the sea] said – "OK."

So – that's what happened.

Tim rowed & the less-nondescript choppered off back to his colleague/to Perry & crabs.

⁎

The seaplane – containing oldest-&-closest-friend John & Lucy/supplies of all sorts & a case of Chivas Regal – circled the channel. They noted – as was to be expected – that the channel was chockers with shipping and that/in addition to the shipping/there was a chopper parked on the blunt end of a ship with a crane. They noted – as was to be expected – that there was another chopper parked on the beach of a nearby atoll. They noted – as was to be expected – a third chopper parked on the beach of the island they were heading for. They – after noting all that there was to be noted – flew on towards/onto & over the island. They landed on the lagoon on the far side of it. It/the seaplane/being of amphibious design/crawled up onto the beach near a burnt-out hut/as well as ones that weren't.

"*At last,*" thought John. "*After all these years.*"

"*I hope,*" thought Lucy – "*we're on the right fucking island.*"

"*Jesus fucking wept, who the fuck's this,*" thought [and then said out loud because that was his default position these days] the 6th Earl – who/after watching the plane land on the lagoon and crawl up on the beach/scurried back to his hidey-hole.

*

Tim – half completing his [so far demi-semi/because it was only necessary to row halfway around it and he'd only rowed halfway around that half of it] circumnavigation of the island – rested on his oars. He watched the seaplane dip down below the tree-line to land. "*Things are getting interesting,*" he thought. He rowed on.

Back on the beach with the chopper/the more-nondescript man – a man so nondescript he made nondescript men appear vulgarly ostentatious/spoke to the less-nondescript man. Perry/tiring of chasing crabs [and having stopped doing so] eagerly awaiting/because there was a thing he wanted to tell him/his father's return.

Tim – being a man who prided himself in maintaining a *corpore sano* to house his *mens sana* – 'worked-out'/'pumped-iron'/'hit-the-gym' [etc.] and one of the [etc.]things he worked out *on* was a rowing machine in his study. His lats were lats for lesser men to dream of. And for this reason he was able to skim/almost aquaplane/his way back to his son/the chopper & the men who melded in well with the beach.

"Daddy, Daddy, I saw a plane with boats on its wheels?"

"I did too."

"It went over there. I think it crashed."

"I don't think so. I think it landed on the sea."

"Planes can't land on the sea, silly Daddy."

"They can if they have boats on their wheels."

"Oh."

"Next move?" asked the less-nondescript men.

"Me row out to the ship with the derrick," said Tim. "See what's going on. You stay here."

He was – without realising it – falling back [with some ease] into his Captain-of-School persona.

"Agreed," said – because he wasn't sure about what to do next – the less-nondescript man.

So – that's what Tim did.

⁎

◎ Now – the story so far is as follows: [Just so that it's clear to everyone – including me.]

1. Annie & Ambrosia & Tom & Macaulay & Jess & Prue & Andy & Zola & Mitzi – and in no particular order of importance – had decided/some time back [at the suggestion of marine biologist Jess] to find a place for a marine-park/university/ eco-resort – etc.

2. Macaulay – now married to Jess – owned by inheritance [A VERDICT ON A LIFE p. 18.] Kawanak Island – more of an atoll – in the Calvados Chain off the tail of New Guinea.

3. Mitzi – by extravagant coincidence – owned/she couldn't remember how/[A JUDGEMENT ON A LIFE p. 241.]/ Matorina Island/an atoll nearby.

4. The 6th Earl of Somewhere-or-other – being down on his luck/as well as pissed & drugged-to-the-eyeballs and having just bonked Lucy/a waitress with [as you know] things that did intriguing things when he did not particularly intriguing things to encourage them to do the intriguing things they did [and as a prelude to other things] – decided to bludgeon his wife to death for her money. Sadly [for Nanny] he bludgeoned Nanny by mistake. Thus &/ needing to disappear/he went to oldest-&-closest-friend John.

5. Oldest-&-closest-friend John – knowing a man called Eli [short for Elijah] Rubenstein – agreed to help.

6. Eli Rubenstein – bad but improving/conceived in Dachau/ but born/only just/in Israel/had inherited [from the late Solomon Hagelstein] an island [a real one] in the Calvados Chain off the tail of New Guinea. And knowing oldest-&-closest-friend John [see above] from other matters – agreed to help. And that's how the 6th Earl of Somewhere-or-other ended up in a cave on an island [a real one] in the Calvados Chain off the tail of New Guinea.

7. Bert – a Sydney boy & reluctant [except when necessary] shark feeder – was *numero uno* in the Aussie narcotics business. He'd recently/some time back/got his hands – although destined for other hands – on half-of-half-a-ton-of-Afghan-best. He'd – after less happy hidings – asked Eli Rubenstein to hide it for him – which/of course/he was happy to do.

8. But Bert – being far from a simple/trusting Aussie boy & wishing to check on the whereabouts of his half-of-half-a-ton-of-Afghan-best – took himself/and others/to an island in the Calvados Chain off the tail of New Guinea.

9. Hai Chang – having escaped from China by way of Zhengzhou [and three years in the arms of his lover & guru] arrived in Hong Kong. He became the right-hand-man to a Mr Woo.

10. Mr Woo – an enthusiastic shark feeder & monkey strangler – was *numero uno* in the HK narcotics business. He was/ he thought/destined to [but dire chance/cruel fate & the general cock-up of life thumbs its nose at destiny] receive the half-of-half-a-ton-of-Afghan-best. And it was the trials & tribulations of thwarted destiny that made Mr Woo not think straight.

11. And that [said Woo's not thinking straight] was what led Hai Chang/a little less reluctantly than reluctantly/to feed – as he

was told by his best-of-the-best-of-the-best that he had been – said Woo to the sharks of the South China Sea and to seek/ because his lover & guru told him to seek/the half-of-half-a-ton-of-Afghan-best. It was what led him [he was following satellitic beepings] to an island in the Calvados Chain off the tail of New Guinea. No one knew/not yet – except for Hai & his long dead lover – what he was going to do when he found it.

12. The post-war apartheid governments of South Africa – appalled to discover how many 'people of colour' there were between themselves and anywhere 'white' – took out the insurance/with the help of Israel/of atomic Armageddon. But – after cooler heads prevailed & Armageddon was Valhalla-ed – 'The Bit' that remained/with the help of Eli Rubenstein/ rose/like Lazarus/from its bed. But unlike Lazarus [who stuck around for the lime-light & sanctification he did nothing to deserve] it then disappeared [with the help of Eli Rubenstein – of course] to an island – of course – in the Calvados Chain off the tail of New Guinea.

13. Noor Coetzee – reared on the veldt & performer of dark & dastardly deeds – wooed/married & deserted Tim Gatting. She went/at the behest of the AWSB/to Israel. She was – such was her mission – to follow Lazarus to his new home. She was – such was her mission – to record *exactly* where 'home' was/ and when sure of *exactly* where home was/terminate – in any way she preferred – the *doos* Rubenstein. But because [once again] the dire chance/cruel fate & general cock-up of life doesn't always do what we expect it to/she found herself in love with the man she was meant to kill. She now found herself/ and in the company of the man she loved/helicoptering to & landing on a ship [one with a crane] nearby an island in the Calvados Chain off the tail of New Guinea.

14. The men of the AWSB – knowing the general whereabouts/ but not the precise whereabouts [and the precise whereabouts

was the thing that mattered] of their 'Bit-Become-Whole' – had already taken themselves to an island in the Calvados Chain off the tail of New Guinea. They awaited Eli & Noor's arrival.

15. Tim – Noor's erstwhile husband – also wished to locate the Armageddon/Lazarus. He – following Noor's beeping handbag – landed/together with his son & non-descript men/on an island in the Calvados Chain off the tail of New Guinea.

16. Boris & Ishmael/convinced of – and confirmed by the 5th Countess – the 6th Earls' continuing existence [and being Scotland Yard's finest] were following oldest-&-closest-friend John's paper trail of money. They – because of that – were in/on a boat skippered by the man who made biannual visits to an island in the Calvados Chain off the tail of New Guinea.

17. Inspector Fang – knowing as much as it was possible to know about Hai Chang – was following/accompanied by Captain Poma and riding in & on the pride of the PNG Navy/the beep from the back cover of Hai Chang's passport. This took them [as you know] to an island in the Calvados Chain off the tail of New Guinea.

18. Oldest-&-best-friend John – enamoured by more than Lucy's enamourable parts &/or what they did when he did what he did to encourage them to do what they did/and knowing the whereabouts of the 6th Earl – landed with [and at the insistence of] Lucy on an island in the Calvados Chain off the tail of New Guinea.

19. Eli Rubenstein [as you know] sported more fingers in more pies than any of us can or could possibly imagine. And because of this [the finger he sported in a pie that was an island in the Calvados Chain off the tail of New Guinea] he – of course he was – was there to keep an eye on the lot of them. His reputation was riding on it.

So – that's all pretty clear. But what was going to happen next?

*

Tim – the only one with a plan of what to do next – pushed the boat off the beach/sculled out through the lagoon and headed across open sea to the ship with the crane. It didn't take him long [certainly not as long as it would you or me] and he was enjoying the exercise.

He was not at all surprised to find Mr Rubenstein there. He was a little – but not overly – surprised to find his wife there. The other people he recognised not. And/because he recognised them not/he wasn't in the slightest surprised to see they were there. But though he recognised them not – as he did/but didn't/ and surprised as he might be/but wasn't – they were as surprising a group of surprising people as a surprisingly surprising group of people could be.

There was the towering woman with the eye of Phoebus. A mutilated face to 'burn the topless towers of Ilium'. He'd never seen a face so destroyed &/or so beautiful – never in the whole of his life. It could & would 'launch a thousand ships' before breakfast.

Aristotle [one of his more ludicrous/but romantic-ish/ideas about the mechanics of sight] poured from her eye. He could feel the gravity of her/the force pulling him into orbit around her. He'd never felt anything like that before.

Then there was the blackest of all black women. Blacker than ever he'd seen before. The blackest of all black people to come from the blackest people of the blackest continent of deepest/ darkest & blackest Africa. And she didn't – but he didn't know that she didn't – even come from there. She was the blackest person in the history of Antigua to ever/in every last bit of the history of Antigua/come from Antigua.

In summary then – she was pretty black.

And she was proud – he could tell [and why shouldn't she be] of being so black.

But the surprisingness of her wasn't the blackness of her. He was/ as everyone was [apart from Maj C M Sanders who'd been too taken with 'the topless towers of Ilium' to notice] surprised/to the very edge of his surprise/by something other than her blackness.

The surprise that surprised him/Tim to the very edge of his surprise was what he saw in her eyes. They weren't the eyes of Phoebus. They were the eyes that gazed the gaze of Leto/the gaze of motherhood. The gaze she gazed upon him was gazed only- &-solely upon him. It was a gaze to take him back to 'first times' – to the first gaze the first mother gazed into the eyes of the first baby. A gaze to see the future-of-man – the good of man/the bad of man & the otherwise of man – written there.

She was Mother Earth. She was his & every man's mother. She was wise beyond the wisdom of the ages. He could feel the gravity of her/the force pulling him into orbit around her. He'd never felt anything like that before. Well – not until just a moment ago.

She rode on the back of an overgrown schoolboy. Tim recognised him. Not 'him' – because he didn't – but he recognised 'the type' of him. He recognised the 'him' as he recognised 'the type'. He/Tim was a 'him' and he was 'the type' too. They were 'hims' from the same tribe and they both/without knowing it/knew it.

So – Tim recognised him [the 'him' who was Tom] as he recognised the 'him' in himself. And so/because of that/Tom recognised him [the 'him' who was Tim] as he recognised the 'him' in himself.

◎   Stuff like that goes on all the time. We just don't notice it.

The surprising thing about the man called Tom/wasn't that Tim recognised the 'him' in him/but more the surprise at finding the things in Tom that weren't to be found in him/Tim.

They weren't earth shattering things to find/or not find – not 'topless towers of Ilium' things/or 'pulling into orbit' things. They were more mundane things. There was a comely & comfortable 'ordinariness' about him/Tom. It was a hard thing for him/Tim to put into words inside his head. Perhaps/he thought/he/Tom was one of those rare beasts – a truly happy man. And – in thinking that thought – he/Tim was right.

Seeing Eli and [because why wouldn't he] wishing to talk to him/Tim said – "I wish to talk to you."

To which Eli replied – "What about?"

To which Tim said – "You know what about."

And Eli – feminine in his powers of perception/something rubbed off from Ruth – knew it was nothing to do with Noor. He knew it was something/if not everything/to do with 'the thing' that brought Noor to Tel Aviv in the first place.

At this point [flash-back/see above] with the ship's Zodiac returning from picking up the ship's chopper pilot – gunfire broke out/lots of it. They went to the rail – of course they did – to see what was going on.

Three fat-and-all-the-rest-of-it men were – while intermittently swigging from bottles of some sort – taking less than steady aim & firing at the Zodiac full [there were only two of them but they were seeing double] of 'darkies' as it passed nearby.

They – the people at the rail of the ship with the crane – watched/with a modicum of pleasure to dilute the more than modicum of horror [i.e. at the things that were going on] when one of the three fat-and-all-the-rest-of-it men/propelled in a retrograde fashion [because we are all subject to Newton's Third Law] by the firing of his weapon/tripped backwards over the forward-hatch and disappeared precipitously & all-of-a-sudden below.

The channel fell very nearly [but not quite] quiet. And the

'very nearly [but not quite]' was because of the continuing stream of invective-filled Afrikaans epithets.

*

Ensign Poma – a convoluted paternal relative of Captain Poma and/because of that/the Captain's 2IC – ordered Seaman 1st Class Poma/his younger brother/to man the 40mm Bofors gun/ which – suffering from an unusually high degree of older brother non-worship [sibling rivalry bordering on dislike/hatred] – he reluctantly did.

Now – a 40mm Bofors gun/when used in the way it was meant to be/can [as well as sending a 2lb explosive shell 40,000 feet into the air] make an awful lot of mess of an awful lot of things. It is not something anyone – least of all a couple of Brahms & Liszt Afrikaans low lifes/least of all ones yelling insults to those at the higher end of the melanotic scale – wants to be standing in front of. And especially when the man with his finger on the trigger of the 40mm Bofors gun is both: A.) From the higher end of the melanotic scale: and B.) Not too happy [being a devotee of Michael Jackson] about being so.

"A short burst in front of the bow, " ordered the Captain.
"A short burst in front of the bow," ordered the 2IC.
"A short burst it is," said the Seaman 1st Class through the gritted teeth of fraternal enmity. And – after taking aim at the offending 70-ish footer – blew the front six-feet-or-so of the sharp end from its literal as well as metaphorical moorings.
"*Fuck*," thought Captain Poma.
"*Fuck*," thought 2IC Poma.
"*Good shooting*," thought Seaman 1st Class Poma/for whom the term 'in front of' was perhaps a little more elastic than it should have been.

Numero due of the Afrikaans low lifes/sobering up rapidly with the turn of events/went below to inspect the damage to both his Comrade-in-Arms and the sharp end. He – unfortunately but not that unfortunately – found said C-in-A impaled on the business end of the spare anchor. There was – of course there was – lots of blood. And some of it/quite a lot of it/was coming out of the man's mouth. He was dead.

"*Fok*," thought the unimpaled man.

"Fok," said the unimpaled man.

But – however hard and inured to death-&-violence and generally unpalatable a man looking upon the transfixed/anchor through the chest/body of an erstwhile colleague may be – he will still experience feelings of regret. And so it was.

He partially regretted the passing of this man & boy he'd grown up with on the veldt. They'd been/always had been/ kindred spirits. They'd enjoyed/always had/the same things. They'd crucified frogs together/fed mice to cats together and bullied their way through puberty & adolescence together. They'd shared the discomforts of their first tattoos and the wonders of mutual masturbation. They weren't the best of men.

But the regret was only partial and – after sweeping his 'partial regret' under the carpet of metaphor – he decided to look/as he seldom did/on the brighter side of life. He would/ at last/no longer need to proceed with care & caution when 'knocking off' his dead colleague's wife & daughters.

And so – in a smallish way – 'relief sprang eternal to his human breast'/but that was only until he came to the cognizance that he was standing up to his ankles & then knees/in water.

Both the skipper of the doomed 70-ish footer and his 'decky' [deck-hand] were 'people of colour'. And – in addition to that

– were from the more colourful end of the colourful spectrum. They were – of course they were – as-black-as.

Becoming aware – as they rapidly had/soon after leaving Moresby – that the men they were transporting were not men for whom 'colour' suggested festival & gaiety [but quite the reverse] they'd strayed seldom from the bridge.

Becoming aware – as they rapidly did – that the recent gunfire from Seaman 1st Class Poma [they knew him from the bars of Moresby's docks] was soon to result in their 'going down by the bows' – they decided – of course they did – to exit-stage-right [although not being chased by a bear].

This feat – exiting-stage-right/starboard [although not being chased by a bear] – was achieved in the boat's Zodiac. They gave no thought – and why should they & why should anyone expect them to – to the fate of their guests.

They – the concept of *sauve qui peut* being a universal one – motored rapidly & with easy conscience to the nearby island. They were met by a boy chasing crabs.

Back aboard the previously 70-ish footer – but now quite a bit shorter than that – the man with the recently relief-sprung-breast/with no intention of emulating Captain Smith of the *Titanic*/scrambled topside. He surveyed the scene. He would need to swim/as his remaining colleague was already doing/to the island. He jumped overboard.

*

Boris & Ishmael – back aboard the 50-ish – heard the Bofors gun. Boris – having been a Cadet Under-Officer in his school's cadet corps – knew about Bofors guns and/because of that/wasn't surprised/not at all/to see the front several feet of the previously offending 70-ish disappear.

They watched as the crew abandoned ship and motored

to the island. They did not see – because it happened on the other side of it – a horrible man/and then another horrible man/ making a swim for it.

They pondered/but not for long. Things were getting interesting.

＊

All the eyes in all of the heads of all of the people on all the boats/ship – of course they were – were on the foundering of the foundering vessel. How could they not be? Where else would they be? It's not every day that you get to see a good founder.

＊

Bert – aware of what was happening – and aware of where his wares were/which were where a helicopter now was/where a seaplane/he assumed [correctly] now was/where the Zodiac from the sinking & soon to be sunken boat now was/where the swimmers from the sunken boat were now swimming to/and soon would be – decided he should get there [to the island] as soon as he could.

He – together with the defrocked Commander – motored/ Zodiaced to the island.

They were met by a boy who said – "My name's Perry, what's yours?"

"Shove off, kid," said Bert.

Perry – being a well-brought-up-boy as well as accustomed to doing what he was told – shoved off/ circled round/came back and – as Bert & the defrocked Commander walked on up the beach – removed both bungs from the bottom of their Zodiac.

＊

Hai – no longer seeing double – was aware that the scene/ *maior est scaena*/was moving to the island. And because of that – decided to go there too. So he did.

"My name's Perry and you're Chinese," said the boy named Perry.

⁎

Boris & Ishmael – keen observers of recent events/as well as men of seasoned thought & considered action/motored to the island.

A boy ran along the beach to greet them.

"My name's Perry," said the boy named Perry.

"My name's Boris," said Boris.

"That's Russian," said Perry.

"We're English," said Boris.

"That's weird," said Perry.

⁎

The first of the horrible men waded ashore. He did not see – because he wasn't looking that way – the remaining horrible man do likewise further up the beach and then shimmy – as much as any [BMI 40+] fat slob can shimmy – his way into the cover of the palm trees.

He saw – because he was looking that way – a child before him.

"My name's Perry," said the child before him.

"Fuck off," said the horrible man.

"Fuck off yourself, you fat-fatty-fatso," shouted Perry over his shoulder as he ran off up the beach.

The horrible man pulled his pistol from his belt/but then – just as a 'fat pansy cunt in a skirt' had some years previously – thought better of it. 'It' being shooting a six-year-old in the back.

It wasn't qualm that calmed his bitter soul/but the knowledge that he would/in all probability/need help from third parties to get what he wanted and then [after having eliminated said third parties] find his way home.

He was not a man of classic intellect/or learning/but he was smart enough. And 'coming home to roost' in his 'smart enough' brain was the realisation that 'eliminating third parties' might prove somewhat more problematic than first thought.

The 'coming home to roost' was bringing consternation to his low & lowering brow.

*

Inspector Fang – aware [because how could he be otherwise] of the sinking of the bow-truncated 70-ish footer – became aware also of the less than well-oiled chain of command aboard the navy's pride-of-the-fleet.

He was happy that his suggestion [the one that they follow the others to the island] was agreed to in both principle & practice.

He was happier-still to hear that he would be accompanied by Captain Poma & 2IC Ensign Poma. He was happier-still to hear that Seaman 1st Class Poma would be left aboard/& with strict instructions from Captain Poma/relayed by 2IC Ensign Poma/to keep well away from the Bofors gun. But sadly – and neither Inspector Fang nor Captain Poma were aware of this – the instructions as given by 2IC Ensign Poma to Seaman 1st Class Poma were given in such a way that only men with older brothers [as well as a bucket full of sibling rivalry bordering on dislike/hatred] would fully appreciate.

To say that the instruction was given & received in a less than ship-shape fashion would be an understatement.

"*OK*," thought Inspector Fang – "*Let's get going.*"

"*No more cock-ups,*" thought Captain Poma after giving a good dressing-down to 2IC Ensign Poma & another to Seaman 1st Class Poma.

"*No more cock-ups,*" thought 2IC Ensign Poma after giving a good dressing-down to Seaman 1st Class Poma.

"*OK,*" thought doubly dressed-down Seaman 1st Class Poma – "*Bofors gun 'no-can-do then', but they didn't mention the 50 cal, now did they... suckers.*"

They motored ashore and Captain Poma – because he was an avid reader of CS Forester – alighted first. And/as he did so/he eased off the safety on his H & K P30.

Inspector Fang followed him. And/as he did so/he eased off the safety on his S & W 45.

Ensign Poma stayed with the dinghy. And/as he did so/and after seeing what the others did/he eased off the safety on his ancient [he'd inherited it from his grandfather who'd been given it on VJ day by a GI who'd taken it off a dead Jap the previous year] Koishikawa Type A.

—
*

Eli – seeing what was going on/and not comfortable with what was going on – bade his farewells to the ship with a crane. He loaded Noor onto the helicopter/kissed Mitzi *au revoir* and flew away to the island. He – soon after lift-off – took a smaller/more easily concealed/Dirty Harriette Thing from his jacket pocket. It was a Glock something-or-other. He handed it to Noor. She looked at it. She asked where 'the safety' was. He said Glock's didn't have one.

◎ Did you know that?

She put it in her bag. He kept another one in his trouser pocket. He instructed the chopper pilot to chopper to the island & chopper down next to the chopper. The chopper pilot said he would and/after saying he would/he did.

Eli didn't – of course he didn't – wish or want to fly to the other side of the island. That was because 'the other side of the island' was where there was a 'thing' [a 'thing' he didn't want other people to know anything about – let alone find].

They landed. A little boy ran up to them.
    "Hello Peregrine called Perry," said Eli.
    "Hello Mr Rubenstein called Eli," said Perry.
    "Hello Perry," said Noor.
    "Hi," said Perry as he turned away.

Eli & Noor looked along the beach. They could see a fat man waddling towards them. They both recognised him. So did Perry/who went and stood behind Eli.
    Noor knew – although she didn't say so – that there was a swastika tattooed on his dick.

*

What no one was noticing were the two unbelievably young-looking heads of the two unbelievably young-looking Chinese girls [twins by the look of it] as they swam through the lagoon to the island.

*

The 6th Earl had heard – of course he had – the firing of the Bofors gun.
    His first instinct was to leave the safety of his sequestered cave and see what was going on. His second instinct was not to. First instincts – as they so often do – won the day.
    He moved his well-placed rocks/pulled aside the curtain of vines and climbed into the light.
    He went to the crow's-nest. He could see the boats in the

channel. He could see the helicopters on the beach. He couldn't see the aeroplane he'd heard.

He could see people on the beach and – even with the help of the –nocular – he didn't recognise any of them.

He knew that oldest-&-closest-friend John knew where he was/ where he'd been all these years/and that was why he was – and had been for all these years – 'fed-&-watered'. He was hoping – just a little hope – that his oldest-&-closest might be among those on the beach. But he was disappointed. He was hoping – just the tiniest sliver of hopes – that the daughter of the Shadow Minister of Something-or-other might be there too. But he was disappointed [even though he never really expected her to be there] that she wasn't.

What the 6th Earl didn't know – because there was no way he could possibly know it – was that [at that very moment] his oldest-&-closest-friend/accompanied by the daughter of the Shadow Minister of Something-or-other/was – after having fully investigated the huts [burned out & otherwise] and noting/with a degree of sadness-but-not-yet-sorrow/the Judeo-Christian burial on the beach – moving up & along the island towards him.

What the 6th Earl did know – or was pretty certain of/ because his years on the island had made him a smarter & more insightful man out of the blinder & more stupid one – was that those on the beach below him were not there by accident or serendipity. They were there for a reason/and the reason/or part of the reason/he felt pretty sure [almost certain] was him.

He also knew – or was pretty certain – that they were there for more than just him. He knew – or was pretty certain – that the metal chests/as well as what the metal chests might contain/ would have something to do with it too.

He – for some time past – would [in his increasingly frequent & more reflective moments] ponder upon the contents of the metal chests.

He was never a reader – avid or otherwise – but he knew the stories of buried treasure and buried bodies. He could [like every other boy of his age] offer his version of Robert Newton's Long John Silver. His 'Aaah Jim laad.' So – while he might not know what the metal chests contained – he knew what they didn't. They weren't full of dog-biscuits.

He returned to his cave/rearranged the greenery and put the rocks back in place. He took two/perhaps three/perhaps more/gulps/big gulps/great big gulps/of Scotch whisky/lay down on his bed and/after barely moments of contemplation/fell into a drunken stupor/sleep.

It wasn't the stupor/sleep of the innocent or the saved/because it wasn't. It was the stupor/sleep of a man who knew his fate to be in the hands of others/and that apart from staying where he was/there was sod-all-else he could do about it all. It was this serenity-of-spirit – a serenity-of-spirit unknown to the spirit of the pre-bludgeoning Earl – together with the two/perhaps three/perhaps more/gulps/big gulps/great big gulps/of Scotch whisky – that allowed stupor & sleep to come upon him like 'the kiss of Somnus'.

But what the 6th Earl didn't know – as he sank into the bosom of Morpheus – was [because there was no way he could] that/with the advancing years & inevitable relaxation of the palatine musculature that comes with it – he snored.

—
*

Eli – knowing full-well the inner nature & animus of the fat man waddling towards them/and if told that there was a tattoo tattooed on his dick wouldn't have been surprised in the slightest that there was – knew/also & full-well/what the man wanted to know/as well as what he planned to do once he knew what he wanted to know. And that was to kill him & Noor and anyone else who might know the thing the AWSB didn't want anyone else to know.

The fat man arrived in front of them. He held a pistol in his hand. He pointed it at both of them. To the surprise/amazement & incredulity of both of them – because both of them knew that the man didn't yet know what he wanted to know/which was something both of *them* knew/and no one else knew/and that [because of that the man wouldn't shoot them until he knew what he wanted to know] which was something neither of them had any intention of telling him – the man shot both of them. Noor first – then Eli.

✱

On board a recently arrived and [because of that] unobserved/ low/sleek/black & futuristic looking craft of some 100-ish feet – sat the Buddha like figure of Mr Woo. He caressed no monkey. The best-of-the-best-of-the-best/both of them/stood behind him.

TO BE CONTINUED.